To Olive Co ...
From Olive Watts
Xmas 1989

**SIMON AND SCHUSTER**
New York   London
Toronto   Sydney
Tokyo

# WHILE MY PRETTY ONE SLEEPS

A Novel by

# MARY HIGGINS CLARK

SIMON AND SCHUSTER
Simon & Schuster Building
Rockefeller Center
1230 Avenue of the Americas
New York, New York 10020

Copyright © 1989 by Mary Higgins Clark

SIMON AND SCHUSTER and colophon are registered trademarks of Simon & Schuster Inc.
Designed by Nina D'Amario/Levavi & Levavi
Manufactured in the United States of America

10   9   8   7   6   5   4   3   2   1

Library of Congress Cataloging in Publication data

Clark, Mary Higgins.
    While my pretty one sleeps.

    I. Title.
PS3553.L287W54   1989      813'.54      89-6078
ISBN 0-671-55665-7

FOR MY NEWEST GRANDCHILDREN,
COURTNEY MARILYN CLARK
AND
DAVID FREDERICK CLARK,
WITH CONTINUING LOVE, AMUSEMENT AND DELIGHT.

1 He drove cautiously up the Thruway toward Morrison State Park. The thirty-five-mile trip from Manhattan to Rockland County had been a nightmare. Even though it was six o'clock, there was no sense of approaching dawn. The snow that had begun during the night had steadily increased until now it was beating relentlessly against the windshield. The overhead

clouds, heavy and gray, were like enormous balloons pumped to the breaking point. The forecast had been for two inches, with "precipitation tapering off after midnight." As usual the weatherman had been wrong.

But he was near the entrance to the park, and, with the storm, there probably wouldn't be anyone hiking or jogging. He'd passed a State Trooper ten miles back, but the car had rushed past him, lights flashing, probably on the way to an accident somewhere. Certainly the cops had no reason to even think about the contents of his trunk, no reason to suspect that under a pile of luggage a plastic bag containing the body of a prominent sixty-one-year-old writer, Ethel Lambston, was wedged in a space-defying squeeze against the spare tire.

He turned off the Thruway and drove the short distance to the parking lot. As he had hoped, it was nearly empty. Only a few cars were scattered around and they were coated with snow. Some damn fools camping out, he supposed. The trick was not to bump into them.

He glanced around carefully as he left the car. No one. The snow was piling in drifts. It would cover the tracks when he left, cover any signs of where he was going to put her. With any luck, by the time she was discovered there wouldn't be much left to find.

First he made his way to the spot alone. His hearing was keen. Now he tried to maximize it, to force it to filter past the sighing of the wind and the creaking of the already heavy branches. Down this way there was a steep path. Past it and on a sharp incline was a pile of rocks layered by heavy loose stones. Very few people bothered to climb there. It was off-limits for riders—the stable didn't want the suburban housewives who were its main customers breaking their necks.

A year ago he had happened to be curious enough to make that climb, and had rested on a boulder-sized rock. His hand had slid across the rock and he'd felt the opening behind it. Not a cave entrance, but a natural formation like the mouth of a cave. Even then, the thought had passed his mind that it would be a great place to hide something.

It was exhausting to reach with the snow turning icy, but, slipping and sliding, he made the climb. The space was still there, a little smaller than he remembered, but he could force the body in. The next step was the worst. Going back to the car, he would have to take infinite caution to avoid any chance of being observed. He'd parked at an angle so that no one who happened to drive in would have a direct view of what he was removing from the trunk, and anyhow a black plastic bag in itself wasn't suspicious.

In life Ethel had been deceptively slim. But as he picked up the plastic-shrouded body he reflected that those expensive outfits had concealed a heavy-boned frame. He tried to heave the bag over his shoulder, but, perverse in death as she had been in life, Ethel must have begun the process of rigor mortis. Her body refused to slide into manageable lines. In the end, he half carried, half dragged the bag as far as the incline, then sheer adrenaline gave him the strength to haul her up the sloping, slippery rocks to the spot.

His original plan had been to leave her in the bag. But at the last minute he changed his mind. Forensics units were getting too damn smart. They could find evidence on anything, fibers from clothes or carpets or human hair that no eye would notice.

Ignoring the cold as the gusting wind seared his forehead and the pellets of snow turned his cheeks and chin into a chunk of ice, he placed the bag in position over the cave and began to rip. It would not give. Two-ply, he thought grimly, remembering all the commercials. Savagely he tugged at it and then grimaced as the bag gave and Ethel's body came into view.

The white wool suit was stained with blood. The collar of her blouse was caught in the gaping hole in her throat. One eye was slightly open. In the gathering dawn it seemed less sightless than contemplative. The mouth that never knew repose in Ethel's life was pursed as though about to start another one of her interminable sentences. The last one she ever got to spit out had been her fatal mistake, he told himself with grim satisfaction.

Even with gloves on, he hated touching her. She'd been dead nearly fourteen hours. It seemed to him there was a faint, sweet odor coming from her body. With sudden disgust he shoved her corpse down and began wedging stones on top of it. The opening was deeper than he'd realized, and the stones dropped neatly in place over her. A casual climber wouldn't dislodge them.

The job was finished. The blowing snow had already covered up his footsteps. Ten minutes after he got out of here, all trace of him and the presence of the car would be obliterated.

He crushed the shredded plastic into a wadded ball and began hurrying toward the car. Now he was frantic to leave, to be far from this exposure to discovery. At the border of the parking lot, he waited. The same cars were there, still untouched. There were no fresh tracks in the lot.

Five minutes later, he was back on the Thruway, the bloodied, torn bag that had been Ethel's shroud jammed under the spare tire. Now there was plenty of room for her suitcases and carry-on and purse.

The roadway was icy now, the commuter traffic beginning, but in a few hours he'd be back in New York, back to sanity and reality. He made his final stop, a lake he remembered not far from the Thruway, that was too polluted now for fishing. It was a good place to dump Ethel's purse and luggage. All four pieces were heavy. The lake was deep, and he knew they'd sink and get caught in the mass of junk that rested on the bottom. People even dumped old cars here.

He tossed Ethel's belongings as far as he could heave them and watched as they disappeared under the dark-gray water. Now the only thing left to do was to get rid of the torn, bloodstained wad of plastic. He decided to stop at a garbage bin when he got off the West Side Highway. It would be lost in the mountain of trash carted off tomorrow morning.

It took three hours to get back into the city. The driving became more treacherous and he tried to keep his distance from other cars. He didn't need a fender bender. Months from now no one would have any reason to know that he'd been out of the city today.

It worked according to plan. He stopped for a split second on Ninth Avenue and got rid of the plastic bag.

At eight o'clock he was delivering the car back to the gas station on Tenth Avenue that rented old cars as a sideline. Cash only. He knew they didn't keep records.

At ten o'clock, freshly showered and changed, he was in his place, gulping straight bourbon and trying to shake the sudden chilling attack of nerves. His mind went over every instant of the time that had elapsed since he'd stood in Ethel's apartment yesterday and listened to her sarcasm, her ridicule, her threats.

Then she'd known. The antique dagger from her desk in his hand. Her face filled with fear and she'd started to back away.

The exhilaration of slashing that throat, of watching her stumble backward through the archway to the kitchen and collapse onto the ceramic-tile floor.

He still was amazed at how calm he'd been. He'd bolted the door so that by some crazy trick of fate the superintendent or a friend with a key couldn't walk in. Everyone knew how eccentric Ethel could be. If someone with a key found that the door was bolted, they'd assume she didn't want to be bothered answering.

Then he had stripped his clothes off down to his underwear and put on his gloves. Ethel had been planning to go away to write a book. If he could get her out of here, people would think she'd left on her own. She wouldn't be missed for weeks, even months.

Now, gulping a mouthful of bourbon, he thought about how he had selected clothes from her closet, changing her from the blood-soaked caftan, pulling her pantyhose on, slipping her arms into the blouse and the jacket, buttoning the skirt, taking off her jewelry, forcing her feet into pumps. He winced as he remembered the way he'd held her up so that blood spurted over the blouse and the suit. But it was necessary. When she was found, if she *was* found, they had to think she'd died in that outfit.

He had remembered to cut out the labels that would have meant immediate identification. He had found the long plastic bag in the closet, probably returned by a cleaner on an evening gown. He had forced her into it, then cleaned the bloodstains that had spattered on the Oriental throw rug, washed the kitchen tile with Clorox, packed the suitcases with clothes and accessories, all the while working frantically against time. . . .

He refilled the glass to the brim with bourbon, remembering when the phone had rung. The answering machine had come on and the sound of Ethel's rapid speech pattern. "Leave a message. I'll get back when and if I feel like it." It had made his nerves scream. The caller broke the connection and he'd turned off the machine. He didn't want a record of people calling, and perhaps remembering broken appointments later.

Ethel had the ground-floor apartment of a four-story brownstone. Her private entrance was to the left of the stoop that led to the main entry. In effect her door was shielded from the view of anyone walking along the street. The only period of vulnerability was the dozen steps from her door to the curb.

In the apartment, he'd felt relatively safe. The hardest part had come when, after he hid Ethel's tightly wrapped body and luggage under her bed, he opened the front door. The air had been raw and damp, the snow obviously about to begin falling. The wind had cut a sharp path into the apartment. He'd closed the door immediately. It was only a few minutes past six. The streets were busy with people coming home from work. He'd waited nearly two hours more, then slipped out, double-locked the door and gone to the cheap car rental. He'd driven back to Ethel's apartment. Luck was with him. He was able to park almost directly in front of the brownstone. It was dark and the street was deserted.

In two trips he had the luggage in the trunk. The third trip was the worst. He'd pulled his coat collar up, put on an old cap he'd found on the floor of the rented car and carried the plastic bag with Ethel's body out of the apartment. The moment when he slammed the trunk down had brought the first sense that he'd surely make it to safety.

It had been hell to go back into the apartment, to make certain that there was no trace of blood, no sign that he'd been there. Every nerve shrieked at him to get to the state park, to dump the body, but he knew that was crazy. The police might notice someone trying to get into the park at night. Instead he left the car on the street six blocks away, followed his normal routine and at 5 A.M. set out with the very early commuters. . . .

It was all right now, he told himself. He was *safe!*

It was just as he was draining the last warming sip of bourbon that he realized the one ghastly mistake he had made, and knew exactly who would almost inevitably detect it.

Neeve Kearny.

**2** | The radio went on at six-thirty. Neeve reached out her right hand, groping for the button to tune out the insistently cheery voice of the newscaster, then stopped as the import of what he was saying sifted into her consciousness. Eight inches of snow had fallen on the city during the night. Do not drive unless absolutely necessary. Alternate-side-of-the-street parking suspended. School closings to be announced. Forecast was for the snow to continue until late afternoon.

Terrific, Neeve thought as she leaned back and pulled the comforter around her face. She hated missing her usual morning jog. Then she winced, thinking of the alterations that had to be completed today. Two of the seamstresses lived in New Jersey and might not get in. Which meant she'd better get to the shop early and see how she could juggle the schedule of Betty, the only other fitter. Betty lived at Eighty-second and Second and would walk the six blocks to the shop no matter how bad the weather.

Hating the moment she abandoned the cozy warmth of the bed, she threw back the covers, hurried across the room and reached into her closet for the ancient terry-cloth robe that her father, Myles, insisted was a relic of the Crusades. "If any of the women who spent those fancy prices buying your dresses could see you in that rag, they'd go back to shopping in Klein's."

"Klein's closed twenty years ago, and anyhow if they saw me in this rag they'd think I'm eccentric," she'd told him. "That would add to the mystique."

She tied the belt around her waist, experiencing the usual fleeting wish that she had inherited her mother's pencil-thin frame instead of the square-shouldered, rangy body of her Celtic forebears, then brushed back the curly coal-black hair that was a trademark of the Rossetti family. She also had the Rossetti eyes, sherry-colored irises, darker at the edges so they blazed against the whites, wide and questioning under sooty lashes. But her skin tone was the milk white of the Celts, with a dotting of freckles against the straight nose. The generous mouth and strong teeth were those of Myles Kearny.

Six years ago when she graduated from college and persuaded Myles that she had no intention of moving out, he'd insisted she redo her bedroom. By haunting Sotheby's and Christie's, she'd assembled an eclectic assortment of a brass bed, an antique armoire and a Bombay chest, a Victorian chaise and an old Persian rug that glowed like Joseph's coat. Now the quilt and the pillows and the dust ruffle were stark white; the reupholstered chaise was covered in turquoise velvet, the same turquoise tone that ribboned through the rug; the stark-white walls were a background for the fine paintings and prints that had come from her mother's family. *Women's Wear Daily* had photographed her in the room, calling it cheerfully elegant, with the peerless Neeve Kearny touch.

Neeve wiggled her feet into the padded slippers Myles called her booties and yanked up the shade. She decided that the weatherman didn't have to be a genius to say this was an important snowstorm. The view from her room in Schwab House at Seventy-fourth Street and Riverside Drive was directly over the Hudson, but now she could barely make out the buildings across the river in New Jersey. The Henry Hudson Parkway was snow-covered and already filled with cautiously moving traffic. The long-suffering commuters had undoubtedly started into town early.

Myles was already in the kitchen and had the coffeepot on. Neeve kissed him on the cheek, willing herself not to remark on how tired he looked. That meant he hadn't slept well again. If only he'd break down and take an occasional sleeping pill, she thought. "How's the Legend?" she asked him. Since his retirement last year, the newspapers constantly referred to him as "New York's legendary Police Commissioner." He hated it.

He ignored the question, glanced at her and assumed an expression of amazement. "Don't tell me you're not all set to run around Central Park?" he exclaimed. "What's a foot of snow to dauntless Neeve?"

For years they had jogged together. Now that he could no longer run, he worried about her early-morning sprints. But then, she suspected, he never *wasn't* worrying about her.

She reached into the refrigerator for the pitcher of orange juice. Without asking she poured out a tall glass for him, a short one for herself, and began to make toast. Myles used to enjoy a hearty breakfast, but now bacon and eggs were off his diet. So were cheese and beef and, as he put it, "half the food that makes you look forward to a meal." His massive heart attack had restricted his diet as well as ending his career.

They sat in companionable silence, by unspoken consent splitting the morning *Times*. But when she glanced up, Neeve realized that Myles wasn't reading. He was staring at the paper without seeing it. The toast and the juice were untouched in front of him. Only the coffee showed any sign of having been tasted. Neeve put section two of the paper down.

"All right," she said. "Let me have it. Is it that you feel rotten? For heaven's sake, I hope you know enough by now not to play the silent sufferer."

"No, I'm all right," Myles said. "Or at least if you mean

have I been having chest pains, the answer is no." He tossed the paper onto the floor and reached for his coffee. "Nicky Sepetti gets out of jail today."

Neeve gasped. "But I thought they refused him parole last year?"

"Last year was the fourth time he came up. He's served every day of his sentence, less time for good behavior. He'll be back in New York tonight." Cold hatred hardened Myles's face.

"Dad, take a look at yourself in the mirror. Keep it up and you'll bring on another heart attack." Neeve realized her hands were trembling. She gripped the table, hoping Myles would not notice and think she was afraid. "I don't care whether or not Sepetti made that threat when he was sentenced. You spent years trying to connect him to . . ." Her voice trailed off, then continued, "And not one shred of evidence has ever come up to tie him to it. And for God's sake don't you dare start worrying about me because he's back on the street."

Her father had been the U.S. Attorney who put the head of the Sepetti Mafia family, Nicky Sepetti, behind bars. At the sentencing, Nicky had been asked if he had anything to say. He'd pointed at Myles. "I hear they think you done such a good job on me, they made you Police Commissioner. Congratu-lations. That was a nice article in the *Post* about you and your family. Take good care of your wife and kid. They might need a little protection."

Two weeks later, Myles was sworn in as Police Commissioner. A month later, the body of his young wife, Neeve's mother, thirty-four-year-old Renata Rossetti Kearny, was found in Central Park with her throat cut. The crime was never solved.

. . .

Neeve did not argue when Myles insisted that he call for a cab to take her to work. "You can't walk in that snow," he told her.

"It isn't the snow, and we both know it," she retorted. As she kissed him goodbye, she put her arms around his neck and hugged him. "Myles, the only thing that we both have to worry about is your health. Nicky Sepetti isn't going to want to go back to prison. I bet if he knows how to pray he's hoping that nothing happens to me for a long, long time. There isn't another person in New York besides you who doesn't think some petty crook attacked Mother and killed her when she wouldn't give up her purse. She probably started screaming at him in Italian and he panicked. So please forget Nicky Sepetti and leave to heaven whoever took Mother from us. Okay? Promise?"

She was only slightly reassured by his nod. "Now get out of here," he said. "The cab meter's ticking and my game shows will be starting any minute."

The snowplows had made what Myles would call a lick-and-a-promise attempt to partially clear the accumulated snow from West End Avenue. As the car crawled and slid along the slippery streets and turned onto the west-to-east transverse road through the park at Eighty-first Street, Neeve found herself wishing the fruitless "if only." If only her mother's murderer had been found. Perhaps in time the loss would have healed for Myles as it had for her. Instead for him it was an open wound, always festering. He was always blaming himself for somehow failing Renata. All these years he had agonized that he should have taken the threat seriously. He could not bear the knowledge that with the immense resources of the New York City Police Department at his command, he had been unable to learn the identity of the thug who had carried out what he was convinced had been Sepetti's order. It was the one unfulfilled need in his life—to find that killer, to make him and Sepetti pay for Renata's death.

Neeve shivered. The cab was cold. The driver must have been glancing in the rearview mirror, because he said, "Sorry, lady, the heater don't work so good."

"It's all right." She turned her head to avoid getting into a conversation. The "if onlys" would not stop running through her mind. If only the killer had been found and convicted years ago, Myles might have been able to get on with his life. At sixty-eight he was still an attractive man, and over the years there had been plenty of women who had a special smile for the lean, broad-shouldered Commissioner with his thick head of prematurely white hair, his intense blue eyes and his unexpectedly warm smile.

She was so deep in thought she did not even notice when the cab stopped in front of the shop. "Neeve's Place" was written in scroll on the ivory-and-blue awning. The display windows that faced both Madison Avenue and Eighty-fourth Street were wet with snowdrops, giving a shimmering look to the flawlessly cut silk spring dresses on the languidly posed mannequins. It had been her idea to order umbrellas that looked like parasols. Sheer raincoats that picked up one color in the print were draped over the mannequins' shoulders. Neeve joked that it was her "don't-be-plain-in-the-rain" look, but it had proved wildly successful.

"You work here?" the cabby asked as she paid him. "Looks expensive."

Neeve nodded noncommittally as she thought, I own this place, my friend. It was a realization that still thrilled her. Six years ago the previous shop at this location had gone bankrupt. It was her father's old friend the famous designer Anthony della Salva who had bullied her into taking it over. "So you're young," he'd said, dropping the heavy Italian accent that was now part of his persona. "That's a plus. You've been working in fashion since you got your first after-school job. Better yet, you've got the know-how, the flair. I'll lend you the money to get started. If it doesn't work, I can use the write-off, but it'll work. You've got what it takes to make a go of it. Besides, I need another place to sell my clothes." That was the last thing Sal needed, and they both knew it, but she was grateful.

Myles had been dead set against her borrowing from Sal. But she had jumped at the chance. Something she had inherited from Renata besides her hair and eyes was a highly developed fashion sense. Last year she had paid back Sal's loan, insisting on adding interest at money-market rates.

She was not surprised to find Betty already at work in the sewing room. Betty's head was bent down, her frown of concentration now a permanent set of lines on her forehead and between her brows. Her hands, slender and wrinkled, handled a needle and thread with the skill of a surgeon. She was hemming an intricately beaded blouse. Her blatantly dyed copper-colored hair accentuated the parchment-thin skin on her face. Neeve hated to realize that Betty was past seventy. She didn't want to visualize the day when she decided to retire.

"Figured I'd better get a jump on things," Betty announced. "We've got an awful lot of pickups today."

Neeve pulled off her gloves and unwound her scarf. "Don't I know it. And Ethel Lambston insists she has to have everything by this afternoon."

"I know. I've got her stuff ready to do when I finish this. It wouldn't be worth listening to her jabbering if every rag she bought isn't ready to go."

"Everybody should be such a good customer," Neeve observed mildly.

Betty nodded. "I suppose so. And, by the way, I'm glad you talked Mrs. Yates into this outfit. That other one she tried on made her look like a grazing cow."

"It also was fifteen hundred dollars more, but I couldn't let her have it. Sooner or later she'd have taken a good look at herself in the mirror. The sequin top is enough. She needs a soft, full skirt."

A surprising number of shoppers braved the snow and slippery sidewalks to come into the store. Two of the saleswomen hadn't made it, so Neeve spent the day on the sales floor. It was the part she enjoyed most about the business, but in the past year she'd been forced to limit herself to handling only a few personal clients.

At noon she went into her office at the back of the shop for a deli sandwich and coffee and dialed home.

Myles sounded more like himself. "I would have won

fourteen thousand dollars and a Champion pickup truck on *Wheel of Fortune*," he announced. "I won so much I might even have had to take that six-hundred-dollar plaster-of-paris Dalmatian they have the gall to call a prize."

"Well, you certainly sound better," Neeve observed.

"I've been talking to the boys downtown. They've got good people keeping tabs on Sepetti. They say he's pretty sick and hasn't much fight left." There was satisfaction in Myles's voice.

"And they also probably reminded you that they don't think he had anything to do with Mother's death." She did not wait for an answer. "It's a good night for pasta. There's plenty of sauce in the freezer. Yank it out, okay?"

Neeve hung up feeling somewhat reassured. She swallowed the last bite of the turkey sandwich, gulped down the rest of the coffee and went back to the sales floor. Three of the six dressing rooms were occupied. With a practiced eye, she took in every detail of the shop.

The Madison Avenue entrance opened into the accessory area. She knew that one of the key reasons for her success was the availability of jewelry, purses, shoes, hats and scarves so that a woman purchasing a dress or a suit didn't have to hunt elsewhere for accessories. The interior of the shop was in shadings of ivory, with accents of blush pink on the upholstered sofas and chairs. Sportswear and separates were contained in roomy alcoves two steps up from the showcases. Except for the exquisitely gowned display mannequins there was no clothing in sight. A potential customer was escorted to a chair, and the sales clerk brought out dresses and gowns and suits for her selection.

It had been Sal who advised Neeve to go that way. "Otherwise you'll have klutzes yanking clothes off the racks. Start exclusive, honey, and stay exclusive," he had said, and as usual he was right.

The ivory and blush had been Neeve's decision. "When a woman looks in the mirror, I don't want the background fighting what I'm trying to sell," she'd told the interior designer who wanted her to go into great splashes of color.

As the afternoon wore on, fewer clients came in. At three o'clock Betty emerged from the sewing room. "Lambston's stuff is ready," she told Neeve.

Neeve assembled Ethel Lambston's order herself. All spring clothes. Ethel was a sixtyish free-lance writer with one best-seller to her credit. "I write on every subject under the sun," she had breathlessly confided to Neeve on the opening day of the shop. "I take the fresh approach, the inquiring look. I'm every woman seeing something for the first time or from a new angle. I write about sex and relationships and animals and nursing homes and organizations and real estate and how to be a volunteer and political parties and . . ." She had run out of breath, her navy-blue eyes snapping, her white-blond hair flying around her face. "The trouble is that I work so hard at what I do, I don't have a minute for myself. If I buy a black dress, I end up wearing brown shoes with it. Say, you have everything here. What a good idea. Put me together."

In the last six years, Ethel Lambston had become a valuable customer. She insisted Neeve pick out every stitch she bought as well as choose accessories and compile lists to tell her what went with what. She lived on the ground floor of a brownstone on West Eighty-second Street, and Neeve stopped there occasionally to help Ethel decide what clothes to keep from year to year and what to give away.

The last time Neeve had gone over Ethel's wardrobe was three weeks ago. The next day Ethel came in and ordered the new outfits. "I've almost finished that fashion article I interviewed you about," she'd told Neeve. "A lot of people are going to be mad at me when it comes out, but you'll love it. I gave you lots of free publicity."

When she made her selections she and Neeve had differed on only one suit. Neeve had started to take it away. "I don't want to sell you that. It's a Gordon Steuber. I refuse to handle anything of his. This one should have gone back. I cannot stand that man."

Ethel had burst out laughing. "Wait till you read what I wrote about him. I crucified him. But I want the suit. His clothes look good on me."

Now, as Neeve carefully placed the garments in heavy protective bags, she felt her lips narrow at the sight of the Steuber outfit. Six weeks ago, the daily maid at the shop had asked her to speak to a friend who was in trouble. The friend, a Mexican, told Neeve about working in an illegal sweatshop in the South Bronx that was owned by Gordon Steuber. "We don't have green cards. He threatens to turn us in. Last week I was sick. He fired me and my daughter and won't pay what he owes us."

The young woman didn't look to be more than in her late twenties. "Your daughter!" Neeve had exclaimed. "How old is she?"

"Fourteen."

Neeve had canceled the order she'd placed with Gordon Steuber and sent him a copy of the Elizabeth Barrett Browning poem which had helped change the child-labor laws in England. She underlined the stanza "But the young, young children, oh my brothers, they are weeping bitterly."

Someone in Steuber's office had tipped off *Women's Wear Daily.* The editors printed the poem on the front page next to Neeve's scathing letter to Steuber and called on other retailers to boycott manufacturers who were breaking the law.

Anthony della Salva had been upset. "Neeve, the word is that Steuber has a lot more than sweatshops to hide. Thanks to what you stirred up, the Feds are nosing around his income-tax returns."

"Wonderful," Neeve had retorted. "If he's cheating at that too, I hope they catch him."

Well, she decided as she straightened the Steuber suit on the hanger, this will be the last thing of his that goes out of my shop. She found herself anxious to read Ethel's fashion article. She knew it was due to come out soon in *Contemporary Woman,* the magazine where Ethel was a contributing editor.

Finally, Neeve made up the lists for Ethel. Blue silk evening suit; wear white silk blouse; jewelry in box A. Pink-and-gray ensemble; gray pumps, matching purse; jewelry in box B. Black cocktail dress . . ." There were eight outfits in all. With the accessories they came to nearly seven thousand dollars. Ethel spent that amount three or four times a year. She'd confided to Neeve that when she was divorced twenty-two years before, she'd gotten a big settlement and invested it wisely. "And I collect a thousand bucks a month alimony from him for life," she'd laughed. "At the time we broke up, he was riding high. He told his lawyers it was worth every cent to get rid of me. In court, he said that if I ever marry again the guy should be stone deaf. Maybe I'd have given him a break if it weren't for that crack. He's remarried and has three kids, and ever since Columbus Avenue got classy his bar's been in trouble. Every once in a while he phones and begs me to let him off the hook, but I tell him I still haven't found anyone who's stone deaf."

At that moment Neeve had been prepared to dislike Ethel. Then Ethel had added wistfully, "I always wanted a family. We separated when I was thirty-seven. The five years we were married, he wouldn't give me a child."

Neeve had made it her business to read Ethel's articles and had quickly realized that even though Ethel might be a talkative, seemingly scatterbrained woman, she was also an excellent writer. No matter what subject she tackled, it was obvious her research was massive.

With the help of the receptionist, Neeve stapled the bottoms of the garment bags. The jewelry and the shoes were packed in individual boxes and then gathered in ivory-and-pink cartons with "Neeve's Place" scrolled along the sides. With a sigh of relief, she dialed Ethel's apartment.

There was no answer. Nor had Ethel left her answering machine on. Neeve decided that Ethel would probably arrive any minute, breathless and with a taxi waiting outside.

At four o'clock there were no customers in the shop and Neeve sent everyone home. Darn Ethel, she thought. She would have liked to go home as well. The snow was still falling steadily. At this rate, she'd never get a cab herself later. She tried Ethel at four-thirty, at five, at five-thirty. Now what? she wondered. Then she had an idea. She'd wait until six-thirty, the usual closing time, then deliver Ethel's things on her way home. Surely she could leave them with the superintendent. That way if Ethel had imminent travel plans, she'd have her new wardrobe.

The taxicab-company starter was reluctant to accept her call. "We're telling all our cars to come in, lady. Driving's a mess. But gimme your name and phone number." When he heard her name, the starter's tone changed. "Neeve Kearny! Why didn't you tell me you're the Commissioner's daughter? You bet we'll get you home."

The cab arrived at twenty of seven. They inched through the now almost impassable streets. The driver was not pleased to make an additional stop. "Lady, I can't wait to pack it in."

There was no answer at Ethel's apartment. Neeve rang in vain for the superintendent. There were four other apartments in the brownstone, but she had no idea who lived in them and couldn't risk leaving the clothes with strangers. Finally she tore a check out of her book and on the back of it wrote a note to slip under Ethel's door: "I have your purchases. Call me when you get in." She put her home phone number under her signature. Then, struggling under the weight of the boxes and bags, she got back into the cab.

. . .

Inside Ethel Lambston's apartment, a hand reached for the note Neeve had pushed under the door, read it, tossed it aside and resumed his periodic search for the hundred-dollar bills that Ethel regularly squirreled away under the carpets or between the cushions of the couch, the money she gleefully referred to as "Seamus the wimp's alimony."

Myles Kearny could not shake off the nagging worry that had been growing in him for weeks. His grandmother used to have a kind of sixth sense. "I have a feeling," she would say. "There's trouble coming." Myles could vividly remember when he was ten and his grandmother had received a picture of his cousin in Ireland. She had cried, "He has death in his eyes." Two hours later the phone had rung. His cousin had been killed in an accident.

Seventeen years ago, Myles had shrugged off Nicky Sepetti's threat. The Mafia had its own code. They never went after the wives or children of its enemies. And then Renata had died. At three o'clock in the afternoon, walking through Central Park to pick up Neeve at Sacred Heart Academy, she'd been murdered. It had been a cold, windy November day. The park was deserted. There were no witnesses to tell who had lured or forced Renata off the path and into the area behind the museum.

He'd been in his office when the principal of Sacred Heart phoned at four-thirty. Mrs. Kearny had not come to pick up Neeve. They'd phoned, but she was not at home. Was anything wrong? When he hung up the phone, Myles had known with sickening certainty that something terrible had happened to Renata. Ten minutes later the police were searching Central Park. His car was on the way uptown when the call came in that her body had been found.

When he reached the park, a cordon of policemen was holding back the curious and the sensation seekers. The media were already there. He remembered how the flash-bulbs had blinded him as he walked toward the spot where her body was lying. Herb Schwartz, his deputy commissioner, was there. "Don't look at her now, Myles," he begged.

He'd shaken Herb's arm off, knelt on the frozen ground and pulled back the blanket they'd put over her. She might have been sleeping. Her face still lovely in that final repose, none of the expression of terror that he'd seen stamped on so many victims' faces. Her eyes were closed. Had she closed them in that final moment or had Herb closed them? At first he thought she was wearing a red scarf. Denial. He was a seasoned viewer of victims, but at that moment his professionalism abandoned him. He didn't want to see that someone had slashed down the length of her jugular vein, then slit her throat. The collar of the white ski jacket she'd been wearing had turned crimson from her blood. The hood had slipped back, and her face was framed by those masses of jet-black hair. Her red ski pants, the red of her blood, the white jacket and the hardened snow under her body—even in death she'd looked like a fashion photograph.

He'd wanted to hold her against him, to breathe life into her, but he knew he should not move her. He'd contented himself with kissing the cheeks and the eyes and the lips. His hand grazed her neck and came away bloodstained, and he'd thought, We met in blood, we part in blood.

He'd been a twenty-one-year-old rookie cop on Pearl Harbor Day, and the next morning he'd enlisted in the Army. Three years later he was with Mark Clark's Fifth Army in the battle for Italy. They'd taken it town by town. In Pontici he'd gone into a church that seemed to be deserted. The next moment he'd heard an explosion, and blood had gushed from his forehead. He'd spun around and seen a German soldier crouched behind the altar in the sacristy. He managed to shoot him before he passed out.

He came to, feeling a small hand shaking him. "Come with me," a voice whispered in his ear in heavily accented English. He could barely think through the waves of pain in his head. His eyes were crusted with dried blood. Outside it was pitch black. The sounds of gunfire were far away, to the left. The child—he realized somehow it was a child—led him down deserted alleys. He remembered wondering where she was taking him, why she was alone. He heard the scraping of his combat boots against the stone steps, the sound of a rusty gate opening, then an intense, rapidly speaking whisper, the child's explanation. Now she was speaking Italian. He couldn't understand what she was saying. Then he felt an arm supporting him, the feeling of being lowered onto a bed. He passed out and awoke intermittently, aware of gentle hands bathing and bandaging his head. His first clear recollection was of an army doctor examining him. "You don't know how lucky you were," he was told. "They drove us back yesterday. It wasn't good for the ones who didn't make it out."

After the war, Myles had taken advantage of the GI Bill of Rights and gone to college. The Fordham Rose Hill campus was only a few miles from where he'd grown up in the Bronx. His father, a police captain, had been skeptical. "It was all we could do to get *you* through high school," he'd observed. "Not that you weren't blessed with a brain, but you never chose to place your nose between the covers of a book."

Four years later, after graduating magna cum laude, Myles went on to law school. His father had been delighted but warned, "You've still got a cop in you. Don't forget that cop when you get all your fancy degrees."

Law school. The DA's office. Private practice. It was then he'd realized it was too easy for a good lawyer to get a guilty defendant off. He didn't have the stomach for it. He'd jumped at the chance to become a U.S. Attorney.

That was 1958. He'd been thirty-seven. Over the years he'd dated plenty of girls and watched them marry off, one by one. But somehow anytime he'd come close, a voice had whispered in his ear, "There is more. Wait a bit."

The notion of going back to Italy was a gradual one. "Being shot at through Europe is not the equivalent of the grand tour," his mother told him when, at a dinner home, he tentatively mentioned his plans. And then she'd asked, "Why don't you look up that family that hid you in Pontici? I doubt you were in any condition to thank them at that time."

He still blessed his mother for that advice. Because when he knocked at their door, Renata had opened it. Renata who was now twenty-three, not ten. Renata tall and slender, so that he was barely half a head over her. Renata who incredibly said, "I know who you are. I brought you home that night."

"How could you have remembered?" he asked.

"My father took my picture with you before they took you away. I've always kept it on my dresser."

They were married three weeks later. The next eleven years were the happiest of his life.

Myles walked over to the window and looked out. Technically, spring had arrived a week ago, but nobody had bothered to pass on the word to Mother Nature. He tried not to remember how much Renata had loved to walk in the snow.

He rinsed the coffee cup and the salad plate and put them into the dishwasher. If all the tunas in the world suddenly vanished, what would people on a diet have for lunch? he wondered. Maybe they'd go back to good, thick hamburgers. The notion made his mouth water. But it did remind him that he was supposed to defrost the pasta sauce.

At six o'clock he began to prepare dinner. He brought out the makings for a salad from the refrigerator and with skillful hands broke lettuce, chopped scallions, sliced green peppers into razor-thin bands of green. Unconsciously he smiled to himself, remembering how, growing up, he'd thought a salad was tomato and lettuce globbed with mayonnaise. His mother had been a wonderful woman, but her calling in life was clearly not as a chef. She'd also cooked meat until "all the germs were killed," so that a pork chop or a steak was dry and hard enough to be karated instead of cut.

It was Renata who had introduced him to the delights of subtle flavors, the joys of pasta, the delicacy of salmon, tangy salads that hinted of garlic. Neeve had inherited her mother's culinary skills, but Myles acknowledged to himself that along the way he'd learned to make a damn good salad.

At ten of seven he began to worry actively about Neeve. Probably few taxis on the road. Dear God, don't let her walk through the park on a night like this. He tried calling the shop, but there was no answer. By the time she struggled in with the bundles of clothes over her arm and dragging the boxes, he'd been ready to call headquarters and ask the police to check the park for her. He clamped his lips together before he admitted that.

Instead as he took the boxes from her arms he succeeded in looking surprised. "Is it Christmas again?" he asked. "From Neeve to Neeve with love? Have you used up today's profits on yourself?"

"Don't be such a wise guy, Myles," Neeve said crossly. "I tell you, Ethel Lambston may be a good customer, but she's also a royal pain in the neck." As she dropped the boxes onto the couch she skimmed through the tale of her attempt to deliver Ethel's clothing.

Myles looked alarmed. "Ethel Lambston! Isn't she the ditsy you had at the Christmas party?"

"You've got it." On impulse, Neeve had invited Ethel to the annual Christmas party she and Myles gave in the apartment. After pinning Bishop Stanton to the wall and

Mary Higgins Clark

explaining why the Catholic Church was no longer rele-
vant in the twentieth century, Ethel had realized Myles
was a widower and hadn't left his side all evening.

"I don't care if you have to camp outside her door for
the next two years," Myles warned. "Don't let that woman
set foot in this place again."

**3** It was not Denny Adler's idea of a good time to be breaking his neck for minimum wages plus tips at the deli on East Eighty-third Street and Lexington. But Denny had a problem. He was on probation. His probation officer, Mike Toohey, was a swine who loved the authority vested in him by the State of New York. Denny knew that if he didn't have a job, he couldn't spend a dime without Toohey asking him what he was living on, so he worked and hated every minute of it.

He rented a dingy room in a fleabag on First Avenue and One Hundred and Fifth Street. What the parole officer *didn't* know was that most of Denny's time away from the job was spent panhandling on the street. He changed both the locations and his disguises every few days. Sometimes he'd dress like a bum, put on filthy clothes and shabby sneakers, smear dirt on his face and hair. He'd prop up against a building and hold a torn piece of cardboard which read, "HELP, I'M HUNGRY."

That was one of the better sucker baits.

Other times he'd put on faded khakis and a gray wig. He'd wear dark glasses, carry a cane, pin a sign to his coat, "HOMELESS VET." At his feet a bowl quickly filled with quarters and dimes.

Denny picked up a lot of loose pocket change that way. Nothing like the thrill of planning a real job, but it was something to keep his hand in. Only once or twice, when he'd come across a wino with a few bucks, had he succumbed to the need to waste someone. But the cops didn't give a damn when a wino or a bum was beaten or stabbed, so it was practically risk-free.

His probation would be finished in three months, then he'd be able to drop out of sight and decide where the best action was to be found. Even the parole officer was relaxing. On Saturday morning, Toohey phoned him at the deli. Denny could just picture Mike, his puny frame hunched over the desk in his sloppy office. "I've been talking to your boss, Denny. He tells me you're one of his most dependable workers."

"Thank you, sir." If Denny had been standing in front

of Toohey's desk he would have twisted his hands in an attitude of nervous gratitude. He'd have forced moisture into his pale-hazel eyes and manipulated his narrow lips to an eager grin. Instead he silently mouthed an obscenity into the phone.

"Denny, you can skip reporting to me on Monday. I've got a heavy schedule and you're one of the men I know I can trust. I'll see you next week."

"Yes, sir." Denny hung up the phone. A caricature of a smile slashed creases below his prominent cheekbones. Half of his thirty-seven years had been spent in custody, beginning with his first break-in when he was twelve. A permanent grayish prison pallor was ground into his skin.

He glanced around the deli, at the sickeningly cute ice-cream tables and wire chairs, the white Formica counter, the luncheon-special signs, the well-dressed regulars deep in their newspapers over French toast or corn flakes. He was interrupted in his dream of what he'd like to do to this place and to Mike Toohey, by the manager shouting, "Hey, Adler, get it moving! Those orders won't deliver themselves."

"Yes, sir!" Countdown on *yes sir!* Denny thought, as he grabbed his jacket and the carton of paper bags.

When he got back to the deli, the manager was just answering the phone. He looked at Denny with his usual sour expression. "I told you no personal calls during business hours." He slammed the receiver into Denny's hand.

The only one who ever called him here was Mike Toohey. Denny snarled his name and heard a muffled "Hello, Denny." He recognized the voice immediately. Big

Charley Santino. Ten years ago Denny had shared a cell in Attica with Big Charley, and from time to time he had done a couple of jobs for him. He knew that Charley had important mob connections.

Denny ignored the "Get on with it" expression on the manager's face. There were only a couple of people at the counter now. The tables were empty. He had the pleasurable glow of knowing that whatever Charley wanted would be interesting. Automatically he turned to the wall and cupped his hand over the speaker. "Yeah?"

"Tomorrow. Eleven o'clock. Bryant Park behind the library. Watch for an '84 black Chevy."

Denny did not realize that he was smiling broadly when the click indicated the connection was broken.

Over the snowy weekend, Seamus Lambston huddled alone in the family apartment on Seventy-first Street and West End Avenue. On Friday afternoon, he called his bartender. "I'm sick. Get Matty to fill in till Monday." He'd slept soundly Friday night, the sleep of the emotionally spent, but he woke up on Saturday with a sense of ultimate dread.

Ruth had driven up to Boston on Thursday and stayed until Sunday. Jeannie, their youngest daughter, was a freshman at the University of Massachusetts. The check Seamus sent for spring semester had bounced. Ruth had gotten an emergency loan from her office and rushed up with the replacement. After Jeannie's distraught call, they'd had a row that must have been heard five blocks away.

"Damn it, Ruth, I'm doing my best," he'd shouted.

"Business is lousy. With three kids in college, is it my fault we're scraping the bottom of the barrel? Do you think I can pull money out of the thin air?"

They'd confronted each other, frightened, exhausted, hopeless. He'd been shamed by the look of distaste in her eyes. He knew he hadn't aged well. Sixty-two years old. He'd built up his five-foot-ten frame with sit-ups and barbells. But now he had a potbelly that wouldn't go away, his once thick sandy hair was thinning and dirty yellow, his reading glasses accentuated the puffiness of his face. He sometimes looked in the mirror, then at the picture of Ruth and himself on their wedding day. Both in handsome suits, both pushing forty, second marriages for both of them, happy, eager for each other. The bar had been going great, and even though he'd mortgaged the hell out of it, he'd been sure he'd be able to recoup in a couple of years. Ruth's quiet, tidy ways were like sanctuary after putting up with Ethel. "Peace is worth every nickel it will cost," he'd told the lawyer who didn't want him to agree to lifetime alimony.

He'd been delighted when Marcy was born. Unexpectedly Linda had followed two years later. They'd been shocked when Jeannie came along as he and Ruth were turning forty-five.

Ruth's slender body had grown stocky. As the rent for the bar doubled and tripled and the old customers moved away, her serene face had taken on a look of perpetual worry. She wanted so much to give things to the girls, things they couldn't afford. Frequently he snapped at her, "Why not give them a happy home instead of a lot of junk?"

These last years with the college expenses had been

excruciating. There just wasn't enough money. And that thousand dollars a month to Ethel until she married or died had become a bone of contention, a bone that Ruth gnawed at incessantly. "Go back into court, for God's sake," she'd nag him. "Tell the judge you can't afford to educate your children and that parasite is making a fortune. She doesn't *need* your money. She's got more than she can spend."

The latest outburst, last week, had been the worst. Ruth read in the *Post* that Ethel had just signed a book contract for a half-million-dollar advance. Ethel was quoted as saying the tell-all book would be a "stick of dynamite thrown into the fashion world."

For Ruth that was the last straw. That and the bounced check. "You go see that, that . . ." Ruth never swore. But the unspoken word might have been shouted. "You tell her that I'm going to go to the columnists and tell *them* she's bleeding you dry. Twelve thousand dollars a year, for over twenty years!" Ruth's voice got shriller with every syllable. "I want to quit working. I'm sixty-two years old. The next thing you know it will be weddings. We'll go to our graves with a choke collar around our necks. You tell her that she'll make news all right! Don't you think her fancy magazines might take exception to one of their feminist editors blackmailing her ex-husband?"

"It's not blackmail. It's alimony." Seamus had tried to sound reasonable. "But yes, I'll see her."

Ruth was due back late Sunday afternoon. At noon on Sunday, Seamus stirred himself from his lethargy and began to clean the apartment. They'd given up the once-a-week cleaning woman two years ago. Now they shared the chores, with Ruth's complaints a running part of the process. "Just what I need after being crushed on the Seventh Avenue subway to spend weekends pushing a vacuum." Last week she'd suddenly burst into tears. "I'm so damn tired."

At four o'clock the apartment was in decent shape. It needed painting. The linoleum in the kitchen was worn. The building had gone co-op, but they hadn't been able to afford to buy the place. Twenty years and nothing to show for it but rent receipts.

Seamus laid out cheese and wine on the cocktail table in the living room. The furniture was faded and shabby, but in the soft light of the late afternoon it didn't look bad. In three years more Jeannie would be finished school. Marcy was a senior this year. Linda a junior. Wishing your life away, he thought.

The closer it came time for Ruth to arrive, the more his hands trembled. Would she notice anything different about *him?*

She got home at five-fifteen. "The traffic was terrible," she announced, her voice querulous.

"Did you give them the certified check and explain about the other one?" he asked, trying to ignore the tone in her voice. It was her let's-have-this-out tone.

"I certainly did. And let me tell you, the bursar was shocked when I told him about Ethel Lambston collecting alimony from you all these years. They had Ethel on a panel at college six months ago, blasting off on women getting equal pay." Ruth accepted the glass of wine he handed her and took a long swallow.

With a shock he realized that somewhere along the way she'd picked up Ethel's habit of licking her lips after she finished an angry sentence. Was it true that you kept marrying the same person? The thought made him want to burst into hysterical laughter.

"Well, let's have it. Did you see her?" Ruth snapped.

A great weariness came over Seamus. The memory of that final scene. "Yes, I saw her."

"And . . ."

He chose his words carefully. "You were right. She doesn't want it to leak out that she's been collecting alimony from me all these years. She's going to let me off the hook."

Ruth set down the wineglass, her face transfigured. "I don't believe it. How did you talk her into it?"

Ethel's taunting, derisive laugh at his threatening and begging words. The jolt of primitive anger that had gone through him, the look of terror in her eyes . . . Her final threat . . . Oh God . . .

"Now when Ethel buys her precious Neeve Kearny clothes and eats high on the hog, *you* won't be paying." Ruth's triumphant laugh pounded against his eardrums as her words sank into his consciousness.

Seamus put down his wineglass. "What made you say that?" he asked his wife quietly.


On Saturday morning the snow was over and the streets were somewhat passable. Neeve brought all Ethel's clothes back to the shop.

Betty rushed to help her. "Don't tell me, she doesn't like *anything*?"

"How would I know?" Neeve asked. "There wasn't hide nor hair of her at her apartment. Honest to God, Betty, when I think of the way we rushed, I could wrap every stitch around her neck."

It was a busy day. They'd run a small ad in the *Times* showing the print dresses and the raincoats, and the response was enthusiastic. Neeve's eyes sparkled as she watched her clerks write up formidable sales slips. Once again, she silently blessed Sal for staking her six years ago.

At two o'clock, Eugenia, a black former fashion model who was now Neeve's second-in-command, reminded Neeve that she hadn't stopped for lunch. "I have some yogurt in the fridge," she offered.

Neeve had just finished helping one of her personal clients select a four-thousand-dollar mother-of-the-bride gown. She smiled quickly. "You know I hate yogurt. Send for a tuna-salad sandwich and a diet Coke, okay?"

Ten minutes later, when the order was delivered to her office, she realized she was starving. "The best tuna salad in New York, Denny," she told the delivery man.

"If you say so, Miss Kearny." His pale face creased into an ingratiating smile.

While she hurried through lunch, Neeve dialed Ethel's number. Once again, Ethel did not answer. Throughout the afternoon the receptionist continued to try to reach her. At the end of the day Neeve told Betty, "I'll take this stuff home once more. I sure don't want to waste my Sunday having to come back here because Ethel suddenly decides she's got a plane to catch and needs everything in ten minutes."

"Knowing her, she'd have the plane make a special trip to the gate if she'd missed it," Betty snapped.

They both laughed, but then Betty said quietly, "You

know those crazy feelings you get sometimes, Neeve. I swear they're catching. Pain in the neck that Ethel is, she never pulled anything like this before."

Saturday night, Neeve and Myles went to the Met to hear Pavarotti. "You should be out on a date," Myles complained as the waiter at the Ginger Man handed them after-theater supper menus.

Neeve glanced at him. "Look, Myles, I go out a lot. You know that. When someone important comes along, I'll know it, just the way you and Mother did. Now why don't you order me some shrimp scampi?"

Myles usually attended early Mass on Sunday. Neeve enjoyed sleeping late and going to the Pontifical Mass at the cathedral. She was surprised to find Myles in the kitchen in his bathrobe when she got up. "Giving up the faith?" she asked.

"No. I thought I'd go with you today." He tried to sound casual.

"Would that have anything to do with Nicky Sepetti's release from prison?" Neeve sighed. "Don't bother to answer."

After church they decided on brunch at Café des Artistes, then caught a movie in the neighborhood theater. When they got back to the apartment, Neeve again dialed Ethel Lambston's number, let the phone ring a half-dozen times, shrugged and raced Myles in their weekly contest to finish the *Times* puzzle first.

"A lovely, unraveling day," Neeve commented as she

bent over Myles's chair to kiss the top of his head after the eleven-o'clock news. She caught the look on his face. "Don't say it," she warned.

Myles pressed his lips together. He knew she was right. He'd been about to say, "Even if it's clear tomorrow, I wish you wouldn't jog alone."

The persistent ringing of the phone in Ethel Lambston's apartment did not go unnoticed.

Douglas Brown, Ethel's twenty-eight-year-old nephew, had moved into the apartment on Friday afternoon. He'd hesitated about taking the risk, but knew he could prove he'd been forced that day out of his illegal sublet.

"I just needed a place to stay while I found a new apartment." That would be his explanation.

He figured it would be better not to answer the phone. The frequent calls irritated him, but he did not want to advertise his presence. Ethel never wanted him to answer her phone. "None of your business who calls me," she'd told him. Other people might have been told the same thing.

He was sure it had been a wise decision not to answer the doorbell on Friday evening. The note slipped under the door into the foyer was about the clothes Ethel had ordered.

Doug smiled unpleasantly. That must have been the errand Ethel had scheduled for him.

Sunday morning Denny Adler waited impatiently in the sharp, gusty wind. Precisely at eleven o'clock, he saw a black Chevy approaching. With long strides, he hurried from the comparative shelter of Bryant Park onto the street. The car pulled over. He opened the passenger door and slid in. The car was moving even as he yanked the door closed.

In the years since Attica, Big Charley had gotten a lot grayer and put on more weight. The steering wheel was burrowed between the folds of his stomach. Denny said, "Hi," not expecting an answer. Big Charley nodded.

The car moved swiftly up the Henry Hudson Parkway and over the George Washington Bridge. Charley turned onto the Palisades Interstate Parkway. Denny noted that while the remaining snow in New York was slushy and soot-filled, the snow on the sides of the parkway was still white. New Jersey, the Garden State, he thought sarcastically.

Past Exit 3 there was a lookout point for people who, as Denny sometimes observed, had nothing better to do than stare at the New York landscape across the Hudson River. Denny was not surprised when Charley pulled into the deserted parking area there. This was where they'd discussed other jobs.

Charley turned off the ignition and reached back over the seat, groaning with the effort of stretching. He pulled up a paper bag containing a couple of cans of beer and dropped it between them. "Your brand."

Denny felt pleased. "Nice of you to remember, Charley." He opened the can of Coors.

Charley swallowed deeply from his own can before he replied, "I forget nothing." He drew an envelope from his inside pocket. "Ten thousand," he told Denny. "The same when the job is finished."

Denny accepted the envelope, taking sensual pleasure in its bulk. "Who?"

"You deliver lunch to her coupla times a week. She lives in Schwab House, that big place on Seventy-fourth between West End and Riverside Drive. Usually walks to and from work coupla times a week. Cuts through Central Park. Grab her handbag and waste her. Clean out the wallet and dump the bag so it looks like a junkie cut her. If you can't nail her in the park, the garment center might be it. She goes there every Monday afternoon. Those streets are packed. Everybody in a rush. Trucks double-parked. Brush by her, shove her in front of a truck. Take your time. It gotta look like an accident or a mugging. Follow her around in one of those panhandler outfits of yours." Big Charley's voice was thick and guttural, as though the rolls of fat around his neck were choking his vocal cords.

For Charley it had been a long speech. He took another deep draught from the beer can.

Denny began to feel uneasy. "*Who?*"

"Neeve Kearny."

Denny shoved the envelope toward Charley as though it contained a ticking bomb. "The Police Commissioner's daughter? Are you nuts?"

"The *ex*-Commissioner's daughter."

Denny could feel the perspiration on his brow. "Kearny was in office for sixteen years. Not a cop in the city who wouldn't risk his life for him. When his wife died they put the heat on everyone who ever stole an apple off a cart. No way."

There was an almost imperceptible change in Big Charley's expression, but his voice was the same guttural

51

monotone. "Denny, I told you I never forget. Remember all those nights in Attica when you used to brag about the jobs you got away with and how you did it? All I need to do is make a no-name-given call to the cops and you won't get to deliver another baloney sandwich. Don't make me a crime-stopper, Denny."

Denny considered and, remembering, cursed his own big mouth. Again he fingered the envelope and thought of Neeve Kearny. He'd been delivering to her shop for nearly a year now. It used to be that the receptionist would tell him to leave the bag with her, but now he went right back to the private office. Even if Kearny was on the phone, she'd wave and smile, a real smile, not that tight-lipped snobby nod that most of his customers gave him. She always told him how great everything tasted.

And she sure was a good-looking babe.

Denny shrugged off the moment of sentiment. It was a job he had to do. Charley wouldn't turn him in to the cops, and they both knew it. His knowledge of the contract had made him too dangerous. To refuse it meant that he'd never make it back to the George Washington Bridge.

He pocketed the money.

"That's better," Charley said. "What are your hours at the deli?"

"Nine to six. Mondays off."

"She leaves for work between eight-thirty and nine. Start hanging around her apartment building. The shop closes at six-thirty. Remember, take your time. *It can't look like a deliberate hit.*"

Big Charley started up the engine for the return trip to New York. Once again he fell into his customary silence, broken only by the grunting sound of his breathing. An overwhelming curiosity was consuming Denny. As Charley turned off the West Side Highway and drove across Fifty-seventh Street, Denny asked, "Charley, got any idea who ordered the job? She don't seem like the kind to get in anyone's way. Sepetti got sprung. Sounds like he's got a memory."

He felt the angry eyes flash in his direction. The guttural voice was now clear, and the words fell with the impact of a rock slide. "You're getting careless, Denny. I don't know who wants her wasted. The guy who contacted me don't know. The guy who contacted *him* don't know. That's how it works, and no questions asked. You're a small-time, small-mind bum, Denny, and some things are none of your business. Now *get out*."

The car stopped abruptly at the corner of Eighth Avenue and Fifty-seventh Street.

Uncertainly, Denny opened the door. "Charley, I'm sorry," he said. "It was just . . ."

The wind was whipping through the car. "Just shut up and make sure that job gets done right."

An instant later, Denny was staring at the back of Charley's Chevy as it disappeared down Fifty-seventh Street. He walked toward Columbus Circle, stopped at a street vendor for a hot dog and a Coke. When he had finished, he wiped his mouth with the back of his hand. His nerves began to settle. His fingers caressed the bulky envelope inside the pocket of his jacket.

"Might as well start earning my keep," he muttered to himself, and began to head up Broadway toward Seventy-fourth Street and West End Avenue.

At Schwab House, he sauntered casually around the

block, noting the Riverside Drive entrance to the building. No chance she'd use that. The West End Avenue one
was much more convenient.

Satisfied, he crossed the street and leaned against the
building directly opposite Schwab House. It would make
a great observation point, he decided. The door opened
near him, and a cluster of residents came out. He didn't
want to be observed, so he casually moved on, reflecting
that his wino outfit would make him blend into the background while he stalked Neeve Kearny.

At two-thirty, as he crossed town toward the East Side,
he passed a line of people waiting to buy tickets for the
movie. His narrow eyes widened. Halfway along the
queue Neeve Kearny was standing next to a white-haired
man whose face Denny recognized. Her father. Denny
hurried by, his head buried in his neck. And I wasn't
even looking for her, he thought. This is going to be the
easiest hit I ever made.

**4** On Monday morning, Neeve was in the lobby, her arms once again filled with Ethel's clothes, when Tse-Tse, a twenty-three-year-old actress, emerged breathlessly from the elevator. Her curly blond hair was early Phyllis Diller. Her eye makeup was violent shades of purple. Her small, pretty mouth had been painted into a Kewpie-doll bow. Tse-Tse, born

Mary Margaret McBride, "After guess who?" as she'd explained to Neeve, was always appearing in off-off-Broadway productions, most of which lasted less than a week.

Neeve had gone to see her several times and had been astonished at how really good Tse-Tse was. Tse-Tse could move a shoulder, droop a lip, change her posture and literally become someone else. She had an excellent ear for accents and could range her voice from a Butterfly McQueen high pitch to a Lauren Bacall throaty drawl. She shared a studio apartment in Schwab House with another aspiring actress and filled out her family's grudgingly small allowance with odd jobs. She'd given up waitressing and dog-walking in favor of cleaning. "Fifty bucks for four hours and you don't have to drag along a pooper-scooper," as she'd explained to Neeve.

Neeve had suggested Tse-Tse to Ethel Lambston, and she knew Tse-Tse cleaned for Ethel several times a month. Now she regarded her as a messenger from heaven. As the cab arrived, she explained her dilemma.

"I'm supposed to go there tomorrow," Tse-Tse explained breathlessly. "Honest to God, Neeve, that place is enough to drive me back to walking pit bulls. No matter how tidy I leave it, the next time it's always in shambles."

"I've seen it." Neeve considered. "Look, if Ethel doesn't pick up this stuff today, I'll take you there in a cab tomorrow morning and leave everything in her closet. You have a key, I guess."

"She gave me one about six months ago. Let me know. See you." Tse-Tse blew Neeve a kiss and started jogging down the street, a flamingo with her permed golden hair, her crazy makeup, her bright purple wooly jacket, red tights and yellow sneakers.

. . .

At the shop, Betty helped Neeve again hang Ethel's purchases on the Will Call rack in the sewing room. "This
has gone beyond Ethel's rattlebrain behavior," she said
quietly, a worried frown creasing the permanent furrows
in her forehead. "Do you think she's been in an accident?
Maybe we should report her missing."

Neeve piled the accessory boxes next to the rack. "I can
ask Myles to check about accident reports," she said, "but
it's too soon to report her missing."

Betty grinned suddenly. "Maybe she's found a boyfriend at last and is off somewhere on an ecstatic weekend."

Neeve glanced through the open door onto the sales
floor. The first customer had arrived, and a new saleswoman was showing her gowns that were absolutely un-
suitable for her. Neeve bit her lip. She knew she had
something of Renata's fiery temperament and had to
watch her tongue. "For Ethel's sake, I hope so," she commented, then with a welcoming smile went over to the
customer and the saleswoman. "Marian, why don't
you bring the green chiffon Della Rosa gown?" she suggested.

It was a briskly busy morning. The receptionist kept
trying Ethel's number. The last time she reported no response, Neeve had the fleeting thought that if Ethel had
met a man and ended up eloping, no one would cheer
louder than Ethel's former husband, who after twenty-
two years was still sending alimony checks every month.

. . .

Monday was Denny Adler's day off. He had planned to spend it following Neeve Kearny, but on Sunday evening there was a call for him at the public phone in the hallway of the rooming house.

The manager of the deli told Denny he'd have to come in to work the next day. The counterman had been fired. "I was figuring out the books and the sonofabitch had his hand in the till. I need you."

Denny swore silently. But it would be stupid to refuse. "I'll be there," he said sullenly. As he hung up, he thought of Neeve Kearny, the smile she'd given him the day before when he delivered lunch, the way that coal-black hair framed her face, the way her breasts filled out the fancy sweater she'd been wearing. Big Charley said that she went to Seventh Avenue on Monday afternoons. That meant there'd be no point trying to catch up with her after work. Maybe just as well. He'd made plans for Monday evening with the waitress at the bar across the street and hadn't wanted to break them.

As he turned to walk the dank, urine-smelling hallway back to his room, he thought, You won't get to be another Monday's child, Kearny.

Monday's child was fair of face. But not after a few weeks in the cemetery.

Monday afternoon was Neeve's usual time to spend on Seventh Avenue. She loved the bizarre bedlam of the Garment District, the crowded sidewalks, the delivery trucks double-parked on the narrow streets, the agile delivery boys manipulating racks of clothes through the traffic, the sense of everyone rushing, no time to spare.

She'd begun coming here with Renata when she was about eight years old. Over Myles's amused objections, Renata had taken a part-time job in a dress shop on Seventy-second Street, just two blocks from their apartment. Before long, the aging owner turned over to her the job of buying for the shop. Neeve could still visualize Renata shaking her head no as an overeager designer tried to persuade her to change her mind about an outfit.

"When a woman sits down in that dress, it will crawl up her back," Renata would say. Whenever she felt strongly, her Italian accent would leap into her voice. "A woman should get dressed, look in the mirror to make sure she doesn't have a run in her stocking, a drooping hem, and then she should forget what she is wearing. Her clothes should fit like a second skin." Renata had pronounced it "skeen."

But she also had an eye for new designers. Neeve still had the cameo pin one of them had presented to Renata. She had been the first to introduce his line. "Your mama, she gave me my first break," Jacob Gold would remind Neeve. "A beautiful lady, and she knew fashion. Like you." It was his highest compliment.

Today as Neeve wended her way from Seventh Avenue through the West Thirties, she realized she was vaguely distressed. There was a throbbing pain somewhere in her psyche, like an emotional sore tooth. She grumbled to herself, Before long, I'll be really one of those superstitious Irish, always getting a "feeling" about trouble around the corner.

At Artless Sportswear, she ordered linen blazers with matching Bermuda shorts. "I like the pastels," she murmured, "but they need a dynamite something."

"We're suggesting this blouse." The clerk, order pad in hand, pointed to a rack of pale nylon blouses with white buttons.

"Uh-uh. They belong under a school jumper." Neeve wandered through the showrooms, then spotted a multi-colored silk T shirt. "That's what I mean." She picked up several of the T shirts in different color patterns and brought them over to the suits. "This with the peach; that one with the mauve. Now we've got something going."

At Victor Costa, she chose romantic boat-necked chiffons that floated on the hangers. And once again Renata drifted into her mind. Renata in a black velvet Victor Costa, going to a New Year's Eve party with Myles. Around her throat she'd worn her Christmas present, a pearl necklace with a cluster of small diamonds.

"You look like a princess, Mommy," Neeve had told her. That moment had been imprinted on her memory. She'd been so proud of them. Myles, straight and elegant with his then prematurely white hair; Renata, so slender, her jet-black hair piled in a chignon.

The next New Year's Eve, a few people came to the apartment. Father Devin Stanton, who was now a bishop, and Uncle Sal, who was still struggling to make his mark as a designer. Herb Schwartz, Myles's deputy commissioner, and his wife. Renata had been dead seven weeks . . .

Neeve realized that the clerk was waiting patiently at her elbow. "I'm woolgathering," she apologized, "and it isn't the season for that, is it?"

She placed her order, went quickly to the next three houses on her list and then, as darkness began to fall, headed for her usual visit to Uncle Sal.

The showrooms of Anthony della Salva were now spread throughout the Garment District. His sportswear line was on West Thirty-seventh Street. His accessories on West Thirty-fifth. His licensing on Sixth Avenue. But Neeve knew she would find him in his main office on West Thirty-sixth. He had started there in a tiny two-room hole-in-the-wall. Now he occupied three sumptuously equipped floors. Anthony della Salva, *né* Salvatore Esposito from the Bronx, was a designer on a par with Bill Blass, Calvin Klein and Oscar de la Renta.

To Neeve's dismay, as she crossed Thirty-seventh Street she came face to face with Gordon Steuber. Meticulously dressed in a tan cashmere jacket over a brown-and-beige Scottish pullover, dark-brown slacks and Gucci loafers, with his blaze of curly brown hair, slender, even-featured face, powerful shoulders and narrow waist, Gordon Steuber could easily have had a successful career as a model. Instead, in his early forties, he was a shrewd businessman with an uncanny knack of hiring unknown young designers and exploiting them until they could afford to leave him.

Thanks to his young designers, his line of women's dresses and suits was exciting and provocative. He makes plenty without having to cheat illegal workers, Neeve thought as she stared coldly at him. And if, as Sal hinted, he was in income-tax trouble, good!

They passed each other without speaking, but it seemed to Neeve that anger emanated from his persona. She thought of hearing that people emitted an aura. I don't want to know the color of that aura right now, she thought as she hurried into Sal's office.

When the receptionist spotted Neeve, she rang through

immediately to the private office. An instant later, Anthony della Salva, "Uncle Sal," came bounding through the door. His cherubic face beamed as he hurried to embrace her.

Neeve smiled as she took in Sal's outfit. He was his own best ad for his spring line of menswear. His version of a safari outfit was a cross between a paratrooper's jumpsuit and Jungle Jim at his best. "I love it. It will be all over East Hampton next month," she said approvingly as she kissed him.

"It already is, darling. It's even the rage of Iowa City. That frightens me a little. I must be slipping. Come. Let's get out of this." On the way to his office, he stopped to greet some out-of-town buyers. "Are you being helped? Is Susan taking good care of you? Wonderful. Susan, show the lazy-time line. It will walk out of the store, I promise you."

"Uncle Sal, do you want to take care of those people?" Neeve asked as they cut through the showroom.

"Absolutely not. They'll waste two hours of Susan's time and end up buying three or four of the cheapest pieces in the place." With a sigh of relief he closed the door of his private rooms. "It's been a crazy day. Where does everyone get the money? I raised my prices again. They're outrageous and people are fighting to put in rush orders."

His smile was beatific. His round face had become puffy in the last years, and now his eyes crinkled till they were lost under his heavy lids. He and Myles and the Bishop had grown up in the same Bronx neighborhood, played stickball together, gone to Christopher Columbus High School together. It was hard to believe that he too was sixty-eight years old.

There was a jumble of swatches on his desk. "Can you beat this? We have an order to design interiors for scale-model Mercedes for three-year-olds. When I was three I had a secondhand red wagon, and one of the wheels kept falling off. Every time it did, my father beat me up for not taking care of my good toys."

Neeve felt her spirits lift. "Uncle Sal, honest to God I wish I had you on tape. I could make a fortune black-mailing you."

"You're too good-hearted. Sit down. Have a cup of coffee. It's fresh, I promise."

"I know you're busy, Uncle Sal. Five minutes only." Neeve unbuttoned her jacket.

"Will you drop the 'uncle' business? I'm getting too old to be treated with respect." Sal eyed her critically. "You look good, as usual. How's business?"

"Great."

"How's Myles? I see Nicky Sepetti got sprung Friday. I suppose that's tearing his guts out."

"He was upset Friday and pretty good over the weekend. Now I'm not sure."

"Invite me up to dinner this week. I haven't seen him for a month."

"You're on." Neeve watched as Sal poured coffee from the Silex on a tray beside his desk. She glanced around. "I love this room."

The wall covering behind the desk was executed in a mural of the Pacific Reef motif, the design that had made Sal famous.

Sal often told her about his inspiration for that line. "Neeve, I was in the Aquarium in Chicago. It was 1972. Fashion was a mess that year. Everyone sick of the miniskirt. Everyone afraid to try something new. The top designers were showing men-tailored suits, Bermuda shorts, skinny unlined suits. Pale colors. Dark colors. Ruffled blouses that belonged in boarding school. Nothing that makes a woman say, 'I want to look like that.' I was just wandering around the Aquarium and went up to the floor with the Pacific Reef exhibit. Neeve, it was like walking underwater. Tanks from floor to ceiling were filled with hundreds of exotic fish and plants and coral trees and shells. The colors on everything—you'd think Michelangelo painted them! The patterns and designs—dozens and dozens, every one unique. Silver blending into blue; coral and red entwined. One fish was yellow, bright as the morning sun, with black markings. And the flow, the grace of movement. I thought, If I can only do this with fabric! I started sketching right on the spot. I knew it was great. I won the Coty Award that year. I turned the fashion industry around. Couturier sales were fantastic. Licenses for the mass market and accessories. And all because I was smart enough to copy Mother Nature."

Now he followed her gaze. "That design. Wonderful. Cheerful. Elegant. Graceful. Flattering. It's still the best thing I ever did. But don't tell anyone. They haven't caught up with me yet. Next week I'll give you a preview of my fall line. The second-best thing I've ever done. Sensational. How's your love life?"

"It isn't."

"What about that guy you had to dinner a couple of months ago? He was crazy about you."

"The fact you can't remember his name says it all. He still makes a pile of money on Wall Street. Just bought a

Cessna and a co-op in Vail. Forget it. He had the personality of a wet noodle. I keep telling Myles and I'll tell you: When Mr. Right comes along, I'll know it."

"Don't wait too long, Neeve. You've been raised on the fairy-tale romance of your mother and father." Sal swallowed the last of his coffee with a great gulp. "For most of us, it don't work like that."

Neeve had a fleeting moment of amusement reflecting that when Sal was with close friends or ready to wax eloquent, the suave Italian accent disappeared and his native jargon took over.

Sal continued. "Most of us meet. We get a little interested. Then not so interested. But we keep seeing each other and gradually something happens. Not magic. Maybe just friendship. We accommodate. We may not like opera, but we go to the opera. We may hate exercise but start playing tennis or jogging. Then love takes over. That's ninety percent of the people in the world, Neeve. Believe me."

"Was that the way it happened for you?" Neeve asked sweetly.

"Four times." Sal beamed. "Don't be so fresh. I'm an optimist."

Neeve finished the coffee and got up feeling immensely cheered. "I think I am, too, but you help bring it out. How's Thursday for dinner?"

"Fine. And remember, I'm not on Myles's diet and don't say I should be."

Neeve kissed him goodbye, left him in his office and hurried through the showroom. With a practiced eye, she studied the fashions on his mannequins. Not brilliant but good. Subtle use of color, clean lines, innovative without being too daring. They'd sell well enough. She wondered about Sal's fall line. Was it as good as he claimed?

She was back in Neeve's Place in time to discuss the next window display with the decorator. At six-thirty, when she closed the shop, she began the now familiar job of carrying home Ethel Lambston's purchases. Once again there had been no message from Ethel; no response to the half-dozen phone calls. But at least there was an end in sight. Tomorrow morning she'd accompany Tse-Tse to Ethel's apartment and leave everything there.

That thought made her mind jump to a line from the poignant Eugene Field poem "Little Boy Blue": "He kissed them and put them there."

As she tightened her hold on the armful of slippery garment bags, Neeve remembered that Little Boy Blue had never returned to his pretty toys.

**5** | The next morning, Tse-Tse met her in the lobby promptly at eight-thirty. Tse-Tse was wearing her hair in braided coils pinned over her ears. A black velvet cape hung loosely from her shoulders to her ankles. Under it she was attired in a black uniform with a white apron. "I just got a part as a parlor-floor servant in a new play," she confided as she took boxes from Neeve's hands. "I thought I'd practice. If Ethel's there she gets a kick out of it when I'm in costume." Her Swedish accent was excellent.

Vigorous bell-ringing did not elicit a response at Ethel's apartment. Tse-Tse fumbled in her purse for the key. When she opened the door, she stepped aside and let Neeve precede her. With a sigh of relief, Neeve dropped the armful of clothes on the couch and started to straighten up. "There is a God," she murmured, then her voice trailed off.

A muscular young man was standing in the entrance of the foyer that led to the bedroom and bath. Obviously in the process of dressing, he was holding a tie in one hand. His crisp white shirt was not yet fully buttoned. His pale-green eyes, set in a face that with a different expression might have been attractive, were narrowed by an annoyed frown. His as yet uncombed hair fell over his forehead in a mass of curls. Neeve's startled response to his presence was replaced by the immediate sense that his tangled hair was the product of a body wave. From behind her, she heard Tse-Tse draw in her breath sharply.

"Who are you?" Neeve asked. "And why didn't you answer the door?"

"I think the first question is mine." The tone was sarcastic. "And I answer the door when I choose to answer it."

Tse-Tse took over. "You are Miss Lambston's nephew," she said. "I have seen your picture." The Swedish accent rose and fell from her tongue. "You are Douglas Brown."

"I know who I am. Would you mind telling me who *you* are?" The sarcastic tone did not abate.

Neeve felt her temper rising. "I'm Neeve Kearny," she said. "And this is Tse-Tse. She does the apartment for Miss Lambston. Do you mind telling me where Miss Lambston is? She claimed she needed these clothes on Friday and I've been carrying them back and forth ever since."

"So you're Neeve Kearny." Now the smile became insolent. "Number-three shoes go with beige suit. Carry number-three purse and wear box-A jewelry. Do you do that for everyone?"

Neeve felt her jaw harden. "Miss Lambston is a very good customer and a very busy woman. And *I'm* a very busy woman. Is she here, and if not, when is she coming back?"

Douglas Brown shrugged. Something of the animosity left him. "I have no idea where my aunt is. She asked me to meet her here Friday afternoon. She had an errand for me."

"Friday afternoon?" Neeve asked quickly.

"Yes. I got here and she wasn't around. I have a key and let myself in. She never came back. I made up the couch and stayed. I just lost my sublet, and the Y isn't my speed."

There was something too glib about the explanation. Neeve looked around the room. The couch on which she'd laid the clothes had a blanket and a pillow piled together at one end. Piles of papers were thrown on the floor in front of the couch. Whenever she'd been here before, the cushions were so covered with files and magazines it was impossible to see the upholstery. Stapled clippings from newspapers were jumbled on the dinette table. Because the apartment was street level, the windows were barred, and even the bars had been used as makeshift files. At the opposite end of the room, she could see into the kitchen. As usual, the countertops looked cluttered. The walls were haphazardly covered with carelessly framed pictures of Ethel, pictures that had been cut from newspapers and magazines. Ethel receiving the Magazine Award of the Year from the American Society of Journalists and Authors. That had been for her scathing article on welfare hotels and abandoned tenements. Ethel at the side of Lyndon and Lady Bird Johnson. She'd worked on his 1964 campaign. Ethel on the dais at the Waldorf with the Mayor the night *Contemporary Woman* had honored him.

Neeve was struck by a thought. "I was here early Friday evening," she said. "What time did you say you arrived?"

"About three. I never pick up the phone. Ethel has a thing about anyone answering it when she's not here."

"That's true," Tse-Tse said. For a moment she forgot her Swedish accent. Then it came back. "Yah, yah, it's true."

Douglas Brown slipped his tie over his neck. "I've got to get to work. Just leave Ethel's clothes, Miss Kearny." He turned to Tse-Tse. "And if you can find some way to clean this place up, that's fine, too. I'll pile my stuff together just in case Ethel decides to favor us with her presence."

Now he seemed in a hurry to get away. He turned and started for the bedroom.

"Just a minute," Neeve said. She waited until he stopped and looked over his shoulder. "You say you came around three o'clock on Friday. Then you must have been here when I was trying to deliver these clothes.

Would you mind explaining why you wouldn't answer the door that night? It could have been Ethel forgetting her key. Right?"

"What time did you get here?"

"Around seven."

"I'd gone out for something to eat. Sorry." He disappeared into the bedroom and pushed the door closed.

Neeve and Tse-Tse looked at each other. Tse-Tse shrugged. "I might as well get busy." Her voice was a singsong. "Yumpin' Yimminy, you could clean Stockholm faster than this place with all the junk around." She dropped the accent. "You don't suppose anything happened to Ethel, do you?"

"I've thought about having Myles call for accident reports," Neeve said. "Although I must say the loving nephew doesn't seem frantic with worry. When he gets out, I'll hang these things in Ethel's closet for her."

Douglas Brown emerged from the bedroom a moment later. Fully dressed in a dark-blue suit, a raincoat over his arm, his hair brushed into a thick, wavy coiffure, he looked sullenly attractive. He seemed surprised and not pleased that Neeve was still there.

"I thought you were so busy," he told her. "Are you planning to help clean?"

Neeve's lips narrowed ominously. "I'm planning to hang these clothes in your aunt's closet, so she'll be able to put her hands on them when she needs them, and then I intend to leave." She tossed her card at him. "You will let me know if you hear from her. I, for one, am getting concerned."

Douglas Brown glanced at the card and pocketed it. "I don't see why. In the two years I've lived in New York, she's pulled the disappearing act at least three times and usually managed to keep me cooling my heels in a restaurant or this place. I'm beginning to think she's certifiably nuts."

"Are you planning to stay until she returns?"

"I don't see that is any of your business, Miss Kearny, but probably yes."

"Do you have a card where I can reach you during business hours?" Neeve felt her temper rising.

"Unfortunately, at the Cosmic Oil Building, they don't have cards made for receptionists. You see, like my dear aunt, I'm a writer. Unfortunately, unlike her, I have not yet been discovered by the publishing world, so I keep body and soul together by sitting at a desk in Cosmic's lobby and confirming the appointments of visitors. It's not the job for a mental giant, but then Herman Melville worked as a clerk on Ellis Island, I believe."

"Do you consider yourself a Herman Melville?" Neeve did not try to conceal the sarcasm in her voice.

"No. I write a different sort of book. My latest is called *The Spiritual Life of Hugh Hefner.* So far no editor has seen the joke in it."

He was gone. Neeve and Tse-Tse looked at each other. "What a creep," Tse-Tse said. "And to think he's poor Ethel's only relative."

Neeve searched her memory. "I don't think she ever mentioned him to me."

"Two weeks ago when I was here, she was on the phone with him and real upset. Ethel squirrels money around the apartment, and she thought some of it was missing. She practically accused him of stealing it."

The dusty, crowded apartment suddenly made Neeve

feel claustrophobic. She wanted out of this place. "Let's get these clothes put away."

If Douglas Brown had slept on the couch the first night, it was clear he had been using Ethel's bedroom since then. There was an ashtray full of cigarettes on the night table. Ethel didn't smoke. The antique-white provincial furniture was, like everything else in the apartment, expensive but lost in clutter. Perfumes and a tarnished silver brush, comb and mirror set were scattered on the dresser. Ethel had notes to herself jammed into the large gold-framed mirror. Several men's suits, sports jackets and slacks were draped over a rose damask chaise longue. A man's suitcase was on the floor, shoved under the chaise.

"Even he didn't have the nerve to disturb Ethel's closet," Neeve observed. The back wall of the fairly large bedroom consisted of an elaborate closet that ran the length of the room. Four years ago when Ethel first asked Neeve to go through her closet, Neeve had told her that it was no wonder she never could put any outfits together. She needed more space. Three weeks later Ethel had invited Neeve back. She had led her to the bedroom and proudly displayed her new acquisition, a custom-built closet that had cost her ten thousand dollars. It had short poles for blouses, high poles for evening gowns. It was sectioned off so that coats hung in one area, suits in another, daytime dresses in another. There were shelves for sweaters and purses; racks for shoes; a jewelry unit with brass extensions shaped like branches of a tree, to hold necklaces and bracelets. A pair of ghoulishly real plaster hands were upraised as though in prayer, the fingers separated.

Ethel had pointed to them. "Don't they look as though they could strangle you?" she'd asked gleefully. "They're for rings. I told the guy from the closet place that I keep everything in marked boxes, but he said I should have this anyhow. Someday I'd be sorry if I didn't take it, he told me."

In contrast to the rest of the apartment, the closet was exquisitely neat. The clothes were hung precisely on the satin hangers. Zippers were fastened up to the top. Jackets were buttoned. "Ever since you started dressing her, people keep commenting on Ethel's clothes," Tse-Tse observed. "Ethel loves it." On the inside of the doors, Ethel had pasted the lists Neeve had given her, which accessories to wear with which outfits.

"I went through everything with Ethel last month," Neeve murmured. "We made room for the new stuff." She laid the clothes on the bed and began to peel the plastic bags from them. "Well, I'll just do what I'd have done if she were standing here. Get this load in place and tack up the list."

As she sorted and hung the new garments, she skimmed the contents of the closet. Ethel's sable coat. Her stone marten jacket. The red cashmere coachman coat. The Burberry. The herringbone cape. The white wraparound with caracul collar. The belted leather. Next came the suits. The Donna Karans, the Beenes, the Ultrasuedes, the— Neeve paused, the hangers with the two new suits still in her hand.

"Wait a minute," she said. She peered up at the top shelf. She knew that Ethel's Vuitton luggage consisted of four matching pieces in a tapestry motif. They were a garment-bag carryall with zippered pockets, a carry-on oversized tote, a large and a medium-sized suitcase. The garment bag, the tote and one suitcase were missing. "Good old Ethel," Neeve said as she hung the new suits in the closet. "She did take off. That beige ensemble with the mink collar is gone." She began poking through the racks. The white wool suit, the green knit, the black-and-white print. "So help me, she just packed up and took off. I swear I could choke her myself." She pushed her hair back from her forehead. "Look," she said, pointing at the list on the door and then the bare spots on the shelves. "She took everything she needed to get all gussied up. I guess the weather was so lousy, she decided she didn't need light spring things. Well, wherever she is, I hope it hits ninety degrees. *Che noiosa spera che muore di caldo*—"

"Easy, Neeve," Tse-Tse said. "Whenever you start lapsing into Italian, you're getting mad."

Neeve shrugged. "The blazes with it. I'll send my bill to her accountant. At least *he* has his head screwed on tight. He doesn't forget to pay on time." She looked at Tse-Tse. "What about *you?* Were you counting on getting paid today?"

Tse-Tse shook her head. "Last time she paid me in advance. I'm okay."


At the shop, Neeve related to Betty what had happened.

"You should charge her your cab fare and for personal-shopper assistance," Betty said. "That woman is the limit."

At noon when Neeve spoke to Myles, she told him what had happened. "And I was about to have you check the accident reports," she said.

"Listen, if a train saw that woman in its path, it would jump the track to duck her," Myles replied.

But, for some reason, Neeve's irritation did not last. Instead, the nagging, persistent feeling that something was wrong about Ethel's sudden departure stayed with her. It accompanied her when she closed up at six-thirty and rushed to the cocktail party in the St. Regis given by *Women's Wear Daily.* In the glitter of the fashionably dressed crowd, she spotted Toni Mendell, the elegant editor in chief of *Contemporary Woman,* and hurried over to her.

"Do you know how long Ethel will be gone?" she managed to ask over the din.

"I'm surprised she isn't here," Toni told her. "She said she was coming, but we all know Ethel."

"When is her fashion article due?"

"She turned it in Thursday morning. I had to have the lawyers go over it to make sure we don't get sued. They made us cut out a few things, but it's still wonderful. You heard about the big contract she has with Givvons and Marks?"

"No."

A waiter offered canapés, smoked salmon and caviar on toast points. Neeve helped herself to one. Toni mournfully shook her head. "Now that waists are back in, I can't afford even an olive." Toni was a size six. "Anyhow, the article is about the great looks of the last fifty years and the designers behind them. Let's face it, the subject has been done and done, but you know Ethel. She makes everything gossipy and fun. Then two weeks ago she got terribly mysterious. I gather the next day she charged into Jack Campbell's office and talked him into a contract for a book on fashion with a six-figure advance. She's probably holed up somewhere writing it."

"Darling, you look divine!" The voice came from somewhere behind Neeve.

Toni's smile revealed every one of her faultlessly capped teeth. "Carmen, I've left a dozen messages for you. Where have you been hiding yourself?"

Neeve began to edge away, but Toni stopped her. "Neeve, Jack Campbell just came in. He's that tall guy in the gray suit. Maybe he knows where you can reach Ethel."

By the time Neeve had made her way across the room, Jack Campbell was already surrounded. She waited, listening to the congratulations he was accepting. From the gist of the conversation, she gathered that he had just been made president and publisher of Givvons and Marks, that he had bought an apartment on East Fifty-second Street, and that he was sure he'd thoroughly enjoy living in New York.

She judged him to be in his late thirties, young for the job. His hair was dark brown and cut short. She suspected that if longer, it would have been quite curly. His body had the lean, taut look of a runner. His face was thin; his eyes were the same dark brown as his hair. His smile seemed genuine. It caused small crinkles to form at the corner of his eyes. She liked the way he bent his head forward to listen to the elderly editor who was speaking to him and then turned to someone else without seeming abrupt.

A real art, Neeve thought, the kind of thing politicians did naturally, but not many businessmen.

It was possible to keep observing him without being obvious. What was there about Jack Campbell that seemed familiar? Something. She'd met him before. But where?

A waiter passed and she accepted another glass of wine. Her second and last, but at least sipping it made her look busy.

"It's Neeve, isn't it?"

In the moment she'd turned her back to him, Jack Campbell had come over to her. He introduced himself. "Chicago, six years ago. You were on your way back from skiing and I'd been on a sales trip. We started talking five minutes before the plane landed. You were all excited about opening a dress shop. How did it work out?"

"Fine." Neeve vaguely remembered the exchange. She'd bolted out of the plane to make her connecting flight. Jobs. That was it. "Weren't you just starting work for a new publisher?"

"Yes."

"Obviously, it was a good move."

"Jack, there are some people I'd like you to meet." The editor in chief of *W* was plucking his sleeve.

"I don't want to keep you," Neeve said quickly. "But just one question. I understand Ethel Lambston is writing a book for you. Do you know where I can reach her?"

"I have her home number. Will that help?"

"Thanks, but I have it, too." Neeve lifted her hand in a quick, self-deprecating gesture. "I mustn't hold you up."

She turned and slipped through the crowd, suddenly

weary of the babble of voices and conscious that it had been a long day.

The usual cluster of people waiting for cabs crowded the sidewalk in front of the St. Regis. Neeve shrugged, walked to Fifth Avenue and started uptown. It was a pleasant enough evening. Maybe she'd cut through the park. A walk home would clear her head. But at Central Park South a cab deposited a fare directly in front of her. She hesitated, then held the door and got in. The idea of walking another mile in high heels was suddenly distinctly unattractive.

She did not see the frustrated expression on Denny's face. He had waited patiently outside the St. Regis and followed her up Fifth Avenue. When she began to head for the park he thought that his opportunity was at hand.

At two o'clock that morning, Neeve awakened from a sound sleep. She had been dreaming. She was standing in front of Ethel's closet, making a list.

A list.

"I hope she melts, wherever she is."

That was it. Coats. The sable. The jacket. The cape. The Burberry. The wraparound. The coachman. They were all there.

Ethel had turned in her article on Thursday. No one had seen her on Friday. Both days had been windy and miserably cold. There'd been a snowstorm on Friday. But every one of Ethel's winter coats was still in place, in her closet. . . .

79

. . .

Nicky Sepetti shivered in the cable-knit cardigan his wife had made for him the year he went to prison. It still fit at the shoulders, but now it hung loosely over his middle. He'd lost thirty pounds in prison.

It was only a block from his home to the boardwalk. Shaking his head impatiently at his wife's fussing—"Put on a scarf, Nicky, you've forgotten how strong the wind is from the ocean"—he pushed open the front door and closed it behind him. The tang of the salty air tickled his nostrils, and he breathed it appreciatively. When he was a kid growing up in Brooklyn, his mother used to take him down on the bus for a swim at Rockaway Beach. Thirty years ago he'd bought the house in Belle Harbor for a summer place for Marie and the kids. She'd moved here for good after his sentencing.

Seventeen years that ended last Friday! His first deep breath outside prison walls brought on waves of chest pain. "Avoid the cold," the doctors had cautioned him.

Marie had had a big dinner cooked, a sign, "Welcome Home, Nicky." He'd been so bushed that halfway through the meal he'd gone to bed. The kids had phoned, Nick Junior and Tessa. "Poppa, we love you," they said.

He hadn't let them visit him in prison. Tessa was just starting college when he went to jail. Now she was thirty-five, had two kids, lived in Arizona. Her husband called her Theresa. Nick Junior had changed his name to Damiano. That was Marie's maiden name. Nicholas Damiano, a CPA who lived in Connecticut.

"Don't come now," Nicky cautioned them. "Wait till the press isn't hanging around."

All weekend, he and Marie stayed in the house, two silent strangers, while the television cameras waited for him to come out.

But this morning they'd been gone. Stale news. That's all he was. A sick ex-con. Nicky breathed in the salt air and felt it fill his lungs.

A baldheaded guy in one of those crazy sweatsuits was jogging toward him, stopped. "Great to see you, Mr. Sepetti. You're looking great."

Nicky frowned. He didn't want to listen to that stuff. He *knew* how he looked. After he had showered, only half an hour ago, he'd studied himself fully and deliberately in the mirror on the bathroom door. Hair completely gone on top, but still thick around the fringes. When he started serving time, it had been black shot with silver: pepper and salt, the barber used to say. Now what was left of it was a faded gray or a dirty white, take your choice. The rest of the self-examination hadn't cheered him any. Protruding eyes that had always annoyed him, even when he was a pretty good-looking younger guy. Now they stuck out like marbles. A faint scar on his cheek that flamed against the pallor of his skin. The weight loss hadn't made him trim. Instead he looked saggy, like a pillow that had lost half its feathers. A man pushing sixty. He'd been forty-two when he went to jail.

"Yeah, I look great," he said. "Thanks." He knew that the guy who was blocking the sidewalk, beaming at him with a nervous, big-toothed smile, lived two or three houses up, but he couldn't remember his name.

He must have sounded annoyed. The jogger looked uncomfortable. "Anyhow. Glad you're back." His smile was forced now. "Terrific day, isn't it? Pretty cool, but you can tell spring is here."

If I want a weather report, I'll turn on the radio, Nicky thought, then raised his hand in a salute. "Yeah, yeah," he muttered. He walked quickly on until he reached the boardwalk.

The wind had whipped the ocean into a mass of churning foam. Nicky leaned on the guardrail remembering how when he was a kid he used to love to ride the waves. His mother was always hollering at him, "Don't go out so far. You'll drown. You'll see."

Restlessly he swung his body around and began walking down toward Beach Ninety-eighth Street. He'd go until he could see the roller coaster and then start back. The guys were coming to pick him up. They'd go to the club first and then have a celebration lunch on Mulberry Street. A sign of respect for him, but he didn't kid himself. Seventeen years was too long to be away. They'd gotten into stuff he never would have let them touch. The word was out that he was sick. They'd complete what they'd started in these last years. Ease him out. Take it or else.

Joey had been sentenced with him. Same amount of time. But Joey got out in six years. Joey was in charge now.

Myles Kearny. He could thank Kearny for those extra eleven years.

Nicky bent his head against the wind, still trying to cope with two bitter pills. His kids might claim they loved him, but they were embarrassed by him. When Marie went to visit them, she told their friends she was a widow.

Tessa. God, she'd been crazy about him when she was a little kid. Maybe he'd been wrong not to let her visit him all these years. Marie went to see her regularly. Out there, and in Connecticut, Marie called herself Mrs. Damiano. He wanted to see Tessa's kids. But her husband thought he should wait.

Marie. Nicky could feel the resentment in her for all the years she'd waited. It was worse than resentment. She tried to act glad to see him, but her eyes were cold and veiled. He could read her mind: "For what you did, Nicky, even among our friends we were outcasts." Marie was only fifty-four and looked ten years older. She worked in the personnel office of the hospital. She didn't have to, but when she took the job she'd told him, "I can't just sit in the house and look at four walls."

Marie. Nick Junior, no, *Nicholas,* Tessa, *no,* Theresa. Would they have been really sorry if he'd had a heart attack in prison? Maybe if he'd gotten out in six years like Joey it wouldn't have been too late. Too late for everything. The extra years he'd served because of Myles Kearny, and he'd still be there if they'd been able to figure a way to keep him in.

Nicky had passed Ninety-eighth Street before he realized he hadn't noticed the lumbering structure that was the ancient roller coaster, then was startled to see it had been torn down. He turned and began retracing his steps, shoving his chilled hands into his pockets, hunching his shoulders against the wind. The taste of bile was in his mouth, blotting out the fresh, salty tang of the sea on his lips. . . .

The car was waiting for him when he got home. Louie was behind the wheel. Louie, the one guy he could always turn his back to. Louie who didn't forget favors. "Any time you're ready, Don Sepetti," Louie said. "It's good to say that to you again." Louie meant it.

Nicky saw the hint of sullen resignation in Marie's eyes when he went into the house and changed his sweater for a suit jacket. He thought of the time in high school when he'd had to do a short-story report. He'd chosen a story about a guy who disappears and his wife thinks he's dead and "she comfortably settled herself into her life as a widow." Marie had comfortably settled herself into a life without him.

Face it. She didn't want him back. His children would be relieved if he vanished, Jimmy Hoffa style. Better yet, they'd like a nice, clean, natural death, one that didn't need explanations for their kids later on. If only they knew how close they were to having it all work out for them.

"Will you want supper when you come home?" Marie asked. "I mean, I'm on the noon-to-nine shift. Should I fix something and leave it in the refrigerator?"

"Forget it."

He was silent on the trip down the Fort Hamilton Parkway, through the Brooklyn–Battery Tunnel, into lower Manhattan. At the club, nothing had changed. Still a shabby storefront exterior. Inside, the card table with chairs grouped ready for the next game; the oversized, tarnished espresso machine; the pay telephone that everyone knew was tapped.

The only difference was in the attitude of the family. Oh sure, they clustered around him, paid their respects, smiled, phony welcoming smiles. But he knew.

He was glad when it was time to go to Mulberry Street.

Mario, the restaurant owner, at least seemed glad to see him. The private room was ready for them. The pastas and the entrees were his favorites from the years before jail. Nicky felt himself start to relax, felt some of the old power flow into his body. He waited until dessert was served, cannoli with rich, black espresso coffee, before he looked from face to face of the ten men who were sitting like two identical rows of tin soldiers. He nodded, acknowledging those on his right side, then those on his left. Two of the faces were new to him. The one was okay. The other was introduced to him as "Carmen Machado."

Nicky studied him carefully. About thirty, dark thick hair and eyebrows, blunt nose, scrawny, but tough. He'd been around three, four years. Been in the slammer for auto theft when Alfie got to know him, they said. Instinctively Nicky did not trust him. He'd button Joey down on how much they really knew about him.

His eyes came to rest on Joey. Joey who had gotten out in six years, who had taken over control while he, Nicky, was locked up. Joey's round face was creased in lines that passed for a smile. Joey looked like the cat who swallowed the canary.

Nicky realized his chest was burning. Suddenly the dinner was lying heavy in his stomach. "Okay, so tell me," he ordered Joey. "What's on your mind?"

Joey continued to smile. "With respect, I got great news for you. We all know how you feel about sonofabitch Kearny. Wait till you hear this. There's a contract out on his daughter. *And it's not ours.* Steuber is gonna waste her. It's almost like a gift to you."

Nicky jumped up and slammed his fist on the table. Awash with rage, he hammered the heavy oak. "You stu-

Mary Higgins Clark

pid bastards!" he shouted. "You stinking, stupid bastards! Get it called off." He had a momentary impression of Carmen Machado, and suddenly knew he was looking into the face of a cop. "Get it called off. I tell you to get it called off, understand?"

Joey's expression turned from fear to concern to pity. "Nicky, you have to know that's impossible. Nobody can cancel a contract. It's too late."

Fifteen minutes later, beside a silent Louie at the driver's wheel, Nicky was on his way home to Belle Harbor. His chest was aflame with waves of pain. The nitroglycerin under his tongue was useless. When Kearny's kid got hit, the cops wouldn't stop till they hung it on him, and Joey knew it.

Drearily he realized he'd been a fool to warn Joey about Machado. "No way that guy worked in Florida for the Palino family," he'd told Joey. "You were too dumb to check him out, right? You stupid bastard, every time you open your mouth you're spilling your guts to a cop."

On Tuesday morning Seamus Lambston woke after four hours of sleep that had been plagued with troubled dreams. He'd closed up the place at two-thirty, read the paper for a while and silently crept into bed trying not to disturb Ruth.

When the girls were young, he'd been able to sleep later, get to the bar at noon, come home for an early dinner with the family and then go back till closing. But in the last years as business fell off in a relentlessly unchanging pattern and the rent doubled and doubled again, he'd let bartenders and waiters go and cut down on the food until now he had only a sandwich menu. He did all the buying himself, got to the place by eight or eight-thirty and, except for a rushed dinner, stayed until closing. And he still couldn't keep his head above water.

Ethel's face had haunted his dreams. The way her eyes bulged when she was angry. The sardonic smile that he'd eradicated from her face.

When he'd arrived at her place on Thursday afternoon, he'd pulled out a snapshot of the girls. "Ethel," he'd pleaded, "look at them. They need the money I'm paying you. Give me a break."

She had taken the picture and studied it carefully. "They should have been mine," she said as she handed it back to him.

Now his stomach squeezed in apprehension. His alimony payment was due on the fifth. Tomorrow. Did he dare not write the check?

It was seven-thirty. Ruth was already up. He could hear the splashing of the shower. He got out of bed and walked into the room that served as den and office. It was already harshly bright from the rays of the early-morning sun. He sat at the rolltop desk that had been in his family for three generations. Ruth hated it. She wanted to be able to replace all their old heavy furniture with modern pieces in light, airy colors. "In all these years, I've never bought so much as a new chair," she liked to remind him. "You left Ethel all your good furniture when you broke up, and I've had to live with the junk from your mother. The only new furniture I ever had were the cribs and beds for the girls and nothing like what I wanted for them."

Seamus put off the agony of decision about Ethel's check by writing some of the others. The gas and electric, the rent, the telephone. They'd canceled cable TV six months ago. That saved twenty-two dollars a month.

From the kitchen he heard the sound of the coffeepot being put on the stove. A few minutes later Ruth came into the den, with a glass of orange juice and a cup of steaming hot coffee on a small tray. She was smiling and for an instant reminded him of the quietly pretty woman he'd married three months after his divorce. Ruth was not given to affectionate gestures, but when she set the tray on the desk she bent down and kissed the top of his head.

"Seeing you write the monthly checks makes it really sink in," she said. "No more money to Ethel. Oh God, Seamus, we can finally begin to breathe. Let's celebrate tonight. Get someone to cover for you. We haven't gone out to dinner in months."

Seamus felt the muscles in his stomach twist. The rich smell of the coffee suddenly made him nauseous. "Honey, I just hope she doesn't change her mind," he faltered. "I mean I haven't got anything in writing. Do you think I should just send the check as usual and let her return it? I really think that would be best. Because then we'd have something legal, I mean, proof that she said it was okay to stop paying."

His voice choked to a gasp as a stinging slap snapped his head over his left shoulder. He looked up and winced at the murderous outrage on Ruth's face. He had seen that look on another face only a few days ago.

Then Ruth's expression dissolved into bright-red spots on her cheekbones and weary tears that welled in her eyes. "Seamus, I'm sorry. I just snapped." Her voice broke. She bit her lip and straightened her shoulders. "But *no more checks.* Let her try to go back on her word. I'll kill her myself rather than let you pay her another dime."

**6** On Wednesday morning, Neeve told Myles about her concern over Ethel. Frowning as she spread cream cheese on a toasted bagel, she voiced the thoughts that had kept her awake half the night. "Ethel is rattlebrained enough to fly off without her new clothes, but she had made a date with her nephew for Friday."

"Or so he claims," Myles interjected.

"Exactly. I do know that on Thursday she turned in the article she was writing. Thursday was freezing cold, and it started to snow late in the day. Friday was like the middle of winter."

"You're turning into a meteorologist," Myles observed.

"Come on, Myles. I think something might be wrong. All of Ethel's warm coats were in her closet."

"Neeve, that woman will live forever. I can just see God and the Devil telling each other, 'Take her, she's yours.' " Myles smiled, enjoying his joke.

Neeve made a face at him, exasperated that he was not taking her concern seriously, but grateful for the bantering tone. The kitchen window was open a few inches, bringing in a breeze from the Hudson, a hint of salt that managed to camouflage the inevitable exhaust fumes of the thousands of cars that traveled the Henry Hudson Parkway. The snow was vanishing in the same abrupt manner it had arrived. Spring was in the air and maybe that fact had helped Myles's spirits. Or was there something else?

Neeve got up, went over to the stove, reached for the coffeepot and freshened both their cups. "You seem pretty chipper today," she commented. "Does that mean you've stopped worrying about Nicky Sepetti?"

"Let's just say I spoke to Herb and I'm satisfied that Nicky won't be able to brush his teeth without one of our boys gazing at his cavities."

"I see." Neeve knew better than to ask Myles any more about that. "Well, as long as you stop fussing over me." She looked at her watch. "I've got to get moving." At the door, she hesitated. "Myles, I know Ethel's wardrobe like the back of my hand. She vanished on Thursday or Friday in bitterly cold weather without a coat. How would you explain that?"

Myles had started to read the *Times*. Now he put it down, his expression patient. "Let's play the pretend game," he suggested. "Let's pretend that Ethel may have seen a coat in someone else's show window and decided it was just what she wanted."

The pretend game had started when Neeve was four and had helped herself to a forbidden can of soda. She'd looked up from the open refrigerator door, where she was blissfully draining the last drop, to see Myles eying her sternly. "I've got a good idea, Daddy," she'd said hurriedly. "Let's play the pretend game. Let's pretend the Coke is apple juice."

Neeve suddenly felt foolish. "That's why you're the cop and I run a dress shop," she said.

But by the time she had showered and dressed, in a boxy cocoa-brown cashmere jacket with bracelet sleeves and turned-back cuffs and a softly gathered black wool midcalf skirt, she had located the fallacy in Myles's thinking. Long ago the Coke hadn't been apple juice, and right now she'd stake everything she had that Ethel hadn't purchased a coat from anyone else.

On Wednesday morning, Douglas Brown awakened early and began to expand his domination over Ethel's apartment. It had been a pleasant surprise on returning from work last night to find it sparkling clean and as reasonably tidy as any human being could make it, given Ethel's massive piles of papers. He'd found some frozen meals in the freezer, selected a lasagna and sipped a cold beer while it heated. Ethel's television set was one of the new massive forty-inch units, and he'd set up a tray in the living room, eating while he watched.

Now, from the luxury of her silk-sheeted four-poster bed, he eyed the contents of the bedroom. His suitcase was still on the chaise, his suits draped over the back on hangers. Screw it. It wouldn't be smart to start using that precious closet of hers, but no reason he couldn't settle into the other one.

The front closet was clearly a catchall. He managed to arrange the photo albums and stacks of catalogues and piles of magazines so that he could use the clothes pole for his suits.

While coffee perked, he showered, appreciating the sparkling white tile, the fact that Ethel's rubble of perfume bottles and lotions was now neatly arranged on the glass tray to the right of the door. Even the towels were folded in the bathroom linen closet. That thought brought on a frown. The money. Had that Swedish kid who cleaned for Ethel found the money?

The thought made Doug jump from the shower, rub his lean body vigorously, wrap the towel around his middle and rush to the living room. He'd left a single hundred-dollar bill under the carpet near the wing chair. It was still there. So either the Swedish kid was honest or she hadn't noticed it.

Ethel was such a dope, he reflected. When that check came in every month from her ex, she had it cashed into one-hundred-dollar bills. "My mad money," she told Doug. That was the money she used when she took him out to dinner in an expensive restaurant. "They're eating beans and we're dining on caviar," she'd say. "Sometimes I go through it all in a month. Sometimes it piles up. Every so often I look around and send the leftover bucks to my accountant toward clothes. Restaurants and clothes. That's what the stupid worm has kept me in all these years."

Doug had laughed with her, clicking glasses as they toasted Seamus the worm. But that night he'd realized that Ethel never kept track of how much cash she had hidden around and so would never miss a couple of hundred bucks a month. Which was what he'd helped himself to these last two years. A couple of times she'd half suspected, but the minute she said anything he'd acted indignant, and she'd always backed right off. "If you'd just write down when you spend that money, you'd *see* where it goes," he'd shouted.

"I'm sorry, Doug," Ethel had apologized. "You know me. I get a bee in my bonnet and start shooting off my mouth."

He blotted out the memory of that last conversation when she'd demanded that he run an errand for her on Friday and told him not to expect a tip. "I took your advice," she said, "and kept track of what I spent."

He'd rushed over here, sure of his ability to sweet-talk her, knowing that if she dumped him she'd have nobody she could order around. . . .

When the coffee was ready, Doug poured a cup, went back into the bedroom and dressed. As he knotted his tie, he surveyed himself critically in the mirror. He looked good. The facials he'd started having with the money he pilfered from Ethel had cleared up his skin. He'd also found a decent barber. The two suits he'd bought recently fitted him the way clothes were supposed to fit. The new receptionist at Cosmic had big eyes for him. He had let her know that he was only doing this crummy desk job because he was writing a play. She knew Ethel's name. "And you're a writer, too," she'd breathed in awe. He wouldn't mind bringing Linda here. But he had to be careful, for a while at least. . . .

Over a second cup of coffee, Doug methodically went through the papers in Ethel's desk. There was one cardboard expansion folder marked "Important." As he flipped through it, his face drained of color. That old windbag Ethel had blue-chip stocks! She had property in Florida! She had a million-dollar insurance policy!

There was a copy of her will in the last section of the folder. He couldn't believe his eyes when he read it.

Everything. Every single dime she had had been left to him. And she was worth a bundle.

He'd be late for work, but it didn't matter. Doug restored his clothes to the back of the chaise, made the bed carefully, got rid of the ashtray, folded a quilt, a pillow and sheets on the couch to suggest he'd slept there, and wrote a note: "Dear Aunt Ethel. Guess you're on one of your unexpected trips. Knew you wouldn't mind if I continue to bunk on the couch until my new place is ready. Hope you've been having fun. Your loving nephew, Doug."

And that establishes the nature of our relationship, he thought as he saluted Ethel's picture on the wall by the front door of the apartment.

At three o'clock on Wednesday afternoon, Neeve left a message at Tse-Tse's answering service. An hour later,

Tse-Tse phoned. "Neeve, we just had a dress rehearsal. I think the play is great," she exulted. "All I do is pass the turkey and say, 'Yah,' but you never know. Joseph Papp might be in the audience."

"You'll be a star yet," Neeve said, meaning it. "I can't wait to brag 'I knew her when.' Tse-Tse, I have to get back into Ethel's apartment. Do you still have her key?"

"Nobody's heard from her?" Tse-Tse's voice lost its lilt. "Neeve, there's something weird going on. That nutty nephew of hers. He's sleeping in her bed and smoking in her room. Either he doesn't expect her back or he doesn't care if she tosses him out on his ear."

Neeve stood up. Suddenly she felt cramped behind her desk, and the samples of gowns and purses and jewelry and shoes strewn about her office seemed terribly unimportant. She'd changed to a two-piece dress from one of her newest designers. It was a pale-gray wool with a silver belt that rested on her hips. The tulip skirt barely skimmed her knees. A silk scarf in tones of gray, silver and peach was knotted at her neck. Two customers had ordered the outfit when they saw her wearing it on the sales floor.

"Tse-Tse," she asked, "would it be possible for you to go to Ethel's apartment again tomorrow morning? If she's there, fine. Admit you were worried about her. If the nephew is around, could you say that Ethel wanted you to do some extra work, clean out the kitchen cabinets or whatever?"

"Sure," Tse-Tse agreed. "I'd love to. This is off-off-Broadway, don't forget. No salary, just prestige. But I have to tell you, Ethel isn't worried about the state of her kitchen cabinets."

"If she turns up and doesn't want to pay you, I will," Neeve said. "I want to go with you. I know she has an appointment book in her desk. I'd just like to have some kind of idea about what plans she may have made before she disappeared."

They agreed to meet at eight-thirty the next morning in the lobby. At closing time, Neeve turned the lock on the Madison Avenue entrance to the store. She went back into her office for a quiet time over desk work. At seven she phoned the Cardinal's residence on Madison Avenue and was put through to Bishop Devin Stanton.

"I got your message," he told her. "I'll be delighted to come up to dinner tomorrow night, Neeve. Sal's coming? Good. The Three Musketeers from the Bronx don't get together enough these days. Haven't seen Sal since Christmas. Has he gotten married again, by any chance?"

Just before he said goodbye the Bishop reminded Neeve that his favorite dish was her pasta al pesto. "The only one who could make it better was your mother, God rest her," he said gently.

Devin Stanton did not usually refer to Renata in a casual phone call. Neeve had a sudden suspicion that he'd been chatting with Myles about Nicky Sepetti's release. He rang off before she could pin him down about that. You'll get your pesto, Uncle Dev, she thought—but you'll also get a flea in your ear. I can't have Myles hovering over me for the rest of my life.

Just before she left, she phoned Sal's apartment. As usual, he was in bubbling good humor. "Of course I haven't forgotten tomorrow night. What are you having? I'll bring the wine. Your father only thinks he knows about wine."

Laughing with him, Neeve replaced the receiver, turned off the lights and went outside. The capricious April weather had turned cool again, but even so she felt the absolute need for a long walk. To appease Myles, she hadn't jogged in nearly a week, and her entire body felt stiff.

She walked rapidly from Madison to Fifth Avenue and decided to cut through the park at Seventy-ninth Street. She always tried to avoid the area behind the museum where Renata's body had been found.

Madison Avenue had still been busy with cars and pedestrians. On Fifth, the taxis and limousines and shiny town cars whizzed by quickly, but on the west side of the street, bordering the park, there were few people. Tossing her head as she approached Seventy-ninth Street, Neeve refused to be deterred.

She was just turning into the park when a squad car pulled up. "Miss Kearny." A smiling sergeant rolled down the window. "How's the Commissioner doing?"

She recognized the sergeant. At one point he had been Myles's driver. She went over to chat with him.


A few paces behind her, Denny stopped abruptly. He was wearing a long, nondescript overcoat with the collar turned up and a stocking cap. His face was almost concealed. Even so he could feel the eyes of the cop at the passenger window of the squad car boring into him. Cops had long memories about faces, could recognize ones they knew even from glimpses of their profiles. Denny knew that. Now he resumed walking, ignoring Neeve, ignoring the cops, but he could still feel eyes following him. There was a bus stand directly ahead. As a bus pulled up, he joined the cluster of waiting people and got on it. When he paid his fare, he could feel the perspiration forming on his forehead. Another second and that cop might have recognized him.

Sullenly Denny took a seat. This job was worth more than he was being paid. When Neeve Kearny went down, forty thousand New York cops would be on a manhunt.

As Neeve entered the park, she wondered whether it was just coincidence that Sergeant Collins had happened to spot her. Or, she speculated as she walked rapidly along the path, has Myles got New York's finest playing guardian angel to me?

There were plentiful joggers, few bicyclers, some pedestrians, a tragic number of homeless resting under layers of newspapers or ragged blankets. They could die there and no one would notice, Neeve thought as her soft Italian boots moved soundlessly along the paths. To her annoyance she found herself glancing over her shoulder. In her teens she had gone to the library and looked up the pictures in the tabloids of her mother's body. Now, as she hurried with increasingly rapid steps, she had the eerie feeling that she was seeing the pictures again. But this time it was her face, not Renata's, that covered the front page of the *Daily News* above the caption "Murdered."

Kitty Conway had joined the riding class at Morrison State Park for only one reason. She needed to fill time.

She was a pretty woman of fifty-eight, with strawberry blonde hair and gray eyes that were enhanced by the fine lines that edged and framed them. There was a time those eyes had always seemed to dance with an amused and impish glow. When she turned fifty, Kitty had protested to Michael, "How come I still feel twenty-two?"

"Because you *are* twenty-two."

Michael had been gone for nearly three years. As Kitty gingerly hoisted herself up on the chestnut mare, she thought of all the activities she'd become involved in during these three years. She now had a real-estate license and was a pretty darn good saleswoman. She'd redecorated the house in Ridgewood, New Jersey, which she and Michael had bought only the year before she lost him. She was active in the Literacy Volunteers. She volunteered one day a week at the museum. She'd made two trips to Japan, where Mike Junior, her only child, a career army officer, was stationed, and had delighted in spending time with her half-Japanese granddaughter. She'd also resumed piano lessons without enthusiasm. Twice a month she drove disabled patients to doctor appointments, and now the latest activity was horseback riding. But no matter what she did, no matter how many friends she enjoyed, she was always haunted by the feeling of aloneness. Even now, as she gamely fell in with the dozen other student riders behind the instructor, she found only profound sadness in observing the aura around the trees, the reddish glow that was a promise of spring. "Oh, Michael," she whispered, "I wish it would get better. I'm really trying."

"How are you making out, Kitty?" the instructor yelled.

"Fine," she shouted.

"If you want to be fine, keep your reins short. Show her you're boss. And keep those heels down."

"Gotcha." Go to hell, Kitty thought. This damn nag is the worst of the lot. I was supposed to have Charley, but of course you assigned him to that sexy-looking new girl.

It was a steep climb up the trail. Her horse stopped to eat every piece of green along the way. One by one, the others in the group passed her. She didn't want to get separated from them. "Come on, damn you," she murmured. She kicked her heels against the horse's flanks.

In a sudden, violent movement, the mare threw back her head, then reared. Startled, Kitty pulled at the reins as the animal swerved down a side path. Frantically she tried to remember not to lean forward. Sit *back* when you're in trouble! She felt the loose stones slide under the hoofs. The uneven canter changed to a full gallop, downhill, over the uneven ground. Dear God, if the horse fell, it would crush her! She tried to slide her boots so that only the tips were still in the stirrups, so as not to get hung up if she fell.

From behind, she heard the instructor yelling, "Don't pull on the reins!" She felt the horse stumble as a rock gave way under its hind leg. It started to pitch forward, then regained its balance. A piece of black plastic flew up and grazed Kitty's cheek. She looked down, and an impression of a hand framed by a bright-blue cuff darted through her mind and was gone.

The horse reached the bottom of the rocky incline and, taking the bit between its teeth, galloped flat out toward the stable. Kitty managed to hang on till the last moment, when she went flying from the saddle as the mare came to an abrupt stop at the watering trough. She felt every bone in her body bounce as she hit the ground, but she was able to pull herself to her feet, shake her arms and legs and move her head from side to side. Nothing seemed to be badly strained or broken, thank God.

The instructor galloped up. "I told you, you gotta *control* her. You're the boss. You okay?"

"Never better," Kitty said. She started for her car. I'll see you in the next millennium."


A half hour later, gratefully reclining in her steaming, churning bathtub Jacuzzi, she began to laugh. So an equestrian I'm not, she decided. That's it for the sport of kings. I'll just jog like a sensible human being from now on. Mentally she relived the harrowing experience. It probably hadn't lasted more than two minutes, she thought. The worst part was when that miserable nag slipped. . . . The image of the plastic flying past her face returned. And then, that impression of a hand in a sleeve. How ridiculous. But still, she *had* seen it, had she not?

She closed her eyes, enjoying the soothing, whirling water, the scent and feel of the bath oil.

Forget it, she told herself.


The sharply cool evening caused the heat to go on in the apartment. Even so, Seamus felt chilled to the soul. After pushing a hamburger and French fries around on his plate, he gave up the pretense of eating. He was aware of Ruth's eyes boring into him across the table. "Did you do it?" she asked finally.

"No."

"Why not?"

"Because it might just be better to let it go."

"I told you to put it in writing. Thank her for agreeing that you need the money and she doesn't." Ruth's voice began to rise. "Tell her that in these twenty-two years you've paid her nearly a quarter of a million dollars on top of a big settlement and it's obscene to want more for a marriage that lasted less than six years. Congratulate her on the big contract she has for her new book and say that you're glad she doesn't need the money but your kids sure do. Then sign the letter, and drop it in her mailbox. We'll keep a copy of it. And if she squawks, there won't be a person alive who doesn't know what a greedy phony she is. I'd like to see how many colleges drape her with honorary degrees if she reneges."

"Ethel thrives on threats," Seamus whispered. "She'd turn a letter like that around. She'd make the alimony payments sound like a triumph for womankind. It's a mistake."

Ruth shoved the plate aside. "Write it!"

They had an old Xerox machine in the den. It took three attempts before they had a clear copy of the letter. Ruth handed Seamus his coat. "Now march yourself over and stick that in her mailbox."

He elected to walk the nine blocks. His head sunk in misery, his hands jammed into his pockets, he fingered the two envelopes he was carrying. One held a check. He had taken it from the back of the checkbook and written it without Ruth's knowledge. The letter was in the other envelope. Which one should he put into Ethel's box? As though she were standing before him, he could see her reaction to the note. With equal clarity, he could visualize what Ruth would do if he left the check.

He turned the corner of West End Avenue onto Eighty-second Street. There were still plenty of people out. Young couples, shopping on the way home from work, their arms filled with groceries. Well-dressed middle-agers, flagging cabs, off to expensive dinners and the theater. Derelicts huddled against brownstones.

Seamus shivered as he reached Ethel's building. The mailboxes were in the vestibule inside the locked main door at the top of the steps. Whenever he was down to the wire with the check, he'd ring the bell for the superintendent, who'd let him in to drop the check into Ethel's mailbox. But today that wasn't necessary. A kid he recognized as living on the fourth floor brushed past him and started up the steps. On impulse he grabbed her arm. She turned, looking scared. She was a bony-looking kid, thin face, sharp features. Maybe about fourteen years old. Not like his girls, Seamus thought. From somewhere in their genes, they'd received pretty faces, warm, loving smiles. A moment of profound regret washed over him as he pulled out one of the envelopes. "Would you mind if I went into the vestibule with you? I have to put something in Miss Lambston's mailbox."

The cautious expression faded. "Oh sure. I know who you are. You're her ex. It must be the fifth of the month. That's when she always says you deliver the ransom." The girl laughed, showing gaping spaces between her teeth.

Wordlessly, Seamus fumbled in his pocket for the envelope and waited as she unlocked the door. The murderous rage washed over him again. So he was the laughingstock of the building!

The mailboxes were directly inside the outer door. Ethel's was fairly full. He still didn't know what to do. Should he leave the check or the letter? The girl waited by the inner door, watching him. "You're just on time," she said. "Ethel told my mother she yanks you right into court when you're late with her check."

Panic swept over Seamus. It would have to be the check. He grabbed the envelope from his pocket and tried to force it down the narrow slit in the mailbox.

When he arrived home, he nodded yes to Ruth's fiercely angry question. He could not at this moment stand the explosion that would occur when he admitted he'd dropped off the alimony. After she stalked out of the room, he hung up his coat and took the second envelope from his pocket. He glanced into it. It was empty.

Seamus sank into a chair, his body trembling, bile rising in his throat, his head in his hands. He had managed to fumble again. He had put the check and the letter into the same envelope, and now they were in Ethel's mailbox.

Nicky Sepetti spent Wednesday morning in bed. The burning in his chest was even worse than last night. Marie was in and out of the bedroom. She brought in a tray with orange juice, coffee, fresh Italian bread spread thick with marmalade. She pestered him to let her call a doctor.

Louie arrived at noon, shortly after Marie went to work. "With respect, Don Nicky, you look real sick," he said.

Nicky told him to watch television downstairs. When he was ready to go to New York, he'd let him know.

Louie whispered, "You were right about Machado. They got him." He smiled and winked.

In early evening, Nicky got up and began to dress. He'd be better off on Mulberry Street, and it wouldn't be good for anyone to guess how sick he really was. As he reached for his jacket, his skin became damp with perspiration. Holding on to the poster of the bed, he eased himself down, loosened his tie and shirt collar and lay back on the bed. For the next hours, the chest pain kept swelling and receding like a giant wave. Under his tongue, his mouth began to burn from the nitroglycerin tablets he kept swallowing. They did nothing to ease the pain, only gave him the familiar sharp, brief headache as they melted.

Faces began drifting past his vision. His mother's face: "Nicky, don't hang around with those guys. Nicky, you're a good boy. Don't get into trouble." Proving himself to the mob. No job too big or too small. But never women. That dumb remark he'd made in the courtroom. Tessa. He'd really like to see Tessa once more. Nicky Junior. No, *Nicholas. Theresa and Nicholas.* They'd be glad he'd died in bed like a gentleman.

From far away he heard the front door open and close. Marie must have come in. Then the doorbell ringing, a hard and demanding sound. Marie's angry voice. "I don't know if he's home. What do you want?"

I'm home, Nicky thought. Yeah. I'm home. The bedroom door swung fully open. Through glazed eyes, he saw the shock on Marie's face, heard her shriek, "Get a doctor." Other faces. Cops. They didn't have to be in uniform. He could smell them even when he was dying. Then he knew why they were there. That undercover guy, the one they'd wasted. Right away the cops had come to him, of course!

"Marie," he said. It came out a whisper.

She bent over, put her ear to his lips, smoothed his forehead. "Nicky!" She was crying.

"On . . . my . . . mother's . . . grave . . . I . . . didn't . . . order . . . Kearny's wife killed." He wanted to say that he'd intended to try to get the contract on Kearny's kid stopped. But all he managed to cry was "Mama" before a last blinding, tearing pain ripped through his chest, and his eyes went out of focus. His head slumped over on the pillow as his agonized breathing filled the house, and abruptly stopped.

How many people had Bigmouth Ethel told that she thought he was helping himself to the money she hid around the apartment? It was a question that haunted Doug Wednesday morning after he arrived at his desk in the lobby of the Cosmic Oil Building. Automatically he verified appointments, wrote names, doled out plastic visitors' cards and collected them back again as people departed. Several times, Linda, the seventh-floor receptionist, stopped by to chat with him. Today he was a little cool to her, which she seemed to find intriguing. What would she think if she knew that he was going to inherit a bundle of money? Where had Ethel *made* all that loot?

There was only one answer. Ethel had told him that she'd taken Seamus for his eyeteeth when he wanted out of the marriage. Besides the alimony, she'd come off with a hefty settlement and had probably been smart enough to invest it. Then that book she wrote five or six years ago had sold well. Ethel, for all her scatterbrained act, had always been pretty shrewd. It was that thought that caused Doug to feel queasy with apprehension. She had known that he was helping himself to money. *How many people had she told?*

After wrestling with the problem until noon, he made his decision. There were just about enough supercheck funds available in his checking account to take out four hundred dollars. Impatiently he waited on the interminable line at the bank and got the money in hundred-dollar bills. He'd stash them in some of Ethel's hiding places, the ones she didn't use most of the time. That way, if anybody searched, the money would be there. Somewhat reassured, he stopped for a hot dog at a food cart and went back to work.

At six-thirty, as Doug was rounding the corner from Broadway to Eighty-second Street, he saw Seamus hurrying down the steps from Ethel's building. He almost laughed out loud. Of course! It was the fifth of the month, and Seamus the wimp was there, right on the button with his alimony check. What a sad sack he was in that shabby coat! Regretfully, Doug realized that it would be a while before he himself could buy any more new clothes. He'd have to be very, very careful from now on.

He'd been collecting the mail every day with the key Ethel kept in a box on top of her desk. The envelope from Seamus was jammed into the box, still sticking out a little. Other than that there was mostly junk mail. Ethel's bills went directly to her accountant. He flipped through the envelopes, then dropped them on the desk. All except the unstamped one, the contribution from Seamus. It hadn't been sealed properly. There was a note inside, and the outline of the check was clearly visible.

It would be easy to open and reseal it. Doug's hand lingered on the flap, then, taking care not to cause a tear, he opened the envelope. The check fell out. Boy, he'd like to have the handwriting on it analyzed. If ever stress showed like a road map, it was in the slanted squiggle that was Seamus' penmanship.

Doug laid the check down, opened the note, read it, reread it and felt his mouth drop in amazement. What the hell . . . Carefully he reinserted the note and the check in the envelope, licked the glued area and pressed the flap firmly down. An image of Seamus with his hands hunched in his pockets, almost running as he crossed the street, loomed like a freeze-time in Doug's mind. Seamus was up to something. What kind of game was he playing, writing to say that Ethel had agreed not to take any more alimony and then including the check?

In a pig's eye she let you off the hook, Doug thought. A chill came over him. Had that note been intended for *his* eyes, not Ethel's?


When Neeve arrived home, she found to her delight that Myles had done a massive grocery shopping. "You even went to Zabar's," she said happily. "I was trying to figure how early I could leave the shop tomorrow. Now I can get everything started tonight." She had warned him that she'd be doing paperwork in the shop after closing hours. She uttered a silent prayer of gratitude that he did not think to ask her how she had gotten across town.

Myles had cooked a small leg of lamb, steamed fresh green beans and made a tomato-and-onion vinaigrette salad. He'd set the small table in the den and had a bottle of burgundy open nearby. Neeve rushed to change into slacks and a sweater, then with a sigh of relief settled into a chair and reached for the wine. "This is very kind of you, Commish," she said.

"Well, since you're feeding the aging Musketeers from the Bronx tomorrow night, I figured one good turn deserves another." Myles began to carve the roast.

Neeve observed him silently. His skin tone was good. His eyes no longer had that sick, heavy look. "I hate to compliment you, but you do realize you look darn healthy," she told him.

"I feel okay." Myles placed the perfectly done slices of lamb on Neeve's plate. "I hope I didn't use too much garlic."

Neeve sampled the first bite. "Great. You have to be feeling better to cook this well."

Myles sipped the burgundy. "Good wine, if I say so myself." His eyes clouded.

Some depression, the doctor had told her. "The heart attack, giving up his job, the bypass . . ."

"And always worrying about me," Neeve had injected.

"Always worrying about you because he can't forgive himself for not worrying about your mother."

"How do I make him stop?"

"Keep Nicky Sepetti in jail. If that's not possible, by spring urge your father to get busy on some project. Right now his guts are torn, Neeve. He'd be lost without you, but he hates himself for depending on you emotionally.

He's a proud guy. And something else. Stop babying him."

That had been six months ago. It was spring now. Neeve knew she had made a real attempt to treat Myles in their old way. They used to have vigorous debates about everything from Neeve's acceptance of the loan from Sal to politics on every level. "You're the first Kearny in ninety years to vote Republican," Myles had exploded.

"It's not quite the same as losing the faith."

"It's getting warm."

And now just when he's on the right track, he's all upset about Nicky Sepetti, she thought, and that could go on forever.

Unconsciously shaking her head, she glanced around, deciding as always that the den was her favorite room in the apartment. The worn Oriental carpeting was in shades of red and blue; the leather couch and the matching chairs were handsome and inviting. Pictures covered the wall. Myles receiving innumerable plaques and honors. Myles with the Mayor, the Governor, the *Republican* President. The windows overlooking the Hudson. The tieback draperies were the ones Renata had hung. Victorian-era, they were a deep warm blue and crimson, a subtle stripe that shimmered in the reflection of the crystal sconces on the wall. Between the sconces were Renata's pictures. The very first one her own father had taken when she was the ten-year-old child who had saved Myles and now looked at him adoringly as he lay, his head bandaged, propped on pillows. Renata with Neeve as a baby, with Neeve as a toddler. Renata and Neeve and Myles snorkeling off Maui. That was the year before Renata died.

Myles asked about the menu for the next night's dinner. "I didn't know what you'd want, so I bought everything," he said.

"Sal told me he doesn't want to eat your diet. The Bishop wants pesto."

Myles grunted. "I can remember when Sal thought a hero sandwich was a rare treat and when Devin's mother sent him to the deli for nickel fish cakes and a can of Heinz spaghetti."

Neeve had coffee in the kitchen as she began to organize the dinner party. Renata's cookbooks were on the shelf over the sink. She reached for her favorite, an old family relic with northern-Italian recipes.

After Renata's death, Myles had sent Neeve to a private tutor to keep up her conversational Italian. Every summer growing up she'd spent a month in Venice with her grandparents, and she'd taken her junior year in college in Perugia. For years she'd avoided the cookbooks, unwilling to see the notations in Renata's bold, curlicued hand. "More pepper. Bake only twenty minutes. Hold the oil." She could see Renata singing to herself as she cooked, letting Neeve stir or mix or measure, exploding, "*Cara,* this is either a misprint or the chef was drunk. Who could put so much oil in this dressing? Better to drink the Dead Sea."

Sometimes Renata had drawn quick sketches of Neeve on the margins of the pages, sketches that were charming, beautifully drawn miniatures: Neeve dressed as a princess sitting at the table, Neeve hovering over a large mixing bowl, Neeve in a Gibson Girl dress sampling a cookie. Dozens of sketches, each one evoking a sense of profound loss. Even now Neeve could not allow herself to do more than skim her eyes over the sketches. The memories they recalled were too painful. She felt sudden moisture in her eyes.

"I used to tell her she should take art lessons," Myles said.

She had not realized he was looking over her shoulder. "Mother liked what she did."

"Selling clothes to bored women."

Neeve bit her tongue. "Exactly how you'd classify me, I guess."

Myles looked conciliatory. "Oh, Neeve, I'm sorry. I'm on edge. I admit it."

"You're on edge, but you also meant it. Now get out of my kitchen."

Deliberately she slammed pots as she measured, poured, cut, sautéed, simmered and baked. Face it. Myles was the world's leading male chauvinist. If Renata had pursued art, if she'd developed into a mediocre painter of watercolors, he would have considered it a ladylike hobby. He simply couldn't understand that helping women select becoming clothing could make a big difference for those women in their social and business lives.

I've been written up in *Vogue, Town and Country, The New York Times* and God knows where else, Neeve thought, but that doesn't cut any ice with him. It's as though I'm stealing from people when I charge them for expensive clothes.

She remembered how annoyed Myles had been when,

during their Christmas party, he found Ethel Lambston in the kitchen browsing through Renata's cookbooks. "Are you interested in cooking?" he'd asked her icily.

Naturally Ethel hadn't noticed his annoyance. "Not at all," she'd told him airily. "I read Italian and happened to notice the books. *Queste desegni sono stupendi.*"

She'd been holding the book with the sketches. Myles had taken it from her hand. "My wife was Italian. I don't speak the language."

That was the point at which Ethel realized Myles was an unattached widower and latched onto him for the evening.

Finally everything was prepared. Neeve put the dishes into the refrigerator, tidied up and set the table in the dining room. She studiously ignored Myles, who was watching television in the den. As she finished placing the serving dishes on the sideboard, the eleven-o'clock news came on.

Myles held out a snifter of brandy to her. "Your mother used to bang the pots and pans when she was mad at me, too." His smile was boyish. It was his apology.

Neeve accepted the brandy. "Too bad she didn't throw them at you."

They laughed together as the phone rang. Myles picked it up. His genial "Hello" was quickly replaced by rapid-fire questions. Neeve watched as his mouth tightened. When he replaced the receiver, he said tonelessly, "That was Herb Schwartz. One of our guys had been planted in Nicky Sepetti's inner circle. He was just found in a garbage dump. Still alive, and there's a chance he'll make it."

Neeve listened, her mouth going dry. Myles's face was

contorted, but she didn't know what she was seeing in it. "His name is Tony Vitale," Myles said. "He's thirty-one years old. They knew him as Carmen Machado. They shot him four times. He should be dead, but somehow he hung on. There was something he wanted us to know."

"What was it?" Neeve whispered.

"Herb was there in the emergency room. Tony told him, 'No contract, Nicky, Neeve Kearny.' " Myles put his hand over his face as though trying to hide the expression on it.

Neeve stared at his anguished face. "You didn't seriously think there would be one?"

"Oh yes I did." Myles's voice rose. "Oh yes I did. And now for the first time in seventeen years, I can sleep at night." He put his hands on her shoulders. "Neeve, they went to question Nicky. Our guys. And they got there just in time to watch him die. The stinking sonofabitch had a heart attack. He's dead. Neeve, Nicky Sepetti is dead!"

He put his arms around her. She could feel the wild beating of his heart.

"Then let his death free you, Dad," she begged. Unconsciously she cupped his face in her palms, and remembered that that was Renata's familiar caress. Deliberately she imitated Renata's accent. *"Caro* Milo, leesten to me."

They both managed shaky smiles as Myles said, "I'll try. I promise."


Undercover detective Anthony Vitale, known to the Sepetti crime family as Carmen Machado, lay in the intensive-care unit of St. Vincent's Hospital. The bullets had lodged in his lung, split the ribs protecting his chest cavity and shattered his left shoulder. Miraculously he was still alive. Tubes invaded his body, dripping antibiotics and glucose into his veins. A respirator had taken over the function of breathing.

In the moments of consciousness that came to him from time to time, Tony could perceive the distraught faces of his parents. I'm tough. I'll try to make it, he wanted to reassure them.

If only he could talk. Had he been able to say anything when they found him? He had tried to tell them about the contract, but it hadn't come out the way he meant it.

Nicky Sepetti and his gang hadn't put a contract on Neeve Kearny. Someone else had. Tony knew he'd been shot on Tuesday night. How long had he been in the hospital? Dimly he remembered fragments of what they'd told Nicky about the contract: You can't call off a contract. The ex-Commissioner will be planning another funeral.

Tony tried to pull himself up. He had to warn them.

"Easy does it," a soft voice murmured.

He felt a prick in his arm and a few moments later slid into a quiet, dreamless sleep.

**7** Thursday morning at eight o'clock, Neeve and Tse-Tse were in a taxi across the street from Ethel Lambston's apartment. On Tuesday, Ethel's nephew had left for work at eight-twenty. Today they wanted to be certain to avoid him. The cabdriver's protest, "I don't get rich on waiting time," was mollified by Neeve's promise of a ten-dollar tip.

It was Tse-Tse who at eight-fifteen spotted Doug. "Look."

Neeve watched as he locked the door of the apartment, glanced around and headed for Broadway. The morning was cool, and he wore a belted trench coat. "That's a real Burberry," she said. "He must get paid awfully well for a receptionist."

The apartment was surprisingly tidy. Sheets and a quilt were stacked under a pillow at the end of the couch. The pillow sham was wrinkled. Clearly it had been slept on. There was no sign of a used ashtray, but Neeve was sure she detected the faint odor of cigarette smoke in the air. "He's been smoking but doesn't want to be caught at it," she observed. "I wonder why."

The bedroom was a model of neatness. The bed was made. Doug's suitcase was on the chaise; hangers with suits, slacks and jackets were laid across it. His note to Ethel was propped against the mirror on the dressing table.

"Who's kidding who?" Tse-Tse asked. "What made him write that and stop using her bedroom?"

Neeve knew that Tse-Tse had an excellent eye for detail. "All right," she said. "Let's start with that note. Has he ever left one for her before?"

Tse-Tse was wearing her Swedish-maid outfit. The coil of braids shook vigorously as she said, "Never."

Neeve walked to the closet and opened the door. Hanger by hanger, she examined Ethel's wardrobe to see whether she had missed any of her coats. But they were all there: the sable, the stone marten, the cashmere, the wraparound, the Burberry, the leather, the cape. At Tse-

Tse's puzzled expression, she explained what she was doing.

Tse-Tse reinforced her suspicions. "Ethel always tells me that she's given up being an impulse buyer since you took over dressing her. You're right. There's no other coat."

Neeve closed the closet door. "I'm not happy snooping around like this, but I have to. Ethel always carries a daily calendar in her purse, but I'm pretty sure she has a ledger-sized one as well."

"Yes she does," Tse-Tse said. "It's on her desk."

The appointment book was lying next to a pile of mail. Neeve opened it. It consisted of a full eleven-by-fourteen page for each day of the month, including December of the previous year. She flipped the pages until she reached March 31. In a bold scrawl, Ethel had written: "Have Doug pick up clothes at Neeve's Place." The slot for three o'clock was circled. The notation next to it was "Doug at the apartment."

Tse-Tse was looking over Neeve's shoulder. "So he's not lying about that," Tse-Tse said. The morning sun had started to pour brightly into the room. Suddenly it vanished behind a cloud. Tse-Tse shivered. "Honest to God, Neeve, this place is starting to spook me."

Without answering, Neeve flipped through the month of April. There were scattered appointments, cocktail parties, lunches. All the pages had a line drawn through. On April first, Ethel had written, "Research/Writing Book."

"She canceled everything. She was planning to go away or at least hole up somewhere and write," Neeve murmured.

"Then maybe she left a day early?" Tse-Tse suggested.

"It's possible." Neeve began to turn the pages backward. The last week of March was crammed with the names of prominent designers: Nina Cochran, Gordon Steuber, Victor Costa, Ronald Altern, Regina Mavis, Anthony della Salva, Kara Potter. "She can't have seen all these people," Neeve said. "I think that she phones to verify quotes just before she turns an article in." She pointed to an entry on Thursday, March 30: "Deadline for *Contemporary Woman* article."

Quickly she skimmed through the first three months of the year, noticing that next to her appointments Ethel had scrawled in the cost of cabs and tips, memos about lunches, dinners and meetings: "Good interview but annoyed if you keep him waiting. . . . Carlos new headwaiter at Le Cygne. . . . Don't use Valet Limo—car smelled like Airwick factory. . . ."

The notes were erratic jottings, the figures often crossed out and changed. Besides that, Ethel was obviously a doodler. Triangles, hearts, swirls and drawings covered every inch of the pages.

On impulse Neeve turned to December 22, the day of the Christmas party she and Myles had given. Ethel had obviously considered the event important. The address of Schwab House and Neeve's name were in block letters and underscored. Swirls and twirls accompanied Ethel's comment: "Neeve's father, single and fascinating." On the side of the page Ethel had drawn a crude imitation of a sketch from Renata's cookbook.

"Myles would have an ulcer if he saw this," Neeve commented. "I had to tell her that he was still too sick to plan any social events. She wanted to invite him to some formal dinner for New Year's. I thought he'd choke."

She turned the pages back to the last week in March and began to copy the names Ethel had listed there. "At least it's a starting place," she said. Two names jumped out at her. Toni Mendell, the editor of *Contemporary Woman*. The cocktail party hadn't been the place to ask her to search her memory for any comment Ethel might have made about a possible writing retreat. The other name was Jack Campbell. Obviously the book contract had been all-important to Ethel. Maybe she had told Campbell more about her plans than he'd realized.

Neeve snapped her notebook shut and zipped up the case. "I'd better get out of here." She reknotted the red-and-blue scarf at her throat. The collar of her coat was high, and her mass of black hair was pulled back in a chignon.

"You look great," Tse-Tse observed. "This morning on the elevator, I heard the guy in Eleven C ask who you were."

Neeve pulled on her gloves. "A Prince Valiant type, I trust."

Tse-Tse giggled. "Somewhere between forty and death. A bad rug. Looks like black feathers on a field of cotton."

"He's yours. Okay, if Ethel pops up or her loving nephew comes home early, you have your story. Do some work on the kitchen cabinets, wash the glasses on the top shelves. Make it look as though you've been busy, but keep your eyes open." Neeve glanced at the mail. "Take a look through that. Maybe Ethel received a letter that made her change her mind. God, I feel like a Peeping

Tom, but this is something we have to do. We both know something's strange, still we can't be marching in and out of here indefinitely."

As she started for the door, Neeve glanced around. "You do manage to make this place look positively livable," she said. "In a way, it reminds me of Ethel. All you usually notice around here is the surface clutter, and it turns you off. Ethel always acts so dizzy you forget she's a very sharp lady."

The wall with Ethel's myriad of publicity pictures was by the door. Her hand on the knob, Neeve studied them carefully. In most of her pictures, Ethel looked as though she'd been photographed in the middle of a sentence. Her mouth was usually slightly open, her eyes blazing with energy, the muscles of her face visibly in motion.

One snapshot caught Neeve's eye. The expression was tranquil, the mouth quiet, the eyes sad. What was it Ethel had once confided? "I was born on Valentine's Day. Easy to remember, huh? But do you know how many years it's been since anyone sent me a card or bothered to phone me? I end up singing 'Happy Birthday' to myself."

Neeve had made a mental note to send Ethel flowers and invite her out to lunch the past Valentine's Day, but she'd been away that week skiing in Vail. I'm sorry, Ethel, she thought. I'm really sorry.

It seemed to her that the mournful eyes in the snapshot were unforgiving.

After his bypass surgery, Myles had begun the habit of taking long afternoon walks. What Neeve did not know was that for the last four months he had also been seeing

a psychiatrist on East Seventy-fifth Street. "You're suffer-
ing from depression," his cardiologist had told him
bluntly. "Most people do, after this kind of operation. It
goes with the territory. But I suspect yours had other
roots." He'd bullied Myles into making the first appointment with Dr. Adam Felton.

Thursday at two was his regular time. He hated the
idea of lying on a couch and instead sat in a deep leather
chair. Adam Felton was not the stereotypical psychiatrist
Myles had expected. In his midforties, he had a crew cut,
somewhat rakish-looking glasses and a slender, wiry
body. By the third or fourth visit, he had won Myles's
trust. Myles no longer felt he was baring his soul. Instead
he had the feeling that when he spoke to Felton it com-
pared with being back in the squad room, laying out all
the aspects of an investigation to his men.

Funny, he thought now as he watched Felton twirl a
pencil between his fingers, it never occurred to me to
talk to Dev instead. But this was not a matter for the
confessional. "I didn't think that shrinks were supposed
to have nervous habits," he observed dryly.

Adam Felton laughed and gave the pencil he was twirl-
ing another deft spin. "I have every right to a nervous
habit when I'm giving up smoking. You seem pretty up-
beat today." The remark could have been made casually
to an acquaintance at a cocktail party.

Myles told him about Nicky Sepetti's death and at Felton's probing questions exclaimed, "We've been through
this territory. I've had seventeen years of feeling as
though something would happen to Neeve the minute
Sepetti got out. I failed Renata. How many damn times
do I have to tell you that? I *didn't take Nicky's threat*

*seriously.* He's a cold-blooded killer. He wasn't out three days before our guy was shot. Nicky probably fingered him. He always said he could smell a cop."

"And now you feel your daughter is safe?"

"I *know* she's safe. Our guy was able to tell us there's no contract on her. It must have been discussed. I know the rest of them wouldn't try. They were going to ease Nicky out anyhow. They'll be happy to drape him in a casket blanket."

Adam Felton began to twirl the pencil again, hesitated and dropped it decisively into the wastebasket. "You're telling me that Sepetti's death has released you from a fear that has haunted you for seventeen years. What does that mean to you? How will it change your life?"

Forty minutes later when Myles left the office and resumed his walk, his step was reminiscent of the brisk pace that at one time was typical of him. He knew that he was almost fully recovered physically. Now that he didn't have to worry about Neeve, he'd take a job. He hadn't told Neeve that he'd had inquiries about his availability to head up the President's Drug Enforcement Agency in Washington. It would mean spending a lot of time there, getting an apartment. But it would be good for Neeve to be on her own. She'd quit spending so much time home and get involved with young people. Before he got sick she used to spend summer weekends in the Hamptons and do a lot more skiing in Vail. In the last year he'd had to force her to go away even for a few days. He wanted her to get married. He wouldn't be around forever. Now, thanks to Nicky's timely heart attack, he could be in Washington with a free mind.

Myles could still remember the awesome pain of his own massive heart attack. It was as though a steamroller with spikes had rolled across his chest. "I hope that's what you felt on the way out, Buster," he thought. Then it was as though he could see his mother's face, sternly fixed on him. *Wish evil to someone else and evil will come to you. What goes around comes around.*

He crossed Lexington Avenue and passed Bella Vita restaurant. The faint delicious aroma of Italian cooking tantalized his nostrils, and he thought with pleasure of the dinner Neeve had prepared for tonight. It would be good to get together with Dev and Sal again. God, how long ago it seemed since they were kids growing up on Tenbroeck Avenue. The way people knocked the Bronx these days! It had been a great place to live in. Only seven houses on the entire block, woods that were thick with birch and oak. They'd made tree houses in them. Sal's parents' truck garden on what was now industrial Williamsbridge Road. The fields where he and Sal and Devin had gone sleigh riding—the Einstein Medical Center covered those fields now. . . . But there were still plenty of good residential areas.

On Park Avenue, Myles walked around a small mound of slushy melting snow. He remembered the time Sal had lost control of his sled and run over Myles's arm, breaking it in three places. Sal had started to cry, "My father will kill me." Dev jumped in to take the blame. Dev's father had come to apologize. "He meant no harm, but he's a clumsy oaf." Devin Stanton. His Grace the Bishop.

Rumor was, the Vatican had its eye on Dev for the next archdiocese opening, and that could mean a cardinal's hat.

When he reached Fifth Avenue, Myles glanced to the right. His eye took in the roof of the massive white structure that was the Metropolitan Museum of Art. He'd always meant to get a better look at the Temple of Dendur. On impulse he walked the six blocks and spent the next hour absorbed in the exquisite remnants of a lost civilization.

It was only when he consulted his watch and decided it was high time to get home and set up the bar that he realized that his real intention in coming to the museum was to visit the site of Renata's death. Forget it, he told himself fiercely. But when he was outside, he could not keep his footsteps from leading him around the back of the museum and to the spot where her body had been found. It was a pilgrimage he made every four or five months.

A reddish haze around the trees in Central Park was the first promise of the greening that would soon take place. There were a fair number of people in the park. Joggers. Nurses pushing baby strollers. Young mothers with energetic three-year-olds. The homeless, pathetic men and women hunched on benches. A steady stream of traffic. Horse-drawn carriages.

Myles stopped at the clearing where Renata had been found. Funny, he thought, she's buried in Gate of Heaven Cemetery, but for me it's as though her body is always here. He stood with his head bowed, his hands in the pockets of his suede jacket. If it had been a day like this, there would have been people in the park. Someone might have seen what was happening. A line from a Tennyson poem ran through his mind: *Dear as remember'd kisses after death ... Deep as first love, and wild with all regret; O Death in Life, the days that are no more.*

But today, for the first time in this place, Myles experienced a tentative sense of healing. "No thanks to me, but at least our girl is safe, *carissima mia*," he whispered. "And I hope that when Nicky Sepetti stood before the Judgment Seat, you were there to point his way to hell."

Myles turned and walked briskly through the park. Adam Felton's final words echoed in his ears: "All right. You don't have to worry about Nicky Sepetti anymore. You experienced a terrible tragedy seventeen years ago. The point is, are you finally ready to get on with your life?"

Myles whispered again the answer he had snapped decisively at Adam. "Yes."


When Neeve arrived at the shop from Ethel's apartment, most of the staff were already in. Besides Eugenia, her assistant manager, she employed seven regular saleswomen and three seamstresses.

Eugenia was dressing the showroom mannequins. "I'm glad ensembles are in again," she said as she expertly adjusted the jacket of a cinnamon silk outfit. "Which purse?"

Neeve stood back. "Hold them up again. The smaller one, I think. The other has too much amber for the dress."

When Eugenia retired from modeling, she'd happily

gone from a size four to a size twelve, but she still retained the graceful movements that had made her a favorite with the designers. She hung the purse on the
mannequin's arm. "You're right as usual," she said
cheerfully. "It's going to be a busy day. I can feel it in my
bones."

"Keep feeling it." Neeve tried to sound casual, but the
effort failed.

"Neeve, what about Ethel Lambston? She still hasn't
shown up?"

"Not a trace." Neeve glanced around the shop. "Look,
I'm going to hole up in the office and make phone calls.
Unless it's absolutely necessary, don't let on that I'm
here. I don't want to be bothered with salesmen today."

Her first call was to Toni Mendell at *Contemporary
Woman*. Toni was at an all-day seminar of magazine editors. She tried Jack Campbell. He was in a meeting. She
left word for him to return her call. "It's rather urgent,"
she told his secretary. She went down the list of the designers whose names had been scribbled in Ethel's book.
The first three she reached hadn't seen Ethel last week.
She'd simply called to confirm the direct quotes she was
attributing to them. Sportswear designer Elke Pearson
summed up the irritation Neeve caught in all their
voices. "Why I let that woman interview me I'll never
know. She kept hammering questions at me till I was
dizzy. I practically had to throw her out, and I have a
hunch I'm not going to like her damn article."

Anthony della Salva was the next name. Neeve didn't
worry when she couldn't reach him. She'd see him tonight for dinner. Gordon Steuber. Ethel had confided
that she'd crucified him in her article. But when was the

last time she saw him? Reluctantly, Neeve dialed Steuber's office and was put through immediately to him.

He did not waste his time on amenities. "What do you want?" he asked stiffly.

She could picture him, leaning back in the ornate leather chair with its elaborate brass nailheads. She made her voice as cold as his. "I've been asked to try to locate Ethel Lambston. It's quite urgent." On a hunch she added, "I know from her appointment book that she met with you last week. Did she give you any indication of where she might be planning to go?"

Long seconds passed in total silence. He's trying to decide what to say, she thought. When Steuber spoke, his tone was detached and even. "Ethel Lambston tried to interview me weeks ago about an article she was writing. I did not see her. I have no time for busybodies. She phoned last week, but I did not accept her call."

Neeve heard a click in her ear.

She was about to dial the next designer on the list when her phone rang. It was Jack Campbell. He sounded concerned. "My secretary said your call was urgent. Is there any problem, Neeve?"

She suddenly felt ridiculous trying to explain to him on the phone that she was worried about Ethel Lambston because Ethel hadn't picked up her new clothes.

Instead she said, "You've got to be awfully busy, but is there any chance I could talk to you for about half an hour very soon?"

"I have a lunch date with one of my authors," he said. "How about three o'clock in my office?"

. . .

Givvons and Marks occupied the top six floors of the building on the southwest corner of Park Avenue and Forty-first Street. Jack Campbell's personal office was a huge corner room of the forty-seventh floor with dazzling views of downtown Manhattan. His oversized desk was finished in black lacquer. The bookshelves on the wall behind the desk were filled with manuscripts. A black leather couch and matching chairs were grouped around a glass cocktail table. Neeve was surprised to see that the room was devoid of personal touches.

It was as though Jack Campbell could read her mind. "My apartment isn't ready yet, so I'm staying at the Hampshire House. Everything I own is still in storage, which is why this place looks like a dentist's waiting room."

His suit jacket was on the back of his desk chair. He was wearing an argyle sweater in tones of green and brown. It suited him, Neeve decided. Autumn colors. His face was too thin and his features were too irregular to be deemed handsome, but were infinitely attractive in their quiet strength. There was good-humored warmth in his eyes when he smiled, and Neeve found herself glad she had changed to one of her new spring ensembles, a turquoise wool dress and matching stroller-length jacket.

"How about coffee?" Jack offered. "I drink too much of it, but I'm still going to have some."

Neeve realized she had skipped lunch and her head was vaguely aching. "I'd love it. Black, please."

While they waited, she commented on the view. "Don't you feel like the king of New York at least?"

"In the month I've been here, I've had to fight to keep my mind on work," he told her. "I became a would-be native New Yorker when I was ten. That was twenty-six years ago and it took all this time to make the Big Apple."

When the coffee came, they sat around the glass table. Jack Campbell lounged on the couch. Neeve perched on the edge of one of the chairs. She knew he had to have pushed off other appointments to see her so quickly. She took a deep breath and told him about Ethel. "My father thinks I'm crazy," she said. "But I've got a weird feeling that something happened to her. The thing is, did she give you any indication that she might be going off by herself? I understand that the book she's writing for you is scheduled for fall release."

Jack Campbell had listened to her with the same attentive posture she had observed at the cocktail party. "No, it isn't," he said.

Neeve felt her eyes widen. "Then how . . . ?"

Campbell sipped the last drops in his coffee cup. "I met Ethel a couple of years ago at the ABA when she was promoting her first book for Givvons and Marks, the one about women in politics. It was darn good. Funny. Gossipy. Sold well. That's why when she wanted to see me, I was interested. She gave me a rundown on the article she was doing and said she might have stumbled across a story that would rock the fashion world and if she wrote a book about it, would I buy it and what kind of advance could she expect?

"I told her I obviously had to know more about it, but, based on the success of the last book, if this one was as explosive as she claimed, we'd buy it and we'd probably be talking a mid-six-figure advance. Last week I read on Page Six in the *Post* that she had a contract with me for a half-million dollars and the book would be on the fall list. The phone's been ringing off the hook. All the soft-cover houses want to have a chance to bid on it. I called Ethel's agent. She never even talked to him about it. I've tried phoning her without success. I've neither con-firmed nor denied the terms. She's a real publicity hound, but if she writes the book and if it's good, all the advance interest is just fine with me."

"And you don't have any idea what she considered a story that would rock the industry?"

"Not a clue."

Neeve sighed and stood up. "I've taken enough of your time. I suppose that I should be reassured. It would be just like Ethel to get hot on a project like this and go hole up in a cabin somewhere. I'd better start minding my own business." She held out her hand to him. "Thank you."

He did not release her hand immediately. His smile was quick and warm. "Do you always make such fast getaways?" he asked. "Six years ago you darted out of the plane like an arrow. The other night when I turned around you'd disappeared."

Neeve withdrew her hand. "Occasionally, I slow down to a jog," she said, "but now I'd better run and pay atten-tion to my own business."

He walked with her to the door. "I hear Neeve's Place is one of the most fashionable shops in New York. Can I get to see it?"

"Sure. You don't even have to buy anything."

"My mother lives in Nebraska and wears sensible clothes."

On her way down in the elevator Neeve wondered

whether that was Jack Campbell's way of telling her that there was no special lady in his life. She found that she was humming softly as she stepped out into the now warm April afternoon and hailed a cab.

When she reached the shop, she found a message to call Tse-Tse at Ethel's apartment immediately. Tse-Tse answered on the first ring. "Neeve, thank God you called. I want to get out of here before that jerky nephew comes home. Neeve, something is really queer. Ethel has a habit of stashing hundred-dollar bills around the apartment. That's how she happened to pay me in advance last time. When I was here Tuesday, I saw one bill under the carpet. This morning I found one in the dish closet and three others hidden in the furniture. *Neeve, they absolutely weren't here on Tuesday.*"

Seamus left the bar at four-thirty. Oblivious of the jostling pedestrians, he darted along the crowded sidewalk up Columbus Avenue. He had to go to Ethel's apartment, and he didn't want Ruth to know he'd been there. Since his discovery last evening that he'd put the check and the note into the same envelope, he'd felt like a trapped animal, leaping wildly, trying to find a way to escape.

There was just one hope. He hadn't stuffed the envelope deep into the mailbox. He could visualize the way the edge of it had been sticking out of the slot. He might be able to retrieve it. It was a one-in-a-million chance. Common sense told him that if the postman had brought more mail, he probably shoved that envelope down. But the possibility still allured him, offering the only course of action.

He turned up Ethel's block, his eyes skimming the passersby, hoping he would not encounter the familiar faces of any of Ethel's neighbors. As he reached her building, his sense of hopeless misery swelled to the point of despair. He couldn't even try to steal a letter without bungling it. You needed a key to get into the vestibule where the mailboxes were located. Last night that obnoxious kid had opened the door for him. Now he'd have to ring for the superintendent, and the super certainly wouldn't let him fool with Ethel's mailbox.

He was in front of the brownstone. Ethel's apartment was the walk-in entrance on the left. There were a dozen steps up to the main entrance. As he stood, uncertain what to do, the fourth-floor window opened. A woman leaned out. Over her shoulder, he could see the face of the kid he'd talked to yesterday.

"She hasn't been around all week," a strident voice told him. "And listen, I almost called the cops last Thursday when I heard you shouting at her."

Seamus turned and fled. His breath came in harsh gasps as he ran unseeingly down West End Avenue. He did not stop until he was safely inside his own apartment and had bolted the door. Only then was he aware of the pounding of his heart, the shuddering sound of his struggle for oxygen. To his dismay, he heard footsteps in the hallway coming from the bedroom. Ruth was home already. Urgently he wiped his face with his hand, tried to pull himself together.

Ruth did not seem to notice his agitation. She was

holding his brown suit over her arm. "I was going to drop this at the cleaners," she told him. "Will you kindly tell me why in the name of God you have a one-hundred-dollar bill in the pocket?"

Jack Campbell stayed in his office for nearly two hours after Neeve left him. But the manuscript which had been messengered to him with an enthusiastic note from an agent he trusted simply could not hold his attention. After valiant efforts to become involved in the story line, he finally shoved it aside with rare irritability. The anger was directed at himself. It wasn't fair to judge someone's hard work when your mind was ninety-nine percent preoccupied.

Neeve Kearny. Funny how six years ago he'd had that moment of regret that he hadn't managed to get her phone number. He'd even looked it up in the Manhattan directory when he was in New York some months later. There were pages of Kearnys in the book. None of them Neeve. She'd said something about a dress shop. He'd looked under Kearny. Nothing.

And then he'd shrugged and put it in the back of his mind. For all he knew she had a live-in boyfriend. But for some reason he'd never quite forgotten her. At the cocktail party, when she approached him, he'd recognized her immediately. She wasn't a twenty-one-year-old kid in a ski sweater anymore. She was a sophisticated, fashionably dressed young woman. But that coal-black hair, the milk-white skin, the enormous brown eyes, the dotting of freckles across the bridge of her nose—all these were the same.

Now Jack found himself wondering whether she had a serious involvement. If not . . .

At six o'clock his assistant poked her head in. "I've had it," she announced. "Is it okay if I warn you that you'll wreck it for everyone else if you keep late hours?"

Jack shoved aside the unread manuscript and got up. "I'm on my way," he said. "Just one question, Ginny? What do you know about Neeve Kearny?"

He mulled over the answer on the walk uptown to his rental apartment on Central Park South. Neeve Kearny had a sensationally successful boutique. Ginny bought her special outfits there. Neeve was well liked, well respected. Neeve had caused an uproar a few months ago when she pulled the plug on a designer who had kids sewing in sweatshops. Neeve could be a fighter.

He'd also asked about Ethel Lambston. Ginny had rolled her eyes. "Don't get me started."

Jack stopped in his apartment long enough to be sure that he didn't feel like fixing his own dinner. Instead he decided that pasta at Nicola's was the right way to go. Nicola's was on Eighty-fourth Street between Lexington and Third.

It was a good decision. As always, there was a line for tables, but after one drink at the bar his favorite waiter, Lou, tapped his shoulder. "All set, Mr. Campbell." Jack found himself relaxing at last over a half bottle of Valpolicella, a watercress-and-endive salad and linguine with frutti di mare. When he ordered a double espresso he also asked for his check.

As he left the restaurant, he shrugged. He had known all evening that he was going to walk over to Madison Avenue and see Neeve's Place. A few minutes later, as a now cooling breeze made him aware that it was still April and that early-spring weather could be capricious, he studied the elegantly dressed windows. He liked what he saw. The delicately feminine soft print dresses and matching umbrellas. The assured poses of the mannequins, the almost arrogant tilt of their heads. Somehow he was sure that Neeve was making a statement with this combination of strength and softness.

But carefully studying the window display made him aware of the elusive thought that had evaded him when he was trying to tell Neeve exactly what Ethel had pitched to him. "There's gossip; there's excitement; there's universality in fashion," Ethel had told him in that hurried, breathless way of hers. "That's what my article is about. But just suppose I can give you a lot more than that. A bombshell. TNT."

He'd been late for an appointment. He'd cut her off. "Send me an outline."

Ethel's insistent, persistent refusal to be dismissed. "How much is a blockbuster scandal worth?"

His almost joking "If it's sensational enough, mid–six figures."

Jack stared at the mannequins holding their parasol-like umbrellas. His eyes shifted to the ivory-and-blue canopy with the scrolled letters, "Neeve's Place." Tomorrow he could call Neeve and tell her exactly what Ethel had said.

As he turned down Madison Avenue, once again finding it necessary to walk off the vague, undefined restlessness, he thought, I'm really reaching for an excuse. Why not just ask her out?

At that moment, he was able to define the cause of the

restlessness. He absolutely did not want to hear that Neeve was involved with someone else.

Thursday was a busy day for Kitty Conway. From nine in the morning till noon she drove elderly people to doctors' appointments. In the afternoon she worked as a volunteer in the small sales shop of the Garden State Museum. Both activities gave her a sense of doing something useful.

Long ago in college she had studied anthropology with some vague idea of becoming a second Margaret Mead. Then she'd met Mike. Now as she helped a sixteen-year-old select a replica of an Egyptian necklace, she thought that maybe in the summer she'd sign up for an anthropology tour.

The prospect was intriguing. As she drove home in the April evening, Kitty realized that she was getting impatient with herself. It was time to get on with the business of living. She turned off Lincoln Avenue and smiled as she saw her house perched high at the bend of Grand View Circle, an impressive white colonial with black shutters.

Inside she walked through the downstairs rooms turning on lights, then lit the gas-fueled fireplace in the den. When Michael was alive, he'd made satisfying, glowing fires, expertly piling logs over the kindling and feeding the flames regularly so that the hickory scent of the wood filled the room. No matter how she tried, Kitty couldn't get a fire started properly, and with apologies to Michael's memory she had had the gas jet installed.

She went upstairs to the master bedroom that she'd redone in apricot and pale green, a pattern copied from a museum tapestry. Peeling off her two-piece gray wool dress, she debated about showering now and getting comfortable in pajamas and a robe. Bad habit, she told herself. It's only six o'clock.

Instead she pulled a teal-blue sweatsuit from the closet and reached for sneakers. "I'm back to jogging as of right now," she told herself.

She followed her usual path. Grand View to Lincoln Avenue, a mile into town, circle the bus station and back home. Feeling pleasantly virtuous, she dropped her sweatsuit and underwear into the bathroom hamper, showered, slipped on lounging pajamas and studied herself in the mirror. She'd always been slim and was holding her shape reasonably well. The lines around her eyes weren't deep. Her hair looked pretty natural. The colorist in the beauty parlor had managed to match her own shade of red. Not bad, Kitty told her reflection, but ye gods, in two years I'll be *sixty*.

It was time for the seven-o'clock news and obviously time for a sherry. Kitty walked across the bedroom toward the hallway and realized she'd left the bathroom lights blazing. Waste not, want not, and anyhow you should conserve electricity. She hurried back and reached for the bathroom light switch. Her fingers turned numb. The sleeve of her blue sweatsuit was dangling from the hamper. Fear, like a cold blade of steel, made Kitty's throat constrict. Her lips went dry. She could feel the hairs on her neck bristle and tighten. That sleeve. There should be a hand on it. Yesterday. When the horse bolted. That scrap of plastic that had hit her face. That blurred image of blue cloth and a hand. She hadn't been crazy. *She had seen a hand.*

Kitty did not remember to turn on the seven-o'clock news. Instead, she sat in front of the fire, hunched forward on the couch, sipping the sherry. Neither the fire nor the sherry could ease the chill that was engulfing her body. Should she call the police? Suppose she was wrong. She'd look like a fool.

I'm *not* wrong, she told herself, but I'll wait until tomorrow. I'll drive back to the park and walk down that embankment. That was a hand I saw, but whoever it belongs to is beyond help now.

"You say Ethel's nephew is in the apartment?" Myles asked as he filled the ice bucket. "So he borrowed some money and then put it back. It's been known to happen."

Once again, Myles's reasonable explanation of the circumstances surrounding Ethel's absence, her winter coats and now the hundred-dollar bills made Neeve feel slightly foolish. She was glad she hadn't yet told Myles about her meeting with Jack Campbell. When she arrived home, she'd changed into blue silk slacks and a matching long-sleeved blouse. She'd expected Myles to say, "Pretty fancy for slinging hash." Instead his eyes had softened when she came into the kitchen, and he'd remarked, "Your mother always looked lovely in blue. You grow more like her as you get older."

Neeve reached for Renata's cookbook. She was serving thinly sliced ham with melon, pasta with pesto, sole stuffed with shrimp, a mélange of baby vegetables, an arugula-and-endive salad, cheese and a tulip pastry. She flipped through the book until she reached the page with the sketches. Again she avoided looking at them. Instead she concentrated on the handwritten instructions Renata had scrawled over the baking time for the sole.

Deciding she was fully organized, she went over to the refrigerator and took out a jar of caviar. Myles watched as she put toast points on a platter. "I never developed a taste for that stuff," he said. "Very plebeian of me, I know."

"You're hardly plebeian." Neeve scooped caviar onto a sliver of toast point. "But you're missing a lot." She studied him. He was wearing a navy jacket, gray slacks, a light-blue shirt and a handsome red-and-blue tie she had given him for Christmas. A good-looking guy, she thought, and best of all, you'd never dream he'd been so sick. She told him that.

Myles reached over and gingerly popped a caviar toast point into his mouth. "I still don't like it," he commented, then added, "I do feel well, and inactivity is getting on my nerves. I had some feelers about heading up the Drug Enforcement Agency in Washington. It would mean spending most of my time there. What do you think?"

Neeve gasped and threw her arms around him. "That's wonderful. Go for it. You could really get your teeth into that job."

She hummed as she brought the caviar and a platter of Brie into the living room. Now if only Ethel Lambston could be tracked down. She was just in the process of wondering how long it would be before Jack Campbell phoned her when the doorbell rang. Their two guests had arrived together.

Bishop Devin Stanton was one of the few prelates who at private functions still seemed more comfortable in a Roman collar than a sports jacket. Traces of now subdued copper-color hair mingled with gray. Behind silver-rimmed glasses, his mild blue eyes radiated warmth and intelligence. His tall, thin body gave an impression of quicksilver when he moved. Neeve always had the uncomfortable impression that Dev could read her mind and the comfortable reaction that he liked what he read. She kissed him warmly.

Once again, Anthony della Salva was resplendent in one of his own creations. He was wearing a charcoal-gray suit of Italian silk. The elegant lines masked the additional weight that had begun creeping onto his always rotund body. Neeve remembered Myles's observation that Sal reminded him of a well-fed cat. It was a description that suited him. His black hair untouched by gray glistened, matching the gloss of his Gucci loafers. It was second nature for Neeve to calculate the cost of clothes. She decided that Sal's suit would retail for about fifteen hundred dollars.

As usual, Sal was bursting with good humor. "Dev, Myles, Neeve, my three favorite people, not counting my present girlfriend but certainly counting my ex-wives. Dev, do you think Mother Church will take me back in when I get old?"

"The prodigal son is supposed to return repentant and in rags," the Bishop observed dryly.

Myles laughed and put his arms around the shoulders of both his friends. "God, it's good to get together with you two. I feel as though we're back in the Bronx. Are you still drinking Absolut vodka or have you found something more trendy?"

The evening began in the usual pleasantly comfortable fashion that had become a ritual. A debate about a second martini, a shrug, and "Why not, we're not together that much" from the Bishop, "I'd better stop" from Myles, a nonchalant "Of course" from Sal. The conversation veered from present-day politics, "Could the Mayor win again?" to problems of the Church, "You can't educate a kid in a parochial school for less than sixteen hundred dollars a year. God, remember when we were at St. Francis Xavier and our parents paid a buck a month? The parish carried the school on Bingo games," to Sal's laments about the foreign imports, "Sure, we should use the union label, but we can get the clothes made in Korea and Hong Kong for a third of the price. If we don't farm some of it out, we outprice ourselves. If we do, we're union busters," to Myles's dry comment, "I still think we don't know the half of how much mob money is on Seventh Avenue."

Inevitably it turned to Nicky Sepetti's death.

"It was too easy for him, dying in bed," Sal commented, the jovial expression gone from his face. "After what he did to your pretty one."

Neeve watched as Myles's lips tightened. Long ago Sal had heard Myles teasingly call Renata "my pretty one" and, to Myles's annoyance, had picked it up. "How's the pretty one?" he would greet Renata. Neeve could still remember the moment at Renata's wake when Sal had knelt at the casket, his eyes flowing with tears, then gotten up, embraced Myles and said, "Try to think your pretty one is sleeping."

Myles had said flatly, "She's not sleeping. She's dead. And, Sal, don't call her that again ever. That was my name for her."

Till now he never had. There was a moment of awkward silence, then Sal gulped the rest of his martini and stood up. "Be right back," he said, beaming, and headed down the hallway to the guest bathroom.

Devin sighed. "He may be a genius designer, but he still has more spit than polish."

"He also gave me my start," Neeve reminded them. "If it weren't for Sal, I'd probably be an assistant buyer in Bloomingdale's right now."

She saw the look on Myles's face and warned, "Don't tell me I'd be better off."

"That never crossed my mind."

When she served dinner, Neeve lit the candles and muted the overhead chandelier. The room was softly shadowed. Each course was pronounced excellent. Myles and the Bishop had seconds of everything. Sal had thirds. "So forget the diet," he said. "This is the best kitchen in Manhattan."

Over dessert inevitably the talk turned to Renata. "This is one of her recipes," Neeve told them. "Prepared especially for you two. I've really just started getting into her cookbooks, and it's fun."

Myles told them about the possibility of heading up the Drug Enforcement Agency.

"I may be keeping you company in the Washington

area," Devin said with a smile, then added, "strictly off the record."

Sal insisted on helping Neeve clear the table and volunteered to prepare the espresso. As he busied himself with the espresso machine, Neeve took from the breakfront the exquisite gold-and-green demitasse cups that had been in the Rossetti family for generations.

The sound of a thud and a cry of pain made them rush to the kitchen. The espresso pot had toppled over, flooding the counter and soaking Renata's cookbook. Sal was running his fiery-red hand under cold water. His face was ghastly white. "The handle on that damn pot came off." He tried to sound nonchalant. "Myles, I think you're trying to get back at me for breaking your arm when we were kids."

It was obvious the burn was nasty and painful.

Neeve scrambled for the eucalyptus leaves Myles always kept for burn emergencies. She patted Sal's hand dry and covered it with the leaves, then wrapped it in a soft linen napkin. The Bishop righted the demitasse pot and began mopping up. Myles was drying the cookbook. Neeve saw the expression in his eyes as he studied Renata's sketches, which were now thoroughly soaked and stained.

Sal noticed as well. He pulled his hand from Neeve's ministrations. "Myles, for God's sake, I'm sorry."

Myles held the book over the sink, drained the puddles of coffee from it and, covering it with a towel, laid it carefully on top of the refrigerator. "What the hell have you got to be sorry about? Neeve, I never saw that damn coffeemaker before. When did you get it?"

145

Neeve began to make fresh espresso in the old pot. "It was a gift," she said reluctantly. "Ethel Lambston sent it to you for Christmas after she was here for the party."

Devin Stanton looked bewildered as Myles, Neeve and Sal burst into wry laughter.

"I'll explain it when we get settled, Your Grace," Neeve said. "My God, no matter what I do, I can't lose Ethel even for the space of a dinner."


Over espresso and Sambuca, she told about Ethel's apparent disappearance. Myles's comment was, "As long as she *stays* out of sight."

Trying not to wince at the pain in his rapidly blistering hand, Sal poured a second Sambuca and said, "There isn't a designer on Seventh Avenue she hasn't bugged about that article. To answer your question, Neeve, she phoned me last week and insisted on being put through. We were in the middle of a meeting. She had a couple of questions like 'Was it true you had the school record for playing hookey at Christopher Columbus High School?' "

Neeve stared at him. "You've got to be joking."

"No joke at all. My guess is Ethel's article is to debunk all the stories we designers pay publicists to grind out about us. That may be hot stuff for an article, but tell me it's worth half a million bucks for a book! It boggles my mind."

Neeve was about to volunteer that Ethel wasn't actually offered the advance, then bit her tongue. Jack Campbell had obviously not meant that to get around.

"By the way," Sal added, "the word is that your tip

about Steuber's sweatshops is really turning up a lot of dirt. Neeve, stay way from that guy."

"What's that supposed to mean?" Myles asked sharply.

Neeve had not told Myles about the rumor that, because of her, Gordon Steuber might be indicted. She shook her head at Sal as she said, "He's a designer I stopped buying from because of the way he does business." She appealed to Sal, "I still say there's something wrong about the way Ethel dropped out of sight. You know she bought all her clothes from me, and every single one of her winter coats is in the closet."

Sal shrugged. "Neeve, I'll be honest, Ethel's such a flake she probably ran out without a coat and never noticed it. Watch and see. She'll show up in something she bought off the rack at J. C. Penney's."

Myles laughed. Neeve shook her head. "You're a big help."

Before they left the table, Devin Stanton offered grace. "We thank Thee, Lord, for good friendship, for the delicious meal, for the beautiful young woman who prepared it, and we ask you to bless the memory of Renata whom we all loved."

"Thank you, Dev." Myles touched the Bishop's hand. Then he laughed. "And if she were here, she'd be telling you to clean up her kitchen, Sal, because you made the mess."

When the Bishop and Sal had left, Neeve and Myles stacked the dishwasher and washed the pots and pans in companionable silence. Neeve picked up the offending espresso pot. "Might as well ditch this before somebody else is scalded," she observed.

"No, leave it alone," Myles told her. "It looks expensive enough, and I can fix it someday when I'm watching *Jeopardy*."

*Jeopardy.* To Neeve the word seemed to hang in the air. Shaking her head impatiently at the thought, she turned off the kitchen light and kissed Myles good night. She glanced around to be sure everything was in order. The light from the foyer shone faintly into the den, and Neeve winced as she watched it fall on the blistered, smeared pages of Renata's cookbook, which Myles had placed on the top of his desk.

**8** On Friday morning, Ruth Lambston left the apartment while Seamus was shaving. She did not say goodbye to him. The memory of the way his face had convulsed in anger when she held out the hundred-dollar bill to him was imprinted on her mind. In these last years, the monthly alimony check had choked off every emotion she felt for him except resentment. Now a new emotion had been added. She was afraid. Of him? For him? She didn't know.

Ruth made twenty-six thousand dollars a year as a secretary. With taxes and Social Security taken out and her expenses for carfare and clothes and lunches, she estimated that her net earnings three days a week just about made up Ethel's alimony. "I'm slaving for that harridan" was a sentence that she regularly threw at Seamus.

Usually Seamus tried to soothe her. But last night his face had convulsed in rage. He'd raised his fist and for a moment she'd flinched, sure he was going to hit her. But he'd snatched the hundred-dollar bill and torn it in half. "You want to know where I got it?" he'd shouted. "That bitch gave it to me. When I asked her to let me off the hook, she told me that she'd be glad to help me. She'd been too busy to eat out much, so this was left over from last month."

"Then she didn't tell you to stop sending the checks?" Ruth cried.

The anger on his face had turned to hatred. "Maybe I convinced her that any human being can take just so much. Maybe it's something you ought to learn, too."

The answer had left Ruth in a temper that still made her breath come in sharp, harsh gasps. "Don't you dare threaten me," she'd shouted and then watched horrified as Seamus burst into tears. Sobbing, he told her how he'd put the check with the letter, how the kid who lived upstairs from Ethel had talked about his delivering the ransom. "Her whole building thinks I'm a joke."

All night Ruth had lain awake in one of the girls' bedrooms, so filled with contempt for Seamus that she could not endure the thought of being near him. Toward morning she realized that the contempt was for herself as well. That woman has turned me into a shrew, she thought. It's got to end.

Now her mouth was set in a harsh, straight line as, instead of turning right toward Broadway and the subway station, she walked straight up West End Avenue. There was a sharp early-morning breeze, but her low-heeled shoes made it possible to move quickly.

She was going to confront Ethel. She should have done it years ago. She'd read enough of Ethel's articles to know that Ethel postured herself as a feminist. But now that she'd signed a big book contract, she really was vulnerable. Page Six of the *Post* would love to print that she was gouging one thousand dollars a month from a man with three daughters in college. Ruth permitted herself a grim smile. If Ethel didn't surrender her alimony rights, Ruth would go for her throat. First the *Post*. Then court.

She'd gone to the personnel office of her company for an emergency loan to cover the tuition check. The personnel director had been shocked to learn about the alimony. "I've got a friend who's a good matrimonial lawyer," she'd said. "She can afford to do pro-bono work and she'd love to have a case like this. The way I understand it, you can't break an irrevocable alimony agreement, but it might be about time to test the law. If you get public outrage going, things might happen."

Ruth had hesitated. "I don't want to embarrass the girls. It would mean admitting the bar is barely making enough money to keep the doors open. Let me think about it."

As she crossed Seventy-third Street, Ruth thought, Either she gives up the alimony or I see that lawyer.

A young woman with a child in a stroller was bearing down on her. Ruth stepped to one side to avoid her and collided with a thin-faced man in a cap that almost covered his face and a filthy overcoat that smelled of stale wine. Wrinkling her nose in disgust, she clutched her pocketbook and scurried to the opposite curb. The sidewalks were so crowded, she thought. Kids rushing with schoolbooks, old-timers making an outing of the daily walk to the newsstand, people on the way to work trying to flag down cabs.

Ruth had never forgotten the house they'd almost bought in Westchester twenty years ago. Thirty-five thousand dollars then and must be worth ten times that now. When the bank saw the alimony payments, the mortgage hadn't been approved.

She turned east on Eighty-second Street, Ethel's block. Squaring her shoulders, Ruth adjusted her rimless glasses, unconsciously preparing herself like a fighter about to enter the ring. Seamus had told her that Ethel had the ground-floor apartment with its own entrance. The name over the bell, "E. Lambston," confirmed that fact.

From inside she could hear the faint sounds of a radio playing. She pressed her index finger firmly on the bell. But there was no response to her first or second ring. Ruth was not to be dissuaded. The third time she rang the bell, she pressed relentlessly.

The loud ringing went on for fully a minute before she was rewarded by the click of the lock turning. The door was yanked open. A young man, his hair tousled, his shirt still unbuttoned, glared at her. "What the hell do you want?" he asked. Then he made a visible attempt to calm down. "I'm sorry. Are you a friend of Aunt Ethel's?"

"Yes, and I must see her." Ruth moved forward, forcing the young man to block her way or let her pass. He stepped back, and she was in the living room. Quickly she glanced around. Seamus always talked about Ethel's messy housekeeping, but this place was spotless. Too many papers around, but they were stacked in neat piles. Fine antique furniture. Seamus had told her about the pieces he had bought for Ethel. And I live with those overstuffed horrors, Ruth thought.

"I'm Douglas Brown." Doug felt clammy apprehension. There was something about this woman, about the way she was sizing up the apartment, that made him nervous. "I'm Ethel's nephew," he said. "Do you have an appointment with her?"

"No. But I insist on seeing her immediately." Ruth introduced herself. "I'm Seamus Lambston's wife and I'm here to collect the last check he gave your aunt. As of now there's no more alimony being paid."

There was a stack of mail on the desk. Near the top of the pile, she saw a white envelope with maroon edging, the stationery the girls had given Seamus for his birthday. "I'll take that," she said.

Before Doug could stop her, the envelope was in her hand. She ripped it open and pulled out the contents. Scanning them, she shredded the check and returned the note to the envelope.

As Doug Brown stared, too startled to protest, she

153

reached into her purse and extracted the pieces of the hundred-dollar bill Seamus had torn. "She isn't here, I gather," she said.

"You have a hell of a nerve," Doug snapped. "I could have you arrested for this."

"I wouldn't try," Ruth told him. "Here." She shoved the torn pieces of the bill into his hand. "You tell that parasite to tape this together and have her final fancy dinner on my husband. Tell her she's not getting another nickel from us and if she tries she'll regret it with every breath she draws for the rest of her life."

Ruth did not give Doug a chance to answer. Instead she walked over to the wall where Ethel's pictures were displayed and studied them. "She postures herself as doing good for all kinds of vague, undefined causes and goes around accepting her damn awards, and yet the one person who ever tried to treat her as a woman, as a human being, she's hounding to his grave." Ruth turned to face Doug. "I think she's despicable. I know what she thinks of you. You eat the food at fancy restaurants that my husband and I and our children are paying for, and, not satisfied with that, you steal from that woman. Ethel told my husband about you. I can only say, you deserve each other."

She was gone. His lips ashen, Doug collapsed onto the couch. Whom else had Ethel, with her big mouth, told about his habit of helping himself to her alimony loot?

When Ruth stepped onto the sidewalk she was hailed by a woman standing on the stoop of the brownstone. She looked to be in her early forties. Ruth observed that her blond hair was fashionably messy, that her pullover sweater and narrow slacks were trendy, and that her expression could only be described as one of unrestrained curiosity.

"I'm sorry to bother you," the woman said, "but I'm Georgette Wells, Ethel's neighbor, and I'm worried about her."

A thin teenager pushed open the house door, clattered down the steps and stood beside Wells. Her sharp eyes looked over Ruth and took in the fact that she was standing in front of Ethel's apartment. "You a friend of Ms. Lambston?" she asked.

Ruth was sure that this was the girl who had taunted Seamus. Intense dislike combined with cold, sinking dread to congeal her stomach muscles. Why was this woman worried about Ethel? She thought of the murderous fury on Seamus' face when he talked about Ethel's thrusting the hundred-dollar bill into his pocket. She thought of the tidy apartment she had just left. How many times over the years had Seamus told her that all Ethel had to do was walk into a room and it was as though the nuclear bomb hit it? Ethel had *not* been in that apartment recently.

"Yes," Ruth said, trying to sound pleasant. "I'm surprised Ethel isn't in, but is there any reason to worry?"

"Dana, get to school," her mother ordered. "You'll be late again."

Dana pouted. "I want to hear."

"All right, all right," Wells said impatiently, and turned back to Ruth. "There's something funny going on. Last week Ethel had a visit from her ex. Usually he only comes on the fifth of the month if he hasn't mailed the alimony.

So when I saw him sneaking around last Thursday afternoon, I thought something was funny. I mean it was only the thirtieth, so why should he pay her early? Well, let me tell you, they had a battle royal! I could hear them shouting at each other like I was in the room."

Ruth managed to keep her voice steady. "What were they saying?"

"Well, what I mean is I could hear shouting sounds. I couldn't hear what they were saying. I started to come downstairs just in case Ethel might be in trouble ...."

No, you wanted to hear better, Ruth thought.

"... but then my phone rang and it was my mother calling from Cleveland about my sister's divorce, and it was an hour before Ma stopped for breath. By then the fight was over. I phoned Ethel. She's really funny about her ex. Her imitation of him is priceless, you know? But she didn't answer, so I figured she'd gone out. You know the kind of person Ethel is—always rushing somewhere. But she usually tells me if she's going to be away for more than a couple of days, and she didn't say a word. Now her nephew is staying at the apartment and that's funny, too."

Georgette Wells folded her arms. "Kind of cold, isn't it? Crazy weather. All that hair spray in the ozone, I guess. Anyhow," she continued as Ruth stared at her and Dana hung on every word, "I have a *very funny feeling* that something happened to Ethel, and that wimp of an ex-husband of hers had something to do with it."

"And don't forget, Mama," Dana interrupted, "he came back on Wednesday and he acted real scared about something."

"I was going to get to that. You saw him Wednesday.

That was the fifth, so that means he was probably delivering the check. Then I saw him yesterday. Will you tell me why he came back? But nobody's seen Ethel. Now, the way I figure it, he might have done something to her and maybe left a clue that's worrying him." Georgette Wells smiled triumphantly, her story completed. "As a good friend of Ethel's," she asked Ruth, "help me decide. Should I call the police and tell them I think my neighbor may have been murdered?"

On Friday morning, Kitty Conway received a call from the hospital. One of the volunteer drivers was sick. Could she possibly fill in?

It was late afternoon before she was able to go home, change to a jogging suit and sneakers and head her car in the direction of Morrison State Park. The shadows were getting longer, and on the way she debated with herself about waiting until morning, then resolutely kept driving until she reached the park. The sunshine of the past few days had dried the macadam surface of the parking lot and the footpaths that arteried from it, but the heavily wooded areas were still damp underfoot.

Kitty walked to the perimeter of the stable, attempting to follow the trail that would retrace the route from which the horse had bolted forty-eight hours ago. But, to her chagrin, she realized that she was totally unsure which trail to follow. "Absolutely no sense of direction," she muttered as a branch slapped her face. She remembered that Mike used to draw painstaking sketches showing crossroads and landmarks whenever she drove alone to an unfamiliar place.

After forty wasted minutes, her sneakers were muddy and soaked, her legs were aching and she had accomplished nothing. She stopped to rest at a clearing where the riding classes from the stable would pause and regroup. There were no other hikers around and she could not hear any sounds of riders on the trails. The sun was almost completely gone. I must be crazy, she thought. This is no place to be alone. I'll come back tomorrow.

She got up and began to retrace her steps. Wait a minute, she thought, it was just past here. We took the fork on the right and went up that incline. Somewhere along there is where that damn nag decided to take off.

She knew she was right. A sense of anticipation combined with mounting dread made her heart pound furiously. During the sleepless night, her mind had been an out-of-control pendulum. She *had* seen a hand ... She *should* call the police ... Ridiculous. It was all her imagination. She'd look like a fool. She should make an anonymous call and stay out of it. No. Suppose she was right and they traced the call somehow. In the end she returned to the original plan. Look for herself.

It took twenty minutes to cover the ground the horses had made in five minutes. "This is where the stupid thing started eating all the junk-food weeds," she remembered. "I tugged the reins and it turned and went straight down here."

"Here" was a steep rocky incline. In the gathering darkness, Kitty began to make her way down it. The rocks slid out from under her sneakers. Once she lost her balance and fell, scraping her hand. I really need this, she thought. Even though it was very cool, beads of perspiration were forming on her forehead. She wiped them away with a hand now soiled from the loose dirt between the rocks. There was no sign of a blue sleeve.

Halfway down she came to a large rock and paused to rest on it. I was crazy, she decided. Thank God I didn't make a perfect fool of myself by calling the police. She'd catch her breath and get home to a hot shower. "Why anybody thinks hiking is fun is beyond me," she said aloud. When her breathing became even, she wiped her hands on her light-green jogging suit. She grasped the side of the rock with her right hand as she prepared to hoist herself up. And felt something.

Kitty looked down. She tried to scream, but no sound came, only a low, disbelieving moan. Her fingers were touching other fingers, manicured, with deep-red polish, help upward by the rocks that had slid around them, framed by the blue cuff that had intruded upon her sub-conscious, a scrap of black plastic, like a mourning band, embracing the slender inert wrist.

Denny Adler, in the guise of a wino, settled at seven o'clock on Friday morning against an apartment building directly across from Schwab House. It was still raw and breezy and he realized the odds were against Neeve Kearny walking to work. But long ago when he was track-ing someone he had learned to be patient. Big Charley had said that Kearny usually left for her shop pretty early, somewhere between seven-thirty and eight.

At about quarter of eight, the exodus started. Kids being picked up by a bus, headed for one of those fancy private schools. I went to a private school, too, Denny thought. Brownsville Reformatory in New Jersey.

Yuppies began to pour out. All in identical raincoats—no, *Burberrys,* Denny thought. Get it straight. Then the gray-haired executives, men and women. All sleek and prosperous-looking. From where he was positioned, he was able to observe them clearly.

At twenty of nine, Denny knew this wasn't his day. The one thing he couldn't risk was the deli manager getting mad at him. He was sure that with his record, he'd be pulled in for questioning when he completed the job. But he knew that even his parole officer would go to bat for him. "One of my best men," Toohey would say. "Never even late for work. He's clean."

Reluctantly Denny stood up, brushed his hands together and glanced down. He was wearing a filthy loose overcoat that smelled of cheap wine, an oversized cap with earmuffs that practically covered his face, and sneakers with holes in the sides. What didn't show was that under the coat he was neatly dressed in his work clothes, a faded denim zip-up jacket and matching jeans. He was carrying a shopping bag. It contained his everyday sneakers, a wet washcloth and a towel. A switchblade knife was in the right-hand pocket of the overcoat.

His plan was to go to the subway station at Seventy-second and Broadway, make his way to the end of the platform, drop the coat and cap into the shopping bag, change the filthy sneakers for the others, and sponge off his face and hands.

If only Kearny hadn't stepped into a cab last night! He could have sworn she was going to walk home. It would have been a great chance to hit her in the park. . . .

Patience born of the absolute certainty that his goal would be achieved, if not this morning, maybe this evening, if not today, maybe tomorrow, sent Denny on his way. He was careful to walk unevenly, to dangle the shopping bag as though he was hardly aware he was carrying it. The few people who bothered to glance at him edged away, the expression on their faces either disgusted or pitying.

As he crossed Seventy-second Street and West End, he collided with an old broad who was walking with her head down, her arm clamped around her pocketbook, her mouth mean and small. It would have been fun to give her a shove and grab that bag, Denny thought, then dismissed the idea. He hurried past her, turned onto Seventy-second Street and headed for the subway station.

A few minutes later he emerged, his face and hands clean, his hair slicked down, his faded denim jacket zipped neatly to his neck, the shopping bag containing the coat, cap, towel and washcloth tied into a neat bundle.

At ten-thirty he was delivering coffee to Neeve's office.

"Hi, Denny," she said when he went in. "I overslept this morning and now I can't get going. And I don't care what everybody else in this place says. Your coffee beats the stuff they brew in the coffeemaker."

"We all gotta oversleep once in a while, Miss Kearny," Denny said as he pulled the container from the bag and solicitously opened it for her.

Friday morning when Neeve awakened, she'd been startled to see that it was quarter to nine. Good Lord, she thought as she tossed back the covers and jumped out of bed, there's nothing like staying up half the night with the kids from the Bronx. She pulled on her robe and hurried into the kitchen. Myles had the coffee perking, juice poured and English muffins ready to be toasted. "You should have called me, Commish," she accused.

"It won't hurt the fashion industry to wait on you for half an hour." He was deep in the *Daily News*.

Neeve leaned over his shoulder. "Anything exciting?"

"A front-page account of the life and times of Nicky Sepetti. He's being buried tomorrow, escorted into eternity from a High Mass at St. Camilla's to interment in Calvary."

"Did you expect them to kick him around until they lost him?"

"No. I was hoping he'd be cremated and I could bid for the pleasure of sliding the coffin into the furnace."

"Oh, Myles, be quiet." Neeve tried to change the subject. "Last night was fun, wasn't it?"

"It *was* fun. Wonder how Sal's hand is. I'll bet he wasn't making love with his latest fiancée last night. Did you hear him say he's thinking of getting married again?"

Neeve downed the orange juice with an all-in-one vitamin. "You're kidding. Who's the lucky lady?"

"I'm not convinced 'lucky' is the word," Myles commented. "He's certainly had a variety of them. Never married till he made it big, and then runs the gamut from a lingerie model to a ballerina to a socialite to a health nut. Moves from Westchester to New Jersey to Connecticut to Sneden's Landing, and leaves them all behind in a fancy house. God knows what it's cost him over the years."

"Will he ever settle down?" Neeve asked.

"Who knows? No matter how many bucks he makes, Sal Esposito is always going to be an insecure kid trying to prove himself."

Neeve popped an English muffin into the toaster. "What else did I miss while I was fussing over a hot stove?"

"Dev's been summoned to the Vatican. That's just between us. He told me as they were leaving, when Sal went to pee—excuse me, your mother forbade me to say that. When Sal went in to wash his hands."

"I heard him say something about Baltimore. The archdiocese there?"

"He thinks it's coming."

"That could mean a red hat."

"It's possible."

"I must say you Bronx boys have been achievers. Must be something in the air."

The toaster popped. Neeve buttered the English muffin, generously spread it with marmalade and bit into it. Even though the day was obviously going to stay gloomy, the kitchen was cheerful with its white-stained oak cabinets and ceramic-tile floor in tones of blue, white and green. The place mats on the narrow butcher-block-top table were mint-green linen squares with matching napkins. The cups and saucers and plates and pitcher and creamer were legacies from Myles's boyhood. The English blue willow pattern. Neeve couldn't conceive of starting the day at home without that familiar china.

She studied Myles carefully. He really looked like himself again. It wasn't just Nicky Sepetti. It was the prospect of getting to work, of doing a job that was needed. She knew how Myles deplored the drug traffic and the carnage it was causing. And who knows? In Washington he might meet someone. He should marry again, and God knows he was a good-looking guy. She told him that.

"You mentioned the same thing last night," Myles told her. "I'm thinking of volunteering to pose for the centerfold of *Playgirl*. Do you think they'll take me?"

"If they do, bimbos will be lining up to seduce you," Neeve told him as she took her coffee back to her room, deciding it was high time to get a move on and go to work.

When he came out from shaving, Seamus realized that Ruth had left the apartment. For a moment he stood irresolute, then lumbered across the foyer into the bedroom, untied the cord of the maroon terry-cloth bathrobe the girls had given him for Christmas, and sank down on the bed. The sense of fatigue was so overwhelming that he could barely keep his eyes open. All he wanted to do was get back into bed, pull the covers over his head and sleep and sleep and sleep.

In all these years with all the problems, Ruth had never *not* slept with him. Sometimes they'd go for weeks, even months on end without touching each other, so strained with the money worries that their guts were torn out, but even so, by mutual unspoken consent they had lain together, both of them bound by the tradition that a woman slept at her husband's side.

Seamus looked around the room, seeing it through Ruth's eyes. The bedroom furniture that his mother had bought when he was ten. Not antique, just old—mahogany veneer, the mirror veering crazily on the supporting posts over the dresser. He could remember how his mother polished that piece of furniture, fussing over it, rejoicing in it. For her the matching set, the bed, dresser and chest, had been an accomplishment, the realized goal of a "nice home."

Ruth used to cut pictures from *House Beautiful* of the kind of rooms she'd like to have. Modern furniture. Pastel shades. Airy open look. Money worries had squeezed hope and brightness from her face, had made her too strict with the girls. He remembered the time she'd shrieked at Marcy, "What do you mean you tore your dress? I *saved* for that dress."

All because of Ethel.

Seamus leaned his head on his hands. The phone call he had made lay on his conscience. No way out. That had been the title of a movie a couple of years ago. *No Way Out.*

Last night he'd almost hit Ruth. The memory of those last few minutes with Ethel, the exact moment when he'd lost all control, when he'd . . .

He slumped back on the pillow. What was the point of going to the bar, of trying to keep up a front? He'd taken a step he wouldn't have believed possible. It was too late to call it off. He knew that. And it wouldn't do any good. He knew that too. He closed his eyes.

He wasn't aware that he'd dozed off, but suddenly Ruth was there. She was sitting on the edge of the bed. The anger seemed to have drained from her face. She looked haunted and panic-stricken, like someone facing a firing squad.

"Seamus," she said, "you've got to tell me everything. What did you do to her?"

. . .

Gordon Steuber arrived at his office on West Thirty-seventh Street at ten o'clock on Friday morning. He had come up in the elevator with three conservatively dressed men whom he instantly recognized as government auditors returning to pore over his books. His staff had only to see the scowl that made his eyebrows meet, the angry stride, to have the word begin to spread. "Watch out!"

He cut through the showroom, ignoring both clients and employees, walked rapidly past his secretary's desk, not deigning to respond to May's timid "Good morning, sir," and entered his private office, slamming the door behind him.

When he sat at his desk and leaned back in the ornate morocco leather chair that always inspired admiring comments, the scowl disappeared and was replaced by a worried frown.

He looked around the office, drinking in the atmosphere he had created for himself: the tooled-leather couches and chairs; the paintings that had cost a king's ransom; the sculptures that his art consultant assured him were of museum quality . . . Thanks to Neeve Kearny, there was a damn good chance he'd be spending more time in court than in his office. Or prison, he reflected, if he wasn't careful.

Steuber got up and walked over to the window. Thirty-seventh Street. The frantic atmosphere of the street peddler. It still had that quality. He remembered how as a kid he'd come directly from school to work for his father, a furrier. Cheap furs. The kind that made I. J. Fox creations look like sables. His father declared bankruptcy every couple of years like clockwork. By the time he was fifteen, Gordon knew he wasn't going to spend his life sneezing over rabbit hairs, talking dopes into thinking they looked good in mangy animal skins.

Linings. He'd figured it out before he was old enough to shave. The one constant. Whether you sold a jacket, a full-length, a fingertip, a stole or a cape, it had to be lined.

That simple realization together with a grudging loan from his father had been the beginning of Steuber Enterprises. The kids he'd hired fresh from FIT or Rhode Island School of Design had imagination and flair. His linings with their exciting patterns had caught on.

But linings didn't make you a byword in a business that hungered for recognition. That was when he started looking for kids who knew how to design suits. He made it his ambition to be the new Chanel.

Once again he'd succeeded. His suits were in the best stores. But he was one of a dozen, two dozen, all competing for the same upscale customer. Not enough money there.

Steuber reached for a cigarette. His gold lighter with his initials blazoned in rubies was on his desk. For an instant after he lit the cigarette, he held the lighter, turning it over and over in his hand. All the Feds had to do was add up how much the contents of this room and this lighter had cost and they'd keep digging till they had enough to indict him on income-tax evasion.

It was the damn unions that kept you from making a real profit, he told himself. Everyone knew that. Every time Steuber saw the ILGWU commercial he wanted to throw something at the television set. All they wanted was more money. Stop all the importing. Hire us.

167

It was only three years ago that he'd started doing what the rest of them did, set up off-the-books places for immigrants without green cards. Why not? The Mexicans were good seamstresses.

And then he'd found where the real money lay. He'd been all set to close out the sweatshops when Neeve Kearny blew the whistle on him. Then that crazy Ethel Lambston had started snooping around. He could still see that bitch bursting in here last week, last Wednesday evening. May was still outside. Otherwise right then . . .

He'd thrown her out, literally taken her shoulders and shoved her across the showroom to the main door, pushed her so she stumbled against the elevator. Even that hadn't fazed her. As he slammed the door, she'd shouted, "In case you haven't found out yet, they're going to get you on income tax as well as sweatshops. And that's just for starters. I know how you've been lining your pockets."

He'd known then that he couldn't let her keep digging into his affairs. She had to be stopped.

The phone rang, a soft purring sound. Annoyed, Gordon picked it up. "What is it, May?"

His secretary sounded apologetic. "I knew you wouldn't want to be disturbed, sir, but the agents from the United States Attorney's office insist on seeing you."

"Send them in." Steuber smoothed the jacket of his light-beige Italian silk suit, flicked a handkerchief over a smudge on his square-cut diamond cufflinks and settled himself in his desk chair.

As the three agents came in, professional and businesslike in their attitude, he remembered for the tenth time in the last hour that all this had begun because

Neeve Kearny had blown the whistle on his illegal factories.

At eleven o'clock on Friday morning, Jack Campbell returned from a staff meeting and again attacked the manuscript he had meant to read the night before. This time he forced himself to concentrate on the spicy adventures of a prominent thirty-three-year-old psychiatrist who falls in love with her client, an over-the-hill film idol. They go off to St. Martin's together on a clandestine vacation. The film idol because of his long and lusty experience with women breaks down the barriers the psychiatrist has built around her femininity. In turn, after three weeks of unending coupling under starry skies, she rebuilds his confidence in himself. He goes back to Los Angeles to accept the role as grandfather in a new situation comedy. She returns to her practice knowing that someday she'll meet a man suitable for a life with her. The book ends as she admits her new client, a handsome thirty-eight-year-old stockbroker who tells her, "I'm too rich, too scared, too lost."

Oh my God, Jack thought as he skimmed through the final pages. He tossed the manuscript on his desk just as Ginny came into the office, a pile of letters in her hand. She nodded in the direction of the manuscript. "How was it?"

"Frightful but it will sell big. Funny, in all those sex scenes in the garden, I kept wondering about love bites from the mosquitos. Is that a sign I'm getting old?"

Ginny grinned. "I doubt it. You know you have a lunch date?"

"I marked it down." Jack stood up and stretched.

Ginny looked at him approvingly. "Do you realize that all the junior editors are twittering about you? They keep asking me if I'm sure you're not involved with someone."

"Tell them you and I are an item."

"I wish. If I were twenty years younger, maybe."

Jack's smile turned to a frown. "Ginny, I just thought of something. How far ahead is the lead time of *Contemporary Woman*?"

"I'm not sure. Why?"

"I'm wondering if I can get a copy of the article Ethel Lambston did for them, the one on fashion? I know Toni usually won't show anything before the magazine's put to bed, but see what you can do, okay?"

"Sure."

An hour later when Jack left for lunch, Ginny called to him. "The article comes out in next week's issue. Toni said as a favor she'll let you see it. She's also going to send Xeroxes of Ethel's notes."

"That's great of her."

"She volunteered them," Ginny said. "She told me the outtakes of Ethel's articles usually make hotter reading than what the lawyers let them print in the magazine. Toni's getting worried about Ethel, too. She says since you're publishing Ethel's fashion book, she doesn't feel as though she's breaking confidentiality."

As Jack went down in the elevator on his way to his lunch date, he realized that he was very, very anxious to get a look at the outtakes in Ethel's file that were too hot to print.

• • •

Neither Seamus nor Ruth went to work on Friday. They sat in the apartment staring at each other like people caught together in quicksand, sinking, unable to reverse the inevitable. At noon, Ruth made strong coffee and grilled-cheese sandwiches. She insisted Seamus get up and dress. "Eat," she told him, "and tell me again exactly what happened."

As she listened, she could only imagine what it would do to the girls. Her hopes for them. The colleges she'd scrimped and sacrificed for. The dancing lessons and singing lessons, the clothes so carefully bought at sales. What good if their father was in prison?

Again Seamus blurted out the story. His round face glistening with perspiration, his hands thick and helpless in his lap, he recounted how he had begged Ethel to let him off the hook, how she'd toyed with him. "Maybe I will and maybe I won't," she'd said. Then she'd searched down behind the cushions of the couch. "Let me see if I can find some of the money my nephew forgot to steal," she told him, laughing, and, finding a hundred-dollar bill, she stuck it into his pocket with the remark that she hadn't had much time to eat out this month.

"I punched her," Seamus said tonelessly. "I never knew I was gonna do it. Her head lobbed to one side. She fell backwards. I didn't know if I'd killed her. She got up and she was scared. I told her if she looked for another dime, I would kill her. She knew I meant it. She said, 'All right, no more alimony.'"

Seamus gulped the rest of his coffee. They were sitting in the den. The day had started gray and cold, and now it was like early evening. Gray and cold. Just the way it had been last Thursday, at Ethel's apartment. The next day the storm broke. The storm would break again. He was sure of it.

"And then you left?" Ruth prompted.

Seamus hesitated. "And then I left."

There was a sense of something unfinished. Ruth looked around the room, at the heavy oak furniture she had despised for twenty years, at the faded machine-made Oriental that she had been forced to live with, and knew that Seamus had not told her the whole truth. She looked down at her hands. Too small. Square. Stubby fingers. All three girls had long, tapering fingers. Genes from whom? Seamus? Probably. Her family pictures showed small, square people. But they were strong. And Seamus was weak. A weak, frightened man who had turned desperate. *How* desperate? "You have not told me everything," she said. "I want to know. I have to know. It's the only way I can help you."

His head burrowed in his hands, he told her the rest. "Oh, my God," Ruth cried. "Oh, my God."

At one o'clock Denny returned to Neeve's Place carrying a cardboard tray containing two tuna-fish sandwiches and coffee. Again the receptionist waved him toward Neeve's office. Neeve was deep in conversation with her assistant, that good-looking black gal. Denny did not give either of them time to dismiss him. He opened the bag, removed the sandwiches and said, "You gonna eat here?"

"Denny, you're spoiling us. This is beginning to feel like room service," Neeve told him.

Denny froze, realizing his mistake. He was getting too visible. But he wanted to hear any plans she might have.

As though in answer to his unspoken request, Neeve told Eugenia, "I'll have to wait until late afternoon to go to Seventh Avenue on Monday. Mrs. Poth is coming in at one-thirty and wants me to help her select some gowns."

"That'll pay the rent for the next three months," Eugenia said briskly.

Denny folded the napkins. *Late afternoon on Monday.* That was good to know. He glanced around the room. Small office. No window. Too bad. If there'd been a window in the outside wall he'd have a direct shot at her back. But Charley had told him it couldn't look like a hit. His eyes swept over Neeve. Really good-looking. Really classy. With all the dogs out there, it was a real shame to have to waste this one. He muttered goodbye and departed, their thanks ringing in his ears. The receptionist paid him, adding the usual generous tip. But two bucks a delivery takes a long time before it adds up to twenty thousand, Denny thought as he opened the heavy glass door and stepped into the street.

While she was nibbling at the sandwich, Neeve dialed Toni Mendell at *Contemporary Woman.* When she heard Neeve's request, Mendell exclaimed, "Ye gods, what is this all about? Jack Campbell's secretary phoned asking for the same thing. I told her I'm worried about Ethel, too. I'll be honest. I let Jack see a copy of Ethel's notes because he's her publisher. Those I can't give you, but you can have the article." She cut through Neeve's attempt to thank her. "But for Pete's sake don't show it around. There'll be enough people in the rag game unhappy as it is when they see it."

An hour later, Neeve and Eugenia were poring over the copy of Ethel's article. It was entitled "The Masters and the Masterful Phonies of Fashion," and even for Ethel it was bitingly sarcastic. She began by naming the three most important fashions of the past fifty years: the New Look by Christian Dior in 1947, the Miniskirt by Mary Quant in the early sixties, and the Pacific Reef Look by Anthony della Salva in 1972.

About Dior, Ethel had written:

In 1947 fashion was in the doldrums, still hung over with the military fashions of the war. Skimpy material; boxy shoulders; brass buttons. Dior, a shy young designer, said that we want to forget all about the war. He dismissed short skirts as a fashion of restriction. Showing what a real genius he was, he had the guts to tell a disbelieving world that the gown of the future for daytime wear would extend to twelve and a half inches from the ground.

It wasn't easy for him. A California klutz tripped over her long skirt getting off the bus and helped fan a national revolt against the New Look. But Dior stuck to his guns, or his scissors, and, season after season, introduced graceful, beautiful clothes—drapery below the décolletage, molded midriffs with unpressed pleats that merged onto slender skirts. And his long-ago prediction was proven in the latest miniskirt disaster. Maybe someday all designers will learn that mystique is an important guideline to fashion.

By the early sixties the times were changing. We can't blame it all on Vietnam or Vatican II, but the wave of change was in the air and an English designer, young and perky, swept onto the scene. She was Mary Quant, the little girl who didn't want to grow up and never, never wanted to wear grown-up clothes. Enter the Miniskirt, the shift, colored stockings, high boots. Enter the premise that the young must *never* on any account look old. When Mary Quant was asked to explain the point of fashion, where it was leading, she brightly answered, "Sex."

In 1972 it was all over for the Miniskirt. Women, tired of being confused by the hemline game, gave up the struggle and switched to menswear.

Enter Anthony della Salva and the Pacific Reef Look. Della Salva began life not in a palace on one of the seven hills of Rome, as his publicist would have you believe, but as Sal Esposito, in a farm on Williamsbridge Road in the Bronx. His sense of color may have been cultivated by helping his father arrange the fruits and vegetables on the truck from which they peddled their wares throughout the neighborhood. His mother, Angelina, not *Countess* Angelina, was famous for her cant-like greeting, "God bless youra momma. God bless youra papa. How about some nicea grapefruit?"

Sal was a mediocre student at Christopher Columbus High School (that's in the Bronx, not Italy), a very mildly talented student at F.I.T. Just one of the crowd, but as fate would have it, eventually one of the blessed. He came up with the collection that put him over the top: the Pacific Reef Look, his one and only original idea.

But what an idea. Della Salva, in a single, magnificent stroke, put fashion back on the track. Anyone who attended that first fashion show in 1972 still remembers the impact of those graceful clothes that seemed to float from the models: the tunic with the drifting shoulder panel, the wool afternoon dresses cut so that they draped and shaped the body, the use of pleated sleeves in tones that shimmered and changed with the light. And his colors. He took the colors of the tropical Pacific ocean life, the coral trees and plants and underwater creatures, and borrowed the patterns nature gave them to create his own exotic designs, some brilliantly bold, some muted like the blues into silvers. The designer of the Pacific Reef Look deserves all the honors the fashion industry can bestow.

At that point, Neeve laughed reluctantly. "Sal will love what Ethel wrote about the Pacific Reef," she said, "but I don't know about the rest. He's lied so much, he's convinced himself he was born in Rome and his mother was a papal countess. On the other hand, from what he said the other night, he's expecting something like it. Everyone's hollering about how tough their parents had it these days. He'll probably find out what ship his folks were on when they sailed to Ellis Island and have a replica made of it."

Having covered the giant fashion looks as she saw them, Ethel proceeded in the article to name the society designers who couldn't tell "a button from a buttonhole" and hired talented young people to plan and execute their lines; to expose the conspiracy among designers to take the easy way out and try to turn fashion upside down every few years, even when it meant dressing aging dowagers like cancan girls; to mock the cowlike followers who plunked down three or four thousand dollars for a suit with barely two yards of gabardine.

Then Ethel turned her guns on Gordon Steuber:

The Triangle Shirtwaist Company fire of 1911 alerted the public to the horrendous working conditions of garment workers. Thanks to the International Ladies Garment Workers Union, the ILGWU, the fashion industry has become a field where talented people can make decent incomes. But some manufacturers have found a way to increase their profits at the expense of the helpless. The new sweatshops are in the South Bronx and Long Island City. Illegal immigrants, many of them hardly more than children, work for pitiful wages because they don't have green cards and are afraid to protest. The king of these cheating manufacturers is Gordon Steuber. Much, much more about Steuber in a future article, but just remember, folks. Every time you put one of his suits on your back, give a thought to the kid who sewed it. She probably can't afford a decent meal.

The article concluded with a paean of praise for Neeve Kearny of Neeve's Place, who started the investigation of Gordon Steuber and who banned his clothes from her shop.

Neeve skimmed the rest of the text about her, then put down the papers. "She's drawn a bead on every major designer in the field! Maybe she scared herself and decided to get away until the heat dies down. I'm beginning to wonder."

"Can't Steuber sue her and the magazine?" Eugenia asked.

"Truth is the best defense. They obviously have all the proof they need. What *really* kills me is that despite all this, Ethel bought one of his suits last time she was here —the one we slipped up on returning."

The phone rang. A moment later the receptionist buzzed on the intercom. "Mr. Campbell for you, Neeve."

Eugenia's eyes raised. "You should see the look on your face." She gathered the remains of the sandwiches with the paper wrappings and the coffee containers and swept them into the wastebasket.

Neeve waited until the door closed before she picked up the phone. She tried to make her voice casual when she said, "Neeve Kearny." Dismayed, she realized she sounded breathless.

Jack came right to the point. "Neeve, can you have dinner with me tonight?" He didn't wait for her answer. "I was planning to tell you that I have some of Ethel Lambston's notes and maybe we could go over them together, but the real fact is I want to see you."

Neeve was embarrassed to realize how her heart was pounding. They agreed to meet at the Carlyle at seven o'clock.

The rest of the afternoon became unexpectedly busy. At four, Neeve went out on the showroom floor and began to take customers. They were all new faces. One young girl who couldn't have been more than nineteen bought a fourteen-hundred-dollar evening gown and a nine-hundred-dollar cocktail dress. She was very insistent that Neeve help her choose. "You know," she confided, "one of my girlfriends works at *Contemporary Woman* and she saw an article that's coming out next week. It says you have more fashion in your little finger than most of the designers on Seventh Avenue and that you never steer people wrong. When I told my mother she sent me over here."

Two other new customers had the same story. Someone knew someone who had told them about the article. At six-thirty, Neeve gratefully put a "CLOSED" sign on the door. "I'm beginning to think we'd better stop knocking poor Ethel," she said. "She's probably hyped business more than if I'd taken ads on every page of *WWD*."

After work Doug Brown stopped at the local superette on his way to Ethel's apartment. It was six-thirty when, as he was turning the key in the lock, he heard the persistent ringing of the phone.

At first he decided to ignore it as he had done all week. But when it relentlessly continued to peal, he debated. It was one thing that Ethel didn't like anyone to answer her phone. But after a week, wouldn't it seem logical that she might be trying to reach him?

He placed the grocery bag in the kitchen. The harsh ringing continued. Finally he picked up the receiver. "Hello."

The voice at the other end was slurred and guttural. "I have to talk to Ethel Lambston."

"She isn't here. I'm her nephew. Do you want to leave a message?"

"You bet I do. Tell Ethel her ex owes a lot of money to the wrong people and can't pay it while he's paying her. If she don't let Seamus off the hook, they're going to teach her a lesson. Tell her she might have a hard time typing with broken fingers."

There was a click and the line went dead.

Doug dropped the receiver onto the cradle and sank onto the couch. He could feel the perspiration on his forehead, in his armpits. He folded his hands to keep them from trembling.

What should he do? Was the call a real threat or a trick? He couldn't ignore it. He didn't want to call the police. They might start asking questions.

*Neeve Kearny.*

She was the one who was worried about Ethel. He'd tell her about the call. He'd be the scared, concerned relative asking for advice. That way, no matter whether it was a trick or for real, he'd have covered himself.

. . .

Eugenia was locking the cases with the fine costume jewelry when the phone rang in the shop. She picked up the receiver. "It's for you, Neeve. Someone sounds terribly upset."

Myles! Another heart attack? Neeve rushed to the phone. "Yes."

But it was Douglas Brown, Ethel Lambston's nephew. There was none of the usual sarcastic insolence in his voice. "Miss Kearny, have you *any* idea where I can try to reach my aunt? I just got back to her place and the phone was ringing. Some guy told me to warn her that Seamus, that's her ex-husband, owes a lot of money and can't pay it while he's paying her. If she doesn't let Seamus off the hook they're going to teach her a lesson. *She might have a hard time typing with broken fingers,* the guy said."

Douglas Brown sounded almost tearful. "Miss Kearny, we have to warn Ethel."

When Doug hung up, he knew he had made the right decision. At the advice of the ex–Police Commissioner's daughter, he would now phone the police and report the threat. In the eyes of the cops, he'd be viewed as a friend of the Kearny family.

He was reaching for the phone when it rang again. This time he picked it up without hesitation.

The police were calling *him.*

. . .

Myles Kearny believed in getting out of the way on Friday whenever it was possible. Lupe, their longtime cleaning woman, was there all day, washing and polishing, vacuuming and scrubbing.

When Lupe arrived, the morning mail in her hand, Myles retreated to the den. There was another letter from Washington, urging him to accept the post as head of the Drug Enforcement Agency.

Myles felt the old adrenaline flowing through his veins. Sixty-eight. It wasn't that old. And to get his teeth into a job that needed doing. Neeve. I fed her too much of love at first sight, he told himself. For most people it just doesn't work like that. Without me around all the time, she'll join the real world.

He leaned back in the desk chair, the old, comfortable leather chair that had been in his office the sixteen years he'd been Police Commissioner. It fits my butt, he thought. If I go to Washington, I'll ship it down.

In the foyer he could hear the sound of the vacuum. I don't want to listen to that all day, he thought. On impulse he phoned his old number, the office of the Commissioner, identified himself to Herb Schwartz's secretary, and a moment later was on the phone with Herb.

"Myles, what are you up to?"

"My question first," Myles responded. "How is Tony Vitale?" He could envision Herb, small stature, small frame, wise and penetrating eyes, tremendous intellect, incredible ability to see the whole picture. And, best of all, true-blue friend.

"We're still not sure. They left him for dead and, be-

Mary Higgins Clark

lieve me, they had a right to think they knew what they were doing. But the kid's tremendous. Against all odds, the doctors think he'll make it. I'm going to see him later. Want to come?"

They agreed to meet for lunch.

Over turkey sandwiches in a bar near St. Vincent's Hospital, Herb briefed Myles on the upcoming Nicky Sepetti funeral. "We've got it covered. The FBI has it covered. The U.S. Attorney's office has it covered. But I don't know, Myles. My guess is that with or without the celestial summons, Nicky was old news. Seventeen years is too long to be out of circulation. The whole world's changed. In the old days the mob wouldn't have touched drugs. Now they're swimming in them. Nicky's world doesn't exist anymore. If he'd stayed, they'd have had him hit."

After lunch they went to the ICU at St. Vincent's. Undercover detective Anthony Vitale was swathed in bandages. Intravenous fluid dripped into his veins. Machines registered his blood pressure, his heartbeats. His parents were in the waiting room.

"They let us see him for a few minutes every hour," his father said. "He's going to make it." There was quiet confidence in his voice.

"You can't kill a tough cop," Myles told him as he gripped his hand.

Tony's mother spoke up. "Commissioner." She was speaking to Myles. He started to indicate Herb, but was stopped by the slight negative movement Herb made. "Commissioner, I think Tony is trying to tell us something."

"He told us what we needed to hear. That Nicky Sepetti didn't put a contract out on my daughter."

Rosa Vitale shook her head. "Commissioner, I've been with Tony every hour for the last two days. That's not enough. There's something else he wants us to know."

There was a round-the-clock guard on Tony. Herb Schwartz beckoned to the young detective who was sitting in the nurses' station of the ICU. "Listen," he told him.

Myles and Herb went down in the elevator together. "What do you think?" Herb asked.

Myles shrugged. "If there's anything I've learned to trust, it's a mother's instinct." He thought of that long-ago day when his mother had told him to look up the nice family who had sheltered him during the war. "There's plenty Tony could have learned that night. They must have been going over everything to make Nicky feel up-to-date." A thought struck him. "Oh, Herb, by the way, Neeve has been pestering me because some writer she knows has dropped out of sight. Tell the guys to keep an eye out for her, will you? About sixty. Five five and a half or six. Dresses well. Dyed silver blonde. Weighs about one-thirty-five. Name is Ethel Lambston. She's probably making someone's life miserable interviewing them for her column, but . . ."

The elevator stopped. They stepped into the lobby, and Schwartz pulled out a pad. "I've met Lambston at Gracie Mansion. She's been giving the Mayor a lot of plugs and he has her there all the time now. Something of an airhead, isn't she?"

"You've got it."

They both laughed.

"Why is Neeve worried about her?"

"Because she swears Lambston left home last Thursday or Friday without a winter coat. She buys all her clothes from Neeve."

"Maybe she was going to Florida or the Caribbean and didn't want to drag one along," Herb suggested.

"That was one of the many possibilities I pointed out to Neeve, but she claims all the clothes missing from Ethel's closet are for winter wear, and Neeve would know."

Herb frowned. "Maybe Neeve is onto something. Go over the description again."

Myles went home to the peace and quiet of the shiningly clean apartment. Neeve's phone call at six-thirty both pleased and disturbed him. "You're going out to dinner. Good. I hope he's interesting."

Then she told him about her call from Ethel's nephew. "You told him to report the threat to the police. That was the right thing to do. Maybe she did get nervous and take off. I spoke to Herb about her today. I'll let him know about this."

Myles settled for fruit and crackers and a glass of Perrier for his own dinner. As he ate and tried to concentrate on *Time* magazine, he found himself increasingly concerned that he had so casually brushed off Neeve's instinct that Ethel Lambston was in serious trouble.

He poured a second Perrier and got to the center of his discomfort. The threatening phone call, as reported by the nephew, did *not* have the ring of truth.

. . .

Neeve and Jack Campbell sat on a banquette in the dining room of the Carlyle. On impulse, she had changed from the sweater dress she'd worn to work to a soft multicolored print. Jack had ordered drinks, a vodka martini straight up with olives for himself, a glass of champagne for Neeve. "You remind me of the song 'A Pretty Girl Is Like a Melody,' " he said. "Or is it all right to call anyone a pretty girl these days? Would you rather be a handsome person?"

"I'll settle for the song."

"Isn't that one of the dresses the mannequins are wearing in your show windows?"

"You're very observant. When did you see them?"

"Last night. And I didn't just happen by. I was overwhelmingly curious." Jack Campbell did not seem uncomfortable disclosing that fact.

Neeve studied him. Tonight he was wearing a dark-blue suit with a faint chalk stripe. Unconsciously she nodded approval at the overall effect, the Hermès tie that exactly picked up the blue, the custom-made shirt, the plain gold cufflinks.

"Will I pass?" he asked.

Neeve grinned. "Very few men manage to wear a tie that really goes with the suit. I've been laying out my father's ties for years."

The waiter arrived with the drinks. Jack waited until he'd left before he spoke. "I wish you'd fill me in a little. Starting with where did you get the name Neeve?"

"It's Celtic. Actually it's spelled N-I-A-M-H and pronounced 'Neeve.' Long ago I gave up trying to explain it, so when I opened the shop I just used the phonetic spelling. You'd be amazed at how much time I've saved myself, to say nothing of the aggravation of being called Nim-ah."

"And who was the original Neeve?"

"A goddess. Some say the exact translation is 'star of the morning.' My favorite legend about her is that she swooped down to earth to pick up the fellow she wanted. They were happy for a long time, then he wanted to visit earth again. It was understood that if his feet touched the ground he would become his real age. You can guess the rest. He slipped from the horse, and poor Niamh left him a bag of bones and returned to the skies."

"Is that what you do to your admirers?"

They laughed together. It seemed to Neeve that it was by mutual consent they were putting off talking about Ethel. She had told Eugenia about the phone call, and, oddly, Eugenia found it reassuring. "If Ethel got a call like that, it says to me that she decided to take off until things cool down. You told her nephew to report it to the police. Your father's on top of it. You can't do anything else. My bet is that good old Ethel is holed up in a spa."

Neeve wanted to believe it. She put Ethel out of her mind as she sipped the champagne and smiled across the table at Jack Campbell.

Over celery rémoulade, they talked about growing up. Jack's father was a pediatrician. Jack had been raised in a suburb of Omaha. He had one older sister, who still lived near his parents. "Tina has five kids. The nights get cold in Nebraska." He had worked in a bookstore summers during high school and become fascinated with publishing. "So after Northwestern, I went to work in

Chicago selling college textbooks. That's enough to prove your manliness. Part of the job is to see if any of the professors you're peddling books to may be *writing* a book. One of them haunted me with her autobiography. Finally I said, 'Madam, let's face it. You've had a very boring life.' She complained to my boss."

"Did you lose your job?" Neeve asked.

"No. They made me an editor."

Neeve glanced around the room. The soft elegance of the ambience; the delicate china, handsome silver and fine damask tablecloths; the flower arrangements; the pleasant murmur of voices from other tables. She felt remarkably, absurdly happy. Over rack of lamb, she told Jack about herself. "My father fought tooth and nail to send me away to college, but I liked being home. I went to Mount St. Vincent and spent one term in England at Oxford, then a year at the University of Perugia. Summers and after school I worked in dress shops. I always knew what I wanted to do. My idea of a good time was to go to a fashion show. Uncle Sal was great. From the time my mother died, he'd send a car to take me when a collection was being unveiled."

"What do you do for fun?" Jack asked.

The question was too casual. Neeve smiled, knowing why he'd asked it. "For four or five summers I had a share in a house in the Hamptons," she told him. "That was great. I skipped last year because Myles was so sick. In the winter, I ski in Vail for at least a couple of weeks. I was there in February."

"Who do you go with?"

"Always my best friend, Julie. The other faces change."

He asked it straight out. "How about men?"

Neeve laughed. "You sound like Myles. I swear he won't be happy till he's playing father of the bride. Sure I've dated a lot. I went with the same guy practically through college."

"What happened?"

"He went to Harvard for an MBA and I got involved with the dress shop. We just drifted into our own worlds. His name was Jeff. Then there was Richard. A really nice person. But he took a job in Wisconsin and I knew there was no way I could leave the Big Apple forever, so it couldn't be true love." She began to laugh. "The nearest I came to getting engaged was a couple of years ago. That was Gene. We broke up at a charity do on the *Intrepid*."

"The ship?"

"Uh-huh. It's docked on the Hudson at West Fifty-sixth. Anyhow, the party's held on Labor Day weekend: black tie, tons of people. I swear I know ninety percent of the regulars at it. Gene and I got separated in the crowd. I didn't worry. I figured we'd catch up eventually. But when we did, he was furious. Thought I should have tried harder to find him. I saw a side of him I knew I didn't want to live with." Neeve shrugged. "The simple truth is I don't think anyone has been right for me."

"So far," Jack smiled. "I'm beginning to think you *are* the legendary Neeve who leaves her admirers behind as she rides away. You haven't been exactly pounding me with questions about myself, but I'll tell you anyhow. I'm a good skier, too. I went to Arosa the past couple of Christmas holidays. I'm planning to look for a summer place where I can have a sailboat. Maybe you'd better show me around the Hamptons. Like you, I came close to settling down a couple of times. In fact, I actually got engaged about four years ago."

"My turn to ask: What happened?" Neeve said.

Jack shrugged. "Once the diamond was on her finger, she became a very possessive young lady. I realized I'd run out of breathing room pretty fast. I'm a great believer in Kahlil Gibran's advice on marriage."

"Something about 'the pillars of the temple stand apart'?" Neeve asked.

She was rewarded by his expression of amused respect. "You've got it."

They waited until they'd finished their raspberries and were sipping espresso before they discussed Ethel. Neeve told Jack about the phone call from Ethel's nephew and the possibility that Ethel was hiding out. "My father is in touch with his department. He'll get them to run down who's making the threats. And, frankly, I have to say I do think Ethel should let that poor guy off the hook. It's disgusting to be collecting from him all these years. She needs that alimony like a hole in the head."

Jack pulled the folded copy of the article from his pocket. Neeve told him she'd already seen it. "Would you call this scandalous?" Jack asked her.

"No. I'd call it funny and bitchy and sarcastic and readable and potentially libelous. There isn't a thing in it that everyone in the business doesn't know already. I'm not sure how Uncle Sal will react, but knowing him I swear he'll turn it into a virtue that his mother peddled fruit. Gordon Steuber I'd worry about. I have a hunch he could be vicious. The other designers Ethel drew a bead on? What can you say? Everyone knows that except for one or two, the society designers can't draw straight. They just love the excitement of playing at working."

Jack nodded. "Next question. Do you think anything in this article would make an explosive book?"

"No. Even Ethel couldn't pull that off."

"I have a file of all the outtakes from the article. I haven't had a chance to study them yet." Jack signaled for the check.

Across the street from the Carlyle, Denny was waiting. It was a long shot. He knew that. He'd followed Neeve when she walked along Madison Avenue to the hotel, but there'd been absolutely no chance to get near her. Too many people. Big guys on their way home from work. Even if he'd been able to waste her, the chances that someone would deck him were too strong. His only hope was that Neeve might come out alone, maybe walk to the crosstown bus, or even walk home. But when she came out, she was with some guy and they got into a cab together.

A sense of frustration made Denny's face turn ugly under the smears of dirt that made him blend in with the other winos in the area. If this weather kept up, she'd always be in cabs. He had to work over the weekend. There was no way he was going to risk drawing attention to himself at the job. So that meant he could only hang around her apartment building early in the morning in case she went to the store or jogged, or after six o'clock.

That left Monday. And the Garment District. Somehow

Denny felt in his bones that that was where he'd end up. He slipped into a doorway, shrugged off the ragged overcoat, wiped his face and hands with a grimy towel, shoved coat and towel into a shopping bag and headed for a bar on Third Avenue. His gut was burning for a boilermaker.

It was ten o'clock when the cab pulled up to Schwab House. "My father will be having a nightcap," Neeve told Jack. "Are you interested?"

Ten minutes later they were in the study, sipping brandy. Neeve knew that something was wrong. There was a look of concern in Myles's expression even while he chatted easily with Jack. She sensed he had something to tell her that he would not discuss now.

Jack was telling Myles about meeting Neeve on the plane. "She ran so fast I couldn't get her number. And she tells me she'd missed her connection."

"I can vouch for that," Myles said. "I waited for her at the airport for four hours."

"I must say I was delighted when she came up to me at the cocktail party the other day and asked about Ethel Lambston. I gather from what Neeve tells me Ethel isn't one of your favorite people, Mr. Kearny."

Neeve gasped at the change in Myles's face. "Jack," he said, "someday I'll learn to listen to Neeve's intuition." He turned to Neeve. "Herb phoned a couple of hours ago. A body was found in Morrison State Park in Rockland County. It answered Ethel's description. They brought Ethel's nephew out and he identified her."

"What happened to her?" Neeve whispered.

"Her throat was cut."

Neeve closed her eyes. "I *knew* something was wrong. I *knew* it!"

"You were right. They already have a hot suspect, it seems. When the upstairs neighbor saw the squad car she came running down. Seems Ethel had a colossal fight with her ex-husband last Thursday afternoon. Apparently no one has seen her since then. On Friday she broke her appointments with you and with her nephew."

Myles swallowed the last of the brandy and got up to refill his glass. "I don't usually have a second brandy, but tomorrow morning the homicide guys from the Twentieth Precinct want to talk to you. And the DA's office in Rockland County has asked if you'd go out and look at the clothing Ethel was wearing. The point is they know the body was moved after death. I told Herb that you spotted the fact that none of her coats was missing and that she bought all her stuff from you. The labels were ripped out of the suit she was wearing. They want to see if you can identify it as one of yours. God *damn* it, Neeve," Myles exclaimed. "I don't like the idea of you being a witness in a murder case."

Jack Campbell reached out his glass for a refill. "Neither do I," he said quietly.

**9** Sometime during the night the wind had shifted, and the low-hanging clouds were blown out over the Atlantic. Saturday dawned with a welcoming golden sun. But the air was still unseasonably cold, and the CBS weatherman warned that the clouds would be back and there might even be snow flurries in the afternoon. Neeve bounded out of bed. She had a date to go jogging with Jack at seven-thirty.

She pulled on a sweatsuit, her Reeboks, and tied her hair back into a ponytail. Myles was already in the kitchen. He frowned.

"I just don't like you jogging alone this early."

"Not alone."

Myles raised his eyes. "I see. Moving fast, aren't we? I like him, Neeve."

She poured orange juice. "Now, don't get your hopes up. You liked the stockbroker too."

"I didn't say I liked that one. I said he seemed respectable. There's a difference." Myles dropped the bantering. "Neeve, I've been thinking. It makes more sense for you to go to Rockland County and talk to those detectives before you sit down with our guys. If you're right, the clothes Ethel Lambston was wearing came from your shop. So that's the first thing we establish. My guess is that after that you should go through her closet with a fine-tooth comb and see exactly what else is missing. We know homicide is going to zero in on the ex-husband, but you can't assume anything."

The intercom rang. Neeve picked up the receiver. It was Jack. "I'll be right down," she told him.

"What time do you want to go to Rockland County?" she asked Myles. "I really have to go to work for a while."

"Midafternoon will be fine." At her surprised expression, Myles added, "Channel Eleven is covering Nicky Sepetti's funeral live. I want a front-row seat."

· · ·

Denny had taken up his position at seven o'clock. At seven-twenty-nine he saw a tall guy in a running suit go into Schwab House. A few minutes later, Neeve Kearny emerged with him. They started jogging toward the park. Denny swore silently under his breath. If she'd only been alone. He had cut through the park on the way over. It was almost deserted. He could have wasted her anywhere. He felt for the pistol in his pocket. Last night when he'd gone back to his room Big Charley had been parked across the street waiting for him. Charley had rolled down the car window and handed out a brown paper bag. Denny had taken it, and his fingers had felt the outline of the gun.

"Kearny is starting to cause real trouble," Big Charley told him. "It don't matter no more if it looks like an accident. Get her any way you can."

Now he was tempted to follow them into the park, to hit the two of them. But Big Charley might not like that.

Denny began to walk in the opposite direction. Today he was wrapped in a bulky sweater that hung to his knees, torn chinos, leather sandals, a stocking cap that had once been bright yellow. Under it he was wearing a gray wig; bits of greasy gray hair were plastered on his forehead. He looked like a mainliner with scrambled brains. In the other getup he looked like a wino. But this way no one would remember that any one guy had been hanging around Neeve Kearny's building.

As Denny put a token into the turnstile at the Seventy-second Street subway, he thought, I oughtta charge Big Charley the money it cost me to change my clothes.

. . .

Neeve and Jack entered the park at Seventy-ninth Street and began jogging east, then north. As they approached the Metropolitan Museum, Neeve instinctively began to cut west again. She did not want to pass the place where her mother had died. But at Jack's puzzled glance she said, "Sorry, you lead."

She tried to keep her eyes resolutely forward but could not resist glancing at the area past the still bare trees. *The day Mother hadn't arrived to pick her up at school. The principal, Sister Maria, had her wait in the office and suggested she begin her homework. It was nearly five o'clock before Myles came for her. By then she'd been sure something was wrong. Mother was never late.*

*The moment when she'd looked up and seen Myles standing over her, his eyes red-rimmed, his expression a mixture of anguish and pity, she'd known. She'd reached up her arms to him. "Is my mother dead?"*

*"You poor little kid," Myles had said as he picked her up and hugged her against him. "You poor little kid."*

Neeve felt tears glisten in her eyes. In a burst of speed she ran past the quiet lane, past the extension of the Met that held the Egyptian collection. She was almost to the reservoir before she slowed down.

Jack had kept pace with her. Now he took her arm. "Neeve." It was a question. As they turned west and then south, now gradually reducing their pace to a fast walk, she told him about Renata.

They left the park at Seventy-ninth Street. The last few blocks to Schwab House they walked side by side, their fingers linked.

. . .

When she turned on the radio at seven o'clock on Saturday morning, Ruth heard the news of Ethel's death. She had taken a sleeping pill at midnight and for the next hours slept a heavy, drugged sleep that was filled with vaguely remembered nightmares. Seamus was arrested. Seamus on trial. That she-devil, Ethel, testifying against him. Years ago Ruth had worked in a law office, and she had a fair knowledge of the kind of charges that could be leveled against Seamus.

But as she listened to the newscast and lowered the teacup from her trembling fingers, she realized that she could add one more count: *murder*.

She shoved her chair back from the table and ran into the bedroom. Seamus was just waking up. Shaking his head, he ran his hand over his face, a characteristic gesture that had always annoyed her.

"You *killed* her!" she screamed. "How can I help you if you won't tell me the truth!"

"What are you talking about?"

She snapped on the radio. The newscaster was describing how and where Ethel had been found. "You took the girls picnicking to Morrison State Park for years," she cried. "You know the place like the back of your hand. *Now tell me the truth! Did you stab her?*"

An hour later, paralyzed with fright, Seamus made his way to the pub. Ethel's body had been found. He knew the police would come for him.

Yesterday, Brian, the day bartender, had worked a double shift. To show his displeasure, he'd left the bar sticky and untidy. The Vietnamese kid who handled the kitchen was already there. At least *he* was a willing worker. "Are you sure you should have come in, Mr. Lambston?" he asked. "You still look real sick."

Seamus tried to remember what Ruth had told him. *"Say you have a touch of flu. You never miss work. They've got to believe you were really sick yesterday, that you were sick last weekend. They've got to believe you never left the apartment last weekend. Did you talk to anyone? Did anyone see you? That neighbor is bound to tell them you were there a couple of times last week."*

"Darn bugs keep coming back on me," he mumbled. "Yesterday was bad, but over the weekend I was *sick*."

Ruth phoned at ten o'clock. Childlike, he listened and repeated word for word what she told him.

He opened the pub at eleven. At noon the old-timers who were still around started drifting in. "Seamus," one of them boomed, his jovial face creased in smiles, "sad news about poor Ethel, but grand that you're off the hook for the alimony. Drinks on the house?"

At two o'clock, shortly after the reasonably busy lunch service was winding down, two men entered the bar. One was in his early fifties, with a beefy build and ruddy complexion, a man who might as well have had a sign on him reading "COP." His partner was a slim Hispanic, in his late twenties. They identified themselves as Detectives O'Brien and Gomez from the Twentieth Precinct.

"Mr. Lambston," O'Brien asked quietly. "Are you aware that your former wife, Ethel Lambston, has been found in Morrison State Park, that she has been the victim of a homicide?"

Seamus gripped the edge of the bar with knuckles that turned white. He nodded, unable to speak.

"Would you mind stepping over to headquarters?" Detective O'Brien asked. He cleared his throat. "We'd like to go over a few things with you."

After Seamus left for the pub, Ruth dialed Ethel Lambston's apartment. The phone was picked up, but no one spoke. Finally she said, "I would like to speak with Ethel Lambston's nephew, Douglas Brown. This is Ruth Lambston."

"What do you want?" It was the nephew's voice. Ruth recognized it.

"I must see you. I'll be right there."

Ten minutes later a cab was dropping her in front of Ethel's apartment. As she stepped out and handed the fare to the driver, Ruth looked up. A curtain moved on the fourth floor. The upstairs neighbor who missed nothing.

Douglas Brown had been watching for her. He opened the door and stepped back to allow her to come into the apartment. It was still inordinately tidy, although Ruth noticed a fine layer of dust on the table. New York apartments needed daily dusting.

Not believing that the thought could even cross her mind at a time like this, she stood directly in front of Douglas, noticing the expensive bathrobe, the silk pajamas that peered out from the hem of the robe. Douglas looked heavy-eyed, as though he'd been drinking. His even features would have been handsome if they were strong. Instead they reminded Ruth of sculptures children made in sand, sculptures that washed away with wind and the tide.

"What do you want?" he demanded.

"I won't waste your time or mine saying I'm sorry Ethel is dead. I want the letter Seamus wrote her, and I want you to put this in its place." She extended her hand. The envelope was unsealed. Douglas opened it. It contained an alimony check dated April 5.

"What are you trying to pull?"

"I'm not pulling anything. I'm making an even exchange. Give me back the letter Seamus wrote Ethel, and get something straight. The reason Seamus came here on Wednesday was to deliver the alimony. Ethel wasn't home and he came back on Thursday because he was worried that he hadn't been able to force the envelope into her mailbox. He knew she'd haul him into court if it wasn't there."

"Why would I do that?"

"Because last year Seamus asked Ethel to whom she was going to leave all her money, that's why. She told him she had no choice—you were her only relative. But last week Ethel told Seamus you were stealing from her and she was planning to change her will."

Ruth watched as Douglas turned a chalky white. "You're lying."

"Am I?" Ruth asked. "I'm giving *you* a break. You give Seamus a break. We'll keep our mouths shut about your being a thief, and you keep your mouth shut about the letter."

Douglas felt grudging admiration for the determined woman who was standing in front of him, handbag clutched under her arm, sensible all-weather coat, sensible shoes, frameless glasses that magnified her pale-blue eyes, thin, rigid mouth. He knew she wasn't bluffing.

He raised his eyes to the ceiling. "You seem to forget that the blabbermouth upstairs is telling everyone who'll listen that Seamus and Ethel had a big fight the day before she didn't show up for her appointments."

"I talked to that woman. She can't quote one single word. Just claims she heard loud voices. Seamus naturally talks loud. Ethel shrieked every time she opened her mouth."

"You seem to have thought of everything," Doug told her. "I'll get the letter." He went into the bedroom.

Ruth moved noiselessly to the desk. Beside the pile of mail, she could see the edge of the red-and-gold-handled dagger Seamus had described to her. In an instant it was in her purse. Was it only her imagination that it felt sticky?

When Douglas Brown emerged from the bedroom carrying Seamus' letter, Ruth glanced at it and shoved it deep into the side pocket of her purse. Before she left, she extended her hand to him. "I am very sorry about the death of your aunt, Mr. Brown," she said. "Seamus has asked me to convey his sympathy. No matter what troubles they had, there was a time when they enjoyed and loved each other. That is the time he will remember."

"In other words," Douglas said coldly, "when the police ask, this is the official reason for the visit."

"That's right," Ruth said. "The unofficial reason is that if you keep your bargain, neither Seamus nor I will even hint to the police that your aunt was planning to disinherit you."

．　．　．

Ruth went home, and in an almost religious fervor began to clean the apartment. Walls were scrubbed, curtains ripped down and left soaking in the bathtub. The twenty-year-old vacuum whined its ineffectual path along the threadbare carpet.

As she worked, Ruth was obsessed with the realization that she had to get rid of the dagger.

She discarded all the obvious places. The incinerator? Suppose the police checked the building trash. She didn't want to drop it into a waste bin on the street. Maybe she was being followed and some cop would retrieve it.

At ten o'clock she phoned Seamus and rehearsed him on what he must say if he was questioned.

She could not delay any longer. She had to decide what to do with the dagger. She took it from her purse, ran it under boiling water and rubbed it with brass polish. Even so it seemed to her that it felt sticky—sticky from Ethel's blood.

She was beyond even a pang of pity for Ethel. All that mattered was to preserve an untainted future for the girls.

She stared with loathing at the dagger. Now it looked brand-new. One of those crazy Indian things, blade sharp as a razor, with an ornate handle, decorated in an intricate pattern of red and gold. Probably expensive.

*Brand-new.*

Of course. So simple. So easy. She knew exactly where to hide it.

At twelve o'clock, Ruth made her way to Prahm and Singh, an Indian artifacts store on Sixth Avenue. She moseyed from display to display, pausing at counters and poring over baskets of trinkets. Finally she found what she was looking for, a large basket of letter openers. The handles were cheap copies of the ornate design of Ethel's antique. Idly, she picked one up. As she'd remembered, in a shabby way it did resemble the one she was carrying.

From her handbag, she extracted Ethel's dagger and dropped it into the basket, then pushed all the contents around until she was sure Ethel's murder weapon was at the bottom of the pile.

"Can I help you?" a clerk asked.

Startled, Ruth looked up. "Oh . . . yes. I was just . . . I mean I'd like to see some coasters."

"They're in aisle three. I'll show you."

At one o'clock Ruth was back in the apartment, making a cup of tea and waiting for her heart to stop pounding. No one will find it there, she promised herself. Never, ever . . .


After Neeve left for her shop, Myles had a second cup of coffee and contemplated the fact that Jack Campbell was going to drive with them to Rockland County. Instinctively he liked Jack very much and wryly acknowledged that for years he'd been urging Neeve not to get hung up on the myth of love at first sight. My God, he thought, is it possible that lightning does strike twice after all?

At quarter of ten, he settled himself in his deep leather chair and watched as television cameras relayed the pageantry of Nicky Sepetti's funeral. Flower cars, three of them overflowing with expensive arrangements, preceded the hearse to St. Camilla's Church. A fleet of hired limousines carried mourners and those who pretended to mourn. Myles knew that the FBI and the U.S. Attorney's office as well as the Police Department racket squad were there, taking down the license numbers of private cars, photographing the faces of the people filing into the church.

Nicky's widow was escorted by a stocky fortyish man and a younger woman who was swathed in a black hooded cape that concealed much of her face. All three were wearing dark glasses. The son and daughter don't want to be recognized, Myles decided. He knew that both had distanced themselves from Nicky's associates. Smart kids.

The coverage continued inside the church. Myles lowered the volume and, keeping one eye on the set, went to the phone. Herb was in his office.

"Have you seen the *News* and the *Post*?" Herb asked. "They're really playing up the Ethel Lambston murder."

"I saw them."

"We're still concentrating on the ex-husband. We'll see what the search of her apartment turns up. That argument the neighbor heard last Thursday might have ended in the stabbing. On the other hand, he may have scared her enough to make her decide to get out of town and then followed her. Myles, you taught me that every murderer leaves a calling card. We'll find this one."

They agreed that Neeve would meet the homicide detectives from the Twentieth Precinct at Ethel's apartment on Sunday afternoon. "Call me if you pick up anything of interest in Rockland County," Herb said. "The Mayor wants to announce that this case is solved."

"What else is new about the Mayor?" Myles asked dryly. "Talk to you, Herb."

Myles turned up the volume of the set and watched as Nicky Sepetti's remains were blessed by the priest. The casket was wheeled out of church as the choir sang "Be Not Afraid." Myles listened to the words, "Be not afraid, I am with you always." *You've* been with me day and night for seventeen years, you sonofabitch, he thought as the pallbearers folded the casket blanket and hoisted the heavy mahogany coffin onto their shoulders. Maybe when I'm sure you're rotting in the ground, I'll be free of you.

Nicky's widow reached the bottom of the church steps, then abruptly turned and walked from her son and daughter to the nearest television commentator. As her face loomed into the camera, a face weary and resigned, she said, "I want to make a statement. A lot of people did not approve of my husband's business dealings, may he rest in peace. He was *sent* to prison for those dealings. But he was *kept* in prison, for many extra years, for a crime he did *not* commit. On his deathbed, Nicky swore to me that he had nothing to do with the murder of Police Commissioner Kearny's wife. Think what you want of him, but don't think of him as the person responsible for that death."

A barrage of unanswered questions followed her as she walked back to stand with her children. Myles snapped off the set. A liar to the end, he thought. But as he pulled on his tie and with quick, deft movements knotted it, he realized that for the first time a seedling of doubt was sprouting in his mind.

After learning that Ethel Lambston's body had been found, Gordon Steuber went into a frenzy of activity. He ordered his last illegal warehouse in Long Island City vacated and the illegal workers warned of the consequences of talking to the police. He then phoned Korea to cancel the expected shipment from one of his factories there. On learning that the shipment was already being loaded at the airport, he threw the phone at the wall in a savage gesture of frustration. Then, forcing himself to think rationally, he tried to assess the damage. How much proof did Lambston have and how much had been bluff? And how could he disentangle himself from her article?

Although it was Saturday, May Evans, his longtime secretary, had come in to catch up on filing. May had a drunk for a husband and a teenage kid who was always in trouble. At least half a dozen times Gordon had bought him out of an indictment. He could count on her discretion. Now he asked May to come into his office.

His calm restored, he studied her, the parchment skin that was already falling into wrinkles, the anxious, downcast eyes, the nervous, eager-to-please manner. "May," he said, "you've probably heard about Ethel Lambston's tragic death?"

May nodded.

"May, was Ethel in here one evening about ten days ago?"

May looked at him for a clue. "There was a night I worked a little late. Everyone was gone except you. I thought I saw Ethel come in and you make her leave. Am I wrong?"

Gordon smiled. "Ethel didn't come in, May."

She nodded. "I understand," she said. "Did you take

her call last week? I mean I thought I put her through, and that you were terribly angry and hung up on her."

"I never took her call." Gordon took May's blue-veined hand in his and squeezed it lightly. "My recollection is that I refused to speak to her, refused to see her, and had no idea what she might have written about me in her forthcoming article."

May withdrew her hand from his grip and backed away from the desk. Her faded brown hair was frizzy around her face. "I understand, sir," she said quietly.

"Good. Close the door on your way out."

Like Myles, Anthony della Salva watched the Nicky Sepetti funeral on television. Sal lived in a penthouse on Central Park South, in Trump Parc, the luxurious apartment building that had been renovated for the very rich by Donald Trump. His penthouse, furnished by the hottest new interior designer, in the Pacific Reef motif, had a breathtaking view of Central Park. Since his divorce from his last wife, Sal had decided to stick to Manhattan. No more boring homes in Westchester or Connecticut or the Island or on the Palisades. He liked the freedom of being able to go out at any hour of the night and find a good restaurant open. He liked first night at the theater and chic parties and being recognized by the people who mattered. "Leave the suburbs to the hicks" had become his motto.

Sal was wearing one of his latest designs, tan doeskin slacks with a matching Eisenhower jacket. Dark-green cuffs and a dark-green collar completed the sportsman look. The fashion critics had not been kind to his last two important collections, but had grudgingly praised his menswear. Of course, the real stardom in the rag game was reserved for the couturiers who revolutionized women's fashion. And no matter what they said or didn't say about any of his collections, they still referred to him as one of the master trendsetters of the twentieth century, the creator of the Pacific Reef look.

Sal thought about the day two months ago when Ethel Lambston had come to his office. That nervous flapping mouth; her habit of speaking so quickly. Listening to her was like trying to follow the numbers on a ticker tape. She had pointed to the Pacific Reef mural on the wall and pronounced, "That is genius."

"Even a nosey journalist like you recognizes truth, Ethel," he had retorted, and they both laughed.

"Come on," she had urged him, "break down and forget the villa-in-Rome crap. What you guys don't understand is that phony nobility is out of style. It's a Burger King world. The man from humble beginnings is hot. I'm doing you a favor when I let people know you came from the Bronx."

"There are a lot of people on Seventh Avenue with more to sweep under the rug than being born in the Bronx, Ethel. I'm not ashamed."

Sal watched Nicky Sepetti's coffin carried down the steps of St. Camilla's. Enough of that, he thought, and was about to turn off the set when Sepetti's widow grabbed the mike and pleaded that Nicky had nothing to do with Renata's murder.

For a while Sal sat with his hands folded. He was sure Myles had been watching. He knew how Myles must be feeling, and decided to phone him. He was relieved to hear Myles sound fairly matter-of-fact. Yes, he'd seen the sideshow, he said.

"My guess is, he hoped his kids would believe him," Sal suggested. "They both married pretty well and won't want the grandchildren to know that Nicky's portrait has a number under it in the police files."

"That's the obvious answer," Myles said. "Although to tell you the truth, my gut says a deathbed confession to save his soul was more Nicky's style." His voice trailed off. "Gotta go. Neeve will be along soon. She has the unpleasant job of seeing if the clothing Ethel was wearing came from her shop."

"I hope not, for her sake," Sal said. "She doesn't need that kind of publicity. Tell Neeve that if she's not careful people will start saying they wouldn't be caught dead in her clothes. And that's all it will take to break the mystique of Neeve's Place."

At three o'clock, Jack Campbell was at the door of apartment 16B in Schwab House. When Neeve returned from the shop, she'd changed from her Adele Simpson navy suit to a red-and-black hip-length ribbed sweater and slacks. The harlequin effect was accentuated by the earrings she had designed for the outfit: the masks of comedy and tragedy in onyx and garnets.

"Her nibs, the checkerboard," Myles said dryly as he shook hands with Jack.

Neeve shrugged. "Myles, you know something? I don't relish what we've got to do. But I have a feeling that Ethel would be pleased if I arrived in a new outfit to talk about the clothes she was wearing when she died. You just can't understand how much pleasure she got from fashion."

The den was brightened by the last of the waning sunshine. The weather forecaster had been on target. Clouds were gathering over the Hudson River. Jack glanced around, appreciating some of the things he had missed the night before. The fine painting of the Tuscany hills that was on the wall to the left of the fireplace. The framed sepia photograph of a toddler in the arms of a dark-haired young woman with a hauntingly beautiful face. He was sure it was Neeve with her mother. He wondered what it would be like to lose the woman you loved to a murderer. Intolerable.

He noticed that Neeve and her father were glaring at each other with exactly the same expression. The similarity was so great he wanted to smile. He sensed that this fashion debate was a running issue between them and had no intention of being caught in the middle. He walked over to the window, where a book that had obviously been damaged was exposed to the sunlight.

Myles had made a fresh pot of coffee and was pouring it into handsome Tiffany china mugs. "Neeve, let me tell you something," he said. "Your friend Ethel is beyond spending a king's ransom on extravagant clothes. Right now she's in her birthday suit, on a slab in the morgue with an ID tag on her big toe."

"Was that the way Mother ended up?" Neeve asked, her voice low and furious. Then she gasped and ran to him, putting her hands on his shoulders. "Oh, Myles, I'm sorry. That was a cheap, rotten thing to say."

Myles stood statue still, the coffeepot in his hand. A

long twenty seconds passed. "Yes," he said, "that was exactly the way your mother ended up. And it was a rotten thing for both of us to say."

He turned to Jack. "Forgive the domestic upheaval. My daughter is either blessed or cursed with the combination of a Roman temperament and Irish thin skin. For my part, I have never found it possible to understand how women can make such a fuss over clothes. My own mother, God rest her soul, did all her shopping in Alexander's on Fordham Road, wore housedresses every day and a flowered print, also from Alexander's, for Sunday Mass and banquets of the Policemen's Glee Club. Neeve and I, like her mother before her, have interesting discussions on the subject."

"I gathered that." Jack lifted a mug from the tray Myles offered to him. "I'm glad somebody else drinks too much coffee," he observed.

"A whiskey or a glass of wine would probably go down better," Myles observed. "But we'll save that for later. I've got an excellent bottle of burgundy that will offer an appropriate warmth at a suitable hour, despite what the doctor told me." He walked over to the wine rack in the bottom section of the bookcase and pulled out a bottle.

"In the old days, I didn't know one from the other," Myles told Jack. "My wife's father had a truly fine wine cellar, and so Renata grew up in a connoisseur's home. She taught me about it. She taught me about many things I'd missed along the way." He pointed to the book on the windowsill. "That was hers. It got drenched the other night. Is there any way of restoring it?"

Jack picked up the book. "What a shame," he said. "These sketches must have been charming. Do you have a magnifying glass?"

"Somewhere."

Neeve scouted through Myles's desk and came up with one. She and Myles watched as Jack studied the stained and crumbled pages. "The sketches really didn't blur," he said. "Tell you what. I'll check with a couple of people on my staff and see if I can come up with the name of a good restorer." He handed the magnifying glass back to Myles. "And, by the way, I don't think it's a great idea to let the sun get at them."

Myles took the book and the magnifying glass and laid them on his desk. "I'd be grateful for anything you can do. Now we'd better get started."

All three sat in the front seat of Myles's six-year-old Lincoln Town Car. Myles drove. Jack Campbell casually threw his arm across the back of the seat. Neeve tried not to be aware of its presence, not to lean against him when the car circled the ramp from the Henry Hudson Parkway to the George Washington Bridge.

Jack touched her shoulder. "Relax," he said. "I don't bite."

The District Attorney's office in Rockland County was typical of district attorneys' offices all over the country. Crowded. Old uncomfortable furniture. Files piled high on cabinets and desks. Overheated rooms except where windows had been opened, and then blasts of chilly air became an unpleasant alternative.

Two detectives from the homicide squad were waiting for them. Neeve noticed how the moment he entered the building, something changed about Myles. His jawline firmed. He walked taller. His eyes took on a hue of flinty blue. "He's in his element," she murmured to Jack Campbell. "I don't know how he's managed the inactivity this past year."

"The District Attorney would like you to drop by, sir." It was clear the detectives were aware they were in the presence of New York City's longest-serving and most highly respected Commissioner.

The District Attorney, Myra Bradley, was an attractive young woman who could not have been more than thirty-six or -seven. Neeve relished the look of astonishment on Myles's face. God, you're a chauvinist, she thought. You have to have known Myra Bradley was elected last year and you chose to block it out.

She and Jack were introduced. Myra Bradley waved them to seats and got to the point. "As you are aware," she said, "there is a matter of jurisdiction. We know the body was moved, but we don't know from where it was moved. She could have been murdered in the park five feet from where she was found. In which case, we take charge."

Bradley indicated the file on her desk. "According to the M.E., death was caused by a violent slash with a sharp instrument which cut her jugular vein and sliced her windpipe. She may have put up a struggle. Her jaw was black and blue and there was a cut on her chin. I might

add, it was a miracle the animals didn't get to her. Probably because she was pretty well covered by the rocks.
She wasn't supposed to be discovered. Burying her there
took careful planning."

"Meaning you're looking for someone who knows the
area," Myles said.

"Exactly. There's no way to pinpoint the exact time of
death, but from what her nephew told us she failed to
meet him last Friday, eight days ago. The body was pretty
well preserved, and when we check the weather we see
that the cold spell started nine days ago, on Thursday. So
if Ethel Lambston died on Thursday or Friday and was
buried shortly thereafter, it would account for the lack of
decomposition."

Neeve was sitting to the right of the District Attorney's
desk. Jack was in the chair beside her. She felt herself
flinch, and his arm went over the back of her chair. *If
only I had remembered her birthday*. She tried to push
away the thought and concentrate on what Bradley was
saying.

"... Ethel Lambston could easily have gone undetected
for months, even to the point where identification would
have been extremely difficult. She wasn't meant to be
found. She wasn't meant to be identified. She was wearing no jewelry; there was no handbag or wallet near her."
Bradley turned to Neeve. "Do the clothes you sell always
have your labels sewn in them?"

"Of course."

"The labels in Ms. Lambston's clothing had all been
removed." The District Attorney got up. "If you don't
mind, Miss Kearny, would you look over the clothing
now?"

They went into an adjoining room. One of the detectives brought in plastic bags filled with rumpled and stained clothing. Neeve watched as the bags were emptied. One of them contained lingerie, a matching bra and panties, both edged with lace, the bra spattered with blood; pantyhose with a wide run up the front of the right leg. Medium-heel pumps of a soft periwinkle-blue leather were held together by a rubber band. Neeve thought of the racks of shoe trees Ethel had been so proud to display in her state-of-the-art closet.

The second bag held a three-piece suit: winter-white wool with periwinkle-blue cuffs and collar, a white skirt and a striped blue-and-white blouse. All three were soaked in blood and smeared with dirt. Neeve felt Myles's hand on her shoulder. Resolutely she studied the garments. Something was wrong, something that went beyond the gruesome end to which these garments and the woman who wore them had come.

She heard the District Attorney ask, "Is this one of the outfits that was missing from Ethel Lambston's closet?"

"Yes."

"Did you sell her this outfit?"

"Yes, around the holidays." Neeve looked up at Myles. "She wore it at the party, remember?"

"No."

Neeve spoke slowly. She felt as though time had dissolved. She was in the apartment and it had been decorated for their annual Christmas cocktail buffet. Ethel had looked particularly attractive. The white-and-blue suit was handsome and very becoming with her dark blue eyes and silver-blond hair. A number of people complimented her on it. Then, of course, Ethel zeroed in on

Myles, talking his ear off, and he spent the rest of the party trying to avoid her. . . .

There was something wrong with the memory. What was it? "She bought that suit with some other clothes in early December. That's a Renardo original. Renardo is a subsidiary of Gordon Steuber Textiles." What was eluding her? She simply didn't know. "Was she wearing a coat?"

"No." The District Attorney nodded to the detectives, who began to fold the clothing and replace it in the plastic bags. "Commissioner Schwartz told me that the reason you began worrying about Ethel was that all her warm coats were in her closet. But isn't it a fact that she could easily have bought a coat from someone other than you?"

Neeve got up. The room seemed to smell faintly of antiseptic. She was not about to make a fool of herself by insisting that Ethel simply didn't shop anywhere except from her. "I'll be glad to do an inventory of Ethel's closet," she said. "I have all the receipts from her purchases in a file. I can tell you exactly what's missing."

"I'd like as full a description as possible. Did she usually wear jewelry with this outfit?"

"Yes. A diamond-and-gold pin. Matching earrings. A wide gold bracelet. She always wore several diamond rings."

"She had no jewelry on. So we may have a simple felony murder."

Jack took her arm as they left the room. "You okay?"

Neeve shook her head. "There's something I'm missing."

One of the detectives had heard her. He gave her his card. "Call anytime."

They headed for the door of the courthouse building. Myles was ahead, chatting with the District Attorney, his silver-white hair a full head over her dark-brown blunt-cut bob. Last year his cashmere overcoat had hung limply from his shoulders. After the operation, he'd looked pale and shrunken. Now his shoulders filled out the coat again. His step was firm and sure. And he was in his element in this situation. Police work was what made sense to him, to his life. Neeve found herself praying that nothing would interfere with that job in Washington.

As long as he works, he'll live to be one hundred, she thought. There was some crazy expression: "If you want to be happy for a year, win the lottery. If you want to be happy for life, love what you do."

Loving his work kept Myles going after Mother died.

And now Ethel Lambston was dead.

The detectives had stayed behind when they left, re-folding the clothes that had been Ethel's shroud, clothing that Neeve knew would someday be seen again at a trial. Last seen wearing . . .

Myles was right. She was a silly fool to come to this place dressed like a checkerboard, those idiotic earrings faintly jangling in this dark place. Neeve was grateful she had not removed the hooded black cape that covered the striking ensemble. A woman was dead. Not an easy woman. Not a popular one. But a highly intelligent woman who fiercely called the shots as she saw them, who wanted to look well but didn't have either the time or the instinct to fend for herself in the fashion world.

Fashion. That was it. There was something about the outfit she was wearing . . .

Neeve felt a tremor go through her body. It was as

though Jack Campbell felt it, too. Suddenly his arm was drawn through hers. "You cared about her a lot, didn't you?" he asked.

"Much more than I realized."

Their footsteps echoed down the long marble corridor. The marble was old and worn, cracks fissured through it like veins beneath flesh.

Ethel's jugular vein. Ethel's neck had been so thin. But unwrinkled. At nearly sixty, a lot of women started to get the telltale signs of age. "The neck goes first." Neeve remembered that that was what Renata would say when a manufacturer tried to persuade her to buy low-cut dresses in mature women's sizes.

They were at the entrance to the courthouse. The District Attorney and Myles were agreeing that Manhattan and Rockland County would cooperate closely in the investigation. Myles said, "I should keep my mouth shut. It gets awfully hard to remember that I'm not pushing the buttons at One Police Plaza anymore."

Neeve knew what she had to say and prayed that she wouldn't sound ridiculous. "I wonder..." The District Attorney, Myles and Jack waited. She began again. "I wonder if I could possibly speak to the woman who found Ethel's body. I don't know why, but I just feel as though I should." She swallowed over a lump in her throat.

She felt their eyes studying her. "Mrs. Conway has made a complete statement," Myra Bradley said slowly. "You can look at that if you want."

"I'd like to talk with her." Don't let them ask why, Neeve thought wildly. "I just have to."

"My daughter is the reason Ethel Lambston has been

identified," Myles said. "If she'd like to speak with this witness, I think she should."

He had already opened the door, and Myra Bradley shivered in the crisp April wind. "More like March," she observed. "Look, I have absolutely no objection. We can give Mrs. Conway a call and see if she's in. We feel she's told everything she knows, but maybe something else will surface. Wait a minute."

A few moments later she returned. "Mrs. Conway is home. She'd be perfectly willing to talk with you. Here's her address and the directions." She smiled at Myles, the smile of two professional cops. "If she happens to remember that she got a good look at the guy who killed Lambston, give us a quick call. Okay?"

Kitty Conway had a fire blazing in the library, a fire that threw pyramids of blue-tipped flame from the glowing logs. "Let me know if it's too warm for you," she said apologetically. "It's just that from the moment I touched that poor woman's hand, I haven't stopped feeling cold." She paused, embarrassed, but the three sets of eyes that were observing her all seemed to signal understanding.

She liked their looks. Neeve Kearny. Better than beautiful. Interesting, magnetic face with those high cheekbones, that milk-white skin accentuating those intense brown eyes. But her face showed strain; the pupils of her eyes were enormous. It was obvious that the young man, Jack Campbell, was concerned about her. When he took her cape he'd said, "Neeve, you're still trembling."

Kitty had a sudden wave of nostalgia. Her son was the

same type as Jack Campbell, a little over six feet tall, broad-shouldered, trim body, strong, intelligent expression. She deplored the fact that Mike Junior lived half a world away.

Myles Kearny. When the District Attorney phoned, she'd known immediately who *he* was. For years his name had appeared regularly in the media. Sometimes she'd seen him when she and Mike used to eat in Neary's Pub on East Fifty-seventh Street. She'd read about his heart attack and retirement, but he looked fine now. A good-looking Irishman.

Kitty was fleetingly grateful that she'd changed from her jeans and ancient oversized sweater to a silk blouse and slacks. When they wouldn't accept drinks, she insisted on making tea. "You need something to warm you up," she told Neeve. Refusing assistance, she disappeared down the corridor to the kitchen.

Myles was sitting in a high-backed wing chair with a striped red-and-burnt-orange upholstery. Neeve and Jack were side by side on a velvet sectional that was placed like a crescent around the fireplace. Myles looked around the room approvingly. Comfortable. There were few people who had the brains to buy couches and chairs in which a tall man could lean his head back. He got up and began to examine the framed family photos. The usual history of a life. The young couple. Kitty Conway hadn't lost her looks along the way, that was for sure. She and her husband with their young son. A collage of the boy's growing years. The last picture was of Kitty, her son, his Japanese wife and their little girl. Myra Bradley had told him that the woman who discovered Ethel's body was a widow.

He heard Kitty's steps in the hallway. Quickly, Myles turned to the bookshelves. One section caught his eye, a collection of well-worn books on anthropology. He began to glance through them.

Kitty placed the silver tray on the round table near the sectional, poured the tea, urged cookies on them. "I baked up a storm this morning; nerves after yesterday, I guess," she said, and walked over to Myles.

"Who's the anthropologist?" he asked.

She smiled. "Strictly amateur. I got hooked in college when the professor said that to know the future we should study the past."

"Something I used to keep reminding my detective squads," Myles said.

"He's turning on the charm," Neeve murmured to Jack. "A most unfamiliar sight."

As they sipped the tea, Kitty told them about the horse bolting down the incline, about the plastic flying into her face, about her blurred impression of a hand in a blue sleeve. She explained about the sleeve of her sweatsuit lapping over the lid of the hamper and how at that moment she'd known she had to go back to the park and investigate.

Throughout, Neeve listened attentively, her head poised to one side as though she were straining to catch every word. She still had the overwhelming feeling that she was missing something, something that was right before her, simply waiting to be pounced on. And then she realized what it was.

"Mrs. Conway, will you describe exactly what you saw when you found the body?"

Mary Higgins Clark

"Neeve?" Myles shook his head. He was building his questions carefully and did not want to be interrupted.

"Myles, I'm sorry, but this is terribly important. *Tell me about Ethel's hand. Tell me what you saw.*"

Kitty closed her eyes. "It was like looking at a mannequin's hand. It was so white and the nails seemed a garish red. The cuff of the jacket was blue. It came to the wrist, and that little piece of black plastic was sticking to it. The blouse was blue and white, but it hardly showed beneath the cuff. It was sort of crumpled. It was crazy, but I almost straightened it."

Neeve let out a long sigh. She leaned forward and rubbed her forehead with her hands. "That's what I couldn't get. That blouse."

"What about the blouse?" Myles asked.

"It . . ." Neeve bit her lip. She was going to sound like a fool to him again. The blouse Ethel had been wearing was a part of the original three-piece ensemble. But when Ethel bought the suit, Neeve had told her she didn't think the blouse was right for it. She'd sold Ethel another blouse, all white, without the distraction of the blue stripes. She'd seen Ethel wear that outfit twice, and both times she'd had the white blouse on.

Why did she wear the blue-and-white one?

"What is it, Neeve?" Myles insisted.

"It's probably nothing. Just I'm surprised she wore that blouse with that suit. It just didn't look right with it."

"Neeve, didn't you tell the police that you recognized the outfit and tell them who the designer was?"

"Yes, Gordon Steuber. It was an ensemble from his workrooms."

222

"I'm sorry, I don't get it." Myles tried to conceal his irritation.

"I think I do." Kitty poured steaming tea into Neeve's cup. "Drink this," she ordered. "You look faint." She looked directly at Myles. "If I'm right, Neeve is saying that Ethel Lambston would not have deliberately dressed in that outfit as it was found on her."

"I *know* she would not have chosen to wear it that way," Neeve said. She looked directly into Myles's disbelieving eyes. "Obviously her body had been moved. Is there any way they can establish whether or not someone dressed her *after* she died?"

Douglas Brown had known that the homicide squad planned to obtain a search warrant for Ethel's apartment. Even so, it was a shock when they arrived with it. A team of four detectives converged on the apartment. He watched as they spread powder over surfaces, as they vacuumed the rugs and floors and furniture, carefully sealing and marking the plastic bags in which they stored the dust and fibers and particles which they collected as they minutely examined and sniffed at the small Oriental rug near Ethel's desk.

Seeing Ethel's body on the slab had left Doug with a queasy stomach; an incongruous reminder of the one boat ride he ever took and how violently seasick he had become. She was covered by a sheet that had been wrapped around her face like a nun's wimple, so at least he didn't have to look at her throat. To avoid thinking about her throat he concentrated on the purple-and-yellow bruise on her cheek. Then he'd nodded his head and bolted for the lavatory.

All night he had lain awake in Ethel's bed, trying to decide what to do. He could tell the police about Seamus, about his desperation to stop the alimony payments. But the wife, Ruth, would be blabbering about him. Cold sweat formed on his forehead as he realized how stupid he'd been to go to the bank the other day and insist on getting the withdrawal in hundred-dollar bills. If the police found that out . . .

Before the police came, he'd agonized about whether to leave the bills hidden around the place. If they weren't there, who could say that Ethel hadn't spent them all?

Someone would know. That crazy kid who had come in to clean might have noticed the ones he'd put back.

In the end, Douglas decided to do absolutely nothing. He'd let the cops find the bills. If Seamus or his wife tried to point a finger at him, he'd call them liars. With the slight comfort of that thought, Douglas turned his mind to the future. This was his apartment now. Ethel's money was his money. He'd get rid of all those stupid clothes and accessories, A goes with A, B goes with B. Maybe he'd pack them all just that way and pitch them into the garbage. The thought brought a grim smile. But no use getting wasteful. All the bucks Ethel spent on her clothes shouldn't go down the drain. He'd find a good second-hand shop and sell them.

When he dressed on Saturday morning, he'd deliberately chosen to wear dark-blue slacks and a tan long-sleeved sport shirt. He wanted to give the impression of subdued grief. The lack of sleep had caused circles to form under his eyes. Today that was all to the good.

The detectives went through Ethel's desk. He watched as they opened the file that read "Important Papers." The will. He still hadn't decided whether to admit he knew about it. The detective finished reading it and looked over at him. "You ever seen this?" he asked, his tone offhand.

On the spur of the moment, Douglas made his decision. "No. Those are my aunt's papers."

"She never discussed her will with you?"

Douglas managed a rueful smile. "She used to kid a lot. She said that if she could only leave me her alimony payments, I'd be set for life."

"Then you didn't know that she seems to have left you a sizable amount of money?"

Douglas swept his hand around the apartment. "I didn't think Aunt Ethel had a sizable amount of money. She bought this place when it went co-op. That must have cost her plenty. She made a good living as a writer, but not big-league."

"Then she must have been very thrifty along the way." The detective had handled the will with gloved hands, holding it at the very edges of the paper. As Douglas stared in dismay, the detective called to the fingerprint expert. "Let's dust this."

Five minutes later, his hands twisting nervously in his lap, Douglas confirmed and then denied any knowledge of the hundred-dollar bills the homicide squad had found secreted in the apartment. To divert them from that subject, he explained that until yesterday he hadn't answered the phone.

"Why?" Detective O'Brien was in charge. The question cut the air like a razor.

"Ethel was funny. I picked up the phone when I was

visiting her once and she took my head off. She told me
it wasn't my business who called her. But then, yesterday, I happened to think maybe she might want to get in
touch with me. So I started answering."

"Could she have reached you at work?"

"I never thought of that."

"And the first call you got was a threat to her. What a
coincidence you got the call almost at the very hour her
body was found." Abruptly, O'Brien cut off the interrogation. "Mr. Brown, do you plan to stay in this apartment?"

"Yes, I do."

"We'll be coming in tomorrow with Miss Neeve Kearny.
She'll be checking Ms. Lambston's closet for missing
items of clothing. We may want to talk to you again. You'll
be here." It was not a request. It was a flat statement.

For some reason Douglas was not relieved that the
questioning was at an end. And then his fears were jus-
tified. O'Brien said, "We may ask you to stop in at headquarters. We'll let you know."

When they left, they took the plastic bags with the
vacuum contents, Ethel's will and appointment book and
the small Oriental carpet. Just before the door closed
behind them, Doug heard one of them say, "No matter
how hard they try, they can't get all the blood off rugs."


In St. Vincent's Hospital, Tony Vitale was still in the intensive-care unit, his condition still critical. But, as the
head surgeon continued to reassure his parents, "He's
young. He's tough. We believe he's going to make it."

Swathed in bandages that covered the gunshot wounds
in his head, shoulder, chest and legs, intravenous fluid

226

dripping into his veins, electronic monitors observing his every bodily change, plastic tubes in his nostrils, Tony drifted from a state of deep coma to fragments of consciousness. Those last moments were coming back to him. *Nicky Sepetti's eyes boring through him. He'd known that Nicky suspected he was a plant. He should have driven to headquarters instead of stopping to call. He should have known that his cover had been blown.*

Tony slid into darkness.

When he groped his way back to consciousness, he heard the doctor say, "Every day shows a little improvement."

*Every day!* How long had he been here? He tried to speak, but no sound came.

Nicky had screamed and pounded his fist on the table and ordered them to get the contract canceled.

Joey had told him it was impossible.

Then Nicky had demanded to know who ordered it.

". . . Someone turned the heat on," Joey had said. "Ruined his operation. Now the Feds are on his tail. . . ." Then Joey had given the name.

As he slid back into unconsciousness, Tony remembered that name:

*Gordon Steuber.*

In the Twentieth Precinct on West Eighty-second Street, Seamus waited, his round, pale face damp with perspiration. He tried to remember all the warnings Ruth had given him, everything she had told him to say.

It was all a blur.

The room he was sitting in was stark. A conference

table, the surface scarred from cigarette burns. Wooden chairs. The one he was sitting on caught the small of his back. A grimy window that overlooked the side street. The traffic outside was hell; cabs and buses and cars blaring at one another. The building was rimmed with squad cars.

How long were they going to keep him here?

It was another half hour before the two detectives came in. A court stenographer followed them and slipped into a chair behind Seamus. He turned and watched as she set up her steno machine on her lap.

The older detective's name was O'Brien. He'd introduced himself and his partner, Steve Gomez, in the bar.

Seamus had expected them to give him the Miranda warning. It was still a shock to hear it read to him, to have O'Brien hand him a printed copy and ask him to read it. He nodded at the question did he understand it? Yes. Did he want his lawyer present? No. Did he realize that he could discontinue answering questions at any point? Yes. Did he realize that anything he said could be used against him?

He whispered, "Yes."

O'Brien's manner changed. It became subtly warmer. His tone was conversational. "Mr. Lambston, it is my duty to tell you that you are considered a possible suspect in the death of your former wife, Ethel Lambston."

Ethel dead. No more alimony checks. No more stranglehold on him and Ruth and the girls. Or had the stranglehold only begun? He could see her hands clawing at him, see the way she'd looked when she fell backward, see the way she'd struggled up and reached the letter opener. He felt the wetness of her blood on his hands.

What was the detective saying in that friendly, conversational tone? "Mr. Lambston, you quarreled with your former wife. She was driving you crazy. The alimony was bankrupting you. Sometimes things get too much for us and we blow our lids. Did that happen?"

Had he gone crazy? He could feel the hatred of that moment, the way bile rose in his throat, the way he'd clenched his fist and aimed it at that mocking, vicious mouth.

Seamus laid his head down on the table and began to cry. Sobs racked his body. "I want a lawyer," he said.

Two hours later, Robert Lane, the fiftyish lawyer Ruth had frantically managed to locate, showed up. "Are you prepared to press formal charges against my client?" he asked.

Detective O'Brien looked at him, his expression sour. "No, we are not. Not at this time."

"Then Mr. Lambston is free to go?"

O'Brien sighed. "Yes, he is."

Seamus had been sure they would arrest him. Not daring to believe what he had heard, he leaned his palms on the table and dragged his body from the chair. He felt Robert Lane put his hand under his arm and guide him from the room. He heard Lane say, "I want a transcript of my client's statement."

"You'll get it." Detective Gomez waited until the door closed, then turned to his partner. "I'd love to have locked up that guy."

O'Brien smiled, a thin, mirthless smile. "Patience. We have to wait for the lab reports. We need to check Lambston's movements on Thursday and Friday. But if you want to bet on a sure thing, bet that we'll have an indictment from the grand jury before Seamus Lambston gets to enjoy the end of his alimony payments."

When Neeve, Myles and Jack got back to the apartment, there was a message on the answering machine. Would Myles please call Police Commissioner Schwartz at his office?

Herb Schwartz lived in Forest Hills, "where ninety percent of the PCs have traditionally dwelt," Myles explained to Jack Campbell as he reached for the phone. "If Herb isn't fussing around his house on Saturday evening, something big is happening."

The conversation was brief. When Myles hung up he said, "It looks as though it's all over. The minute they brought in the ex-husband and started questioning him, he cried like a baby and demanded a lawyer. It's only a matter of time till they have enough to indict him."

"What you're saying is that he didn't confess," Neeve said. "Isn't that right?" As she spoke, she began turning on table lamps until the room was bathed in a soft, warm glow. Light and warmth. Was that what the spirit yearned for after witnessing the harsh reality of death? She could not shake off the feeling of something ominous surrounding her. From the moment she had seen Ethel's clothing laid out on that table, the word *shroud* had danced in her head. She realized now that she had immediately wondered what *she* would be wearing when she died. Intuition? Irish superstition? The feeling that someone was walking on her grave?

Jack Campbell was watching her. He knows, she thought. He senses that there's more than just the clothes. Myles had pointed out that if the blouse Ethel usually wore with the suit was at the cleaners, she would automatically choose as a substitute the one that belonged with the ensemble.

All the answers Myles came up with made such sense. Myles. He was standing in front of her; his hands were on her shoulders. "Neeve, you haven't heard a word I said. You asked me a question and I answered it. What's the matter with you?"

"I don't know." Neeve tried to smile. "Look, it's been a rotten afternoon. I think we should have a drink."

Myles scrutinized her face. "I think we should have a *stiff* drink, and then Jack and I should take you out for dinner." He looked up at Jack. "Of course, you may have plans."

"No plans except, if I may, to fix us that drink."

The scotch, like the tea at Kitty Conway's, did the job of temporarily taking from Neeve the sense of being swept along by a dark current. Myles repeated what the Commissioner had told him: The homicide detectives felt that Seamus Lambston was on the verge of admitting guilt.

"Do they still want me to go through Ethel's closet tomorrow?" Neeve wasn't sure whether she wanted to be relieved of the task.

"Yes. I don't think it's going to matter one way or the other whether Ethel had planned to go away and packed for herself or if he killed her and then tried to make it look as though she was off on one of her trips, but we don't leave loose ends."

"But wouldn't he have to keep sending the alimony indefinitely if people thought she was away? I remember Ethel told me once that if he was late with the check she'd have her accountant call and threaten suit. If Ethel's body wasn't discovered, they'd have been after him to keep paying for seven years before she'd be declared legally dead."

Myles shrugged. "Neeve, the percentage of homicides that are the result of domestic violence is awesome. And don't credit people with too many brains. They act impulsively. They go off the deep end. Then they try to cover their tracks. You've heard me say it over and over. 'Every killer leaves his calling card.' "

"If that's true, Commish, I'd be interested to know what calling card Ethel's murderer left."

"I'll tell you what I think the calling card is. That bruise on Ethel's jaw. You didn't see the autopsy report. I did. As a kid, Seamus Lambston was a darn good Golden Glover. The bruise almost broke Ethel's jaw. With or without a confession, I'd have started looking for someone with a boxing background."

"The Legend has spoken. And you're dead wrong."

Jack Campbell sat on the leather couch sipping Chivas Regal, and for the second time in one day decided to keep his own counsel as Neeve and her father argued. Listening to them was not unlike watching a game of tennis between two well-matched opponents. He almost smiled but, observing Neeve, felt another stab of worry. She was still very pale, and the coal-black hair that framed her face accentuated the milk-white luster of her skin. He had seen those wide sherry-colored eyes brighten with amusement, but tonight it occurred to him that there was a sadness in them that went beyond Ethel Lambston's death. Whatever happened to Ethel isn't finished, Jack thought, and it has to do with Neeve.

Impatiently he shook his head. His Scottish forebears with claims of their own to second sight were getting to him. He had asked to accompany Neeve and her father to the District Attorney's office in Rockland County for the simple reason that he wanted to spend the day with Neeve. When he left her this morning, he'd gone to his place, showered, changed and headed for the Mid-Manhattan Library. There on microfilm he had read the seventeen-year-old newspapers with the screaming headlines POLICE COMMISSIONER'S WIFE MURDERED IN CENTRAL PARK. He'd absorbed every detail; studied the pictures of the funeral procession from St. Patrick's Cathedral. Neeve, ten years old, in a dark coat and bonnet-shaped hat, her small hand lost in Myles's hand, her eyes shimmering with tears. Myles's face carved in granite. The rows upon rows of policemen. They seemed to stretch the length of Fifth Avenue. The editorials that linked convicted mobster Nicky Sepetti to the execution of the Police Commissioner's wife.

Nicky Sepetti had been buried this morning. That had to have yanked both Neeve and her father back to the full memory of Renata Kearny's death. The microfilms of the old newspapers had been filled with speculation about whether Nicky Sepetti from his prison cell had also ordered Neeve's death. This morning Neeve had told Jack that her father had been dreading Nicky's release because he was worried about her, that she believed that Nicky Sepetti's death had freed Myles from that obsessive fear.

Then why am I worried about you, Neeve? Jack wondered.

The answer came into his thoughts as simply as though he'd asked the question aloud. Because I love her. Because I've been looking for her since that first day when she ran away from me on the plane.

Jack realized that all their glasses were empty. He got up and reached for Neeve's glass. "Tonight I don't think you should fly on one wing."

With the second cocktail they watched the evening news. Excerpts of Nicky Sepetti's funeral came on, including his widow's impassioned statement. "What do you think?" Neeve asked Myles quietly.

Myles snapped off the set. "What I think isn't printable."

They had dinner at Neary's Pub on East Fifty-seventh Street. Jimmy Neary, a twinkly-eyed Irishman with a leprechaun's smile, rushed to greet them. "Commissioner, it's grand to see you." They were ushered to one of the prize corner tables Jimmy reserved for his special guests. Jimmy was introduced to Jack and pointed out to him the pictures that framed the walls. "There's himself." Former Governor Carey's picture was placed where it could not be missed. "Only the cream of New York up there," Jimmy told Jack. "See where the Commissioner is." Myles's picture was directly opposite Governor Carey's.

It was a good evening. Neary's was always the gathering place for politicians and the clergy. Repeatedly people stopped at the table to greet Myles. "It's great to see you again, Commissioner. You're looking fit."

"He loves this," Neeve murmured to Jack. "He hated being sick and just about dropped out of sight this last year. I think he's ready to join the real world."

Senator Moynihan came over. "Myles, I hope to God you're taking over the Drug Enforcement Agency," he said. "We *need* you. We've got to get rid of this drug scum, and you're the man we want in charge."

When the Senator left, Neeve raised her eyes. "You talked about 'feelers.' It's gone this far!"

Myles was studying the menu. Margaret, his longtime favorite waitress, came over. "How's the shrimp Creole, Margaret?"

"Brilliant."

Myles sighed. "I knew it would be. In honor of my diet, bring me broiled flounder, please."

They ordered, and as they sipped wine Myles said, "It means spending a lot of time in Washington. It means renting an apartment there. I don't think I could have left you here alone, Neeve, if Nicky Sepetti was walking the streets. But now I do feel safe about you. The gang hated Nicky for ordering your mother's death. We kept the heat on them until most of the old crowd was up there with him."

"Then you don't believe the deathbed statement?" Jack asked.

"It's hard for those of us who were raised believing that deathbed repentance might slip you into heaven to witness a man going out with a false oath on his lips. But in Nicky's case I'll stand by my first reaction. That was a

farewell gesture for his family, and obviously they fell for
it. And now it's been a grueling enough day. Let's talk
about something interesting. Jack, have you been in New
York long enough to decide if the Mayor will win another
election?"

As they were finishing coffee, Jimmy Neary stopped
back at the table. "Commissioner, did you know that the
Lambston woman's body was found by one of my old
customers, Kitty Conway? She used to come in here with
her husband. She's a grand lady."

"We met her today," Myles said.

"If you see her again, give her my best and tell her not
to be such a stranger."

"Maybe I'll do better than that," Myles said casually.
"Maybe I'll bring her in myself."

Jack's apartment was the first stop for the cab. As he
said good night, Jack asked, "Look, I know this sounds
pushy, but would there be any objection if I went along
with you tomorrow to Ethel's apartment?"

Myles raised his eyebrows. "Not if you promise to fade
into the background and keep your mouth shut."

"Myles!"

Jack grinned. "Your dad's absolutely right, Neeve. I accept the conditions."


When the cab pulled up to Schwab House, the doorman
opened the door for Neeve. She stepped out as Myles
waited for change from the driver. The doorman went
back to stand at the entrance to the lobby. The night had
become clear. The sky was filled with stars. Neeve walked

236

away from the cab. She raised her head and looked up to admire the galaxy.

Across the street, Denny Adler was propped against an apartment house, a wine bottle by his side, his head sunk on his chest. Through narrowed eyes he observed Neeve step from the cab. He inhaled sharply. He had a clear shot at her and could be gone before anyone saw him. Denny reached into the pocket of the raggedy sweater-jacket he was wearing tonight.

Now.

His finger touched the trigger. He was about to pull the gun from his pocket when the door to his right opened. An elderly woman emerged from the building, holding a leash from which a small poodle strained forward. The poodle lunged toward Denny.

"Don't be afraid of Honey Bee," the woman said. "She's a friendly darling."

Outrage built like erupting lava within Denny as he watched Myles Kearny step from the cab and walk behind Neeve into Schwab House. His fingers went for the poo-dle's throat, but in time he managed to control the gesture and let his hand drop onto the pavement.

"Honey Bee loves to be petted," the elderly woman encouraged, "even by strangers." She dropped a quarter onto Denny's lap. "I hope this will help."

# 10

On Sunday morning, Detective O'Brien phoned and asked for Neeve.

"Why do you want her?" Myles asked sharply.

"We'd like to talk to the cleaning woman who was in the Lambston apartment last week, sir. Does your daughter have her number?"

"Oh." Myles did not know why he experienced instant relief. "That's easy. I'll get it from Neeve."

Five minutes later, Tse-Tse called. "Neeve, I'm a witness." Tse-Tse sounded thrilled. "But could I have them meet me in your apartment at one-thirty? I've never been interviewed by the police before. I'd kind of like you and your dad to be around." Her voice lowered. "Neeve, they don't think I killed her, do they?"

Neeve smiled into the receiver. "Of course not, Tse-Tse. Sure. Dad and I are going to the twelve at St. Paul's. One-thirty will be fine."

"Should I tell them about the creepy nephew taking the money and putting it back and Ethel threatening to disinherit him?"

Neeve was shocked. "Tse-Tse, you said that Ethel was mad at him. You didn't say she threatened to disinherit him. Of course you've got to tell them that."

When she hung up the receiver, Myles was waiting, his eyebrows raised. "What was that all about?"

She told him. Myles emitted a soundless whistle.


When Tse-Tse arrived, her hair was in a prim bun. Her makeup was understated except for her false eyelashes. She was wearing a granny dress and flat shoes. "This is the costume I wore when I played the housekeeper on trial for poisoning her employer," she confided.

Detectives O'Brien and Gomez were announced a few minutes later. When Myles greeted them, Neeve thought, You'd never guess he wasn't still top man at One Police Plaza. They're practically genuflecting.

But when Tse-Tse was introduced, O'Brien looked bewildered. "Douglas Brown told us that the cleaning woman was Swedish."

His eyes bulged as Tse-Tse earnestly explained how she used different personas depending upon her current off-off-Broadway roles. "I've been playing a Swedish maid," she concluded, "and I sent a personal invitation to Joseph Papp to come to the show last night. It was closing night. My astrologer said that Saturn was on the cusp of Capricorn, so my career aspects were very strong. I really had a feeling he'd show." She shook her head sadly. "He didn't come. In fact, nobody came."

Gomez coughed vigorously. O'Brien swallowed a smile. "I'm sorry about that. Now, Tse-Tse—if I may call you that?" He began to question her.

The questioning became a dialogue as Neeve explained why she had gone with Tse-Tse to Ethel's apartment, why she had gone back to check the coats in the closet, to look over Ethel's daily calendar. Tse-Tse told about Ethel's angry phone call to her nephew a month ago, about the money that had been replaced last week.

At two-thirty O'Brien snapped his notebook closed. "You've both been very helpful. Tse-Tse, would you mind accompanying Miss Kearny to the Lambston apartment? You know the place well. I'd like to have your impressions of anything that might be missing. Come over in about an hour, if you will. I'd like to have another little chat with Douglas Brown."

Myles had been sitting in his deep leather chair, his forehead furrowed. "So now a greedy nephew enters the picture," he said.

Neeve smiled wryly. "What do you think his calling card would be, Commish?"

. . .

At three-thirty, Myles, Neeve, Jack Campbell and Tse-Tse entered Ethel's apartment. Douglas Brown was sitting on the couch, his hands twisting in his lap. When he looked up, his expression was unfriendly. His sullenly handsome face was damp with perspiration. Detectives O'Brien and Gomez were sitting across from him, their notebooks open. The surfaces of the tables and the desk appeared sooty and unkempt.

Tse-Tse murmured to Neeve, "This place was spotless when I left it."

Neeve whispered an explanation that the smear was caused by the homicide squad dusting for fingerprints, then said quietly to Douglas Brown, "I'm terribly sorry about your aunt. I liked her very much."

"Then you were one of the few," Brown snapped. He stood up. "Look, anyone who knew Ethel can swear to how irritating and demanding she could be. So she bought me a bunch of dinners. There were plenty of nights I gave up being with my friends because she wanted company. So she slipped me some of those hundred-dollar bills she kept around here. Then she'd forget where she hid the rest of them and say I took them. Then she'd find them and say she was sorry. And that's the whole of it." He stared at Tse-Tse. "What the hell are you doing in that getup, paying off a bet? If you want to make yourself useful, why don't you get out the vacuum and clean up this place?"

"I worked for Miss Lambston," Tse-Tse said with dignity, "and Miss Lambston is dead." She looked at Detective O'Brien. "What do you want me to do?"

"I'd like Miss Kearny to itemize the clothing that is missing from the wardrobe, and I'd like you to generally look around and see if there's anything missing that you notice."

Myles murmured to Jack, "Why don't you go in with Neeve? Maybe you can take notes for her." He chose to sit in a straight chair near the desk. From there he could clearly see the wall that was Ethel's photo gallery. After a moment he got up to study the pictures and was grudgingly surprised to see a montage showing Ethel at the last Republican convention on the dais with the President's immediate family; Ethel giving the Mayor a hug at Gracie Mansion; Ethel receiving the annual award for the best magazine article from the American Society of Journalists and Authors. There had obviously been more to the woman than I realized, Myles thought. I dismissed her as a rattlebrain.

The book Ethel had proposed to write. There was plenty of mob money being laundered through the fashion industry. Had Ethel stumbled on that? Myles made up his mind to ask Herb Schwartz if there was any big undercover investigation going on that had to do with the rag trade.

Although the bed was neatly made and there was nothing out of order in the room, the bedroom had the same soiled appearance as the rest of the apartment. Even the closet looked different. Obviously every garment and accessory had been pulled out, examined and haphazardly put back. "Terrific," Neeve told Jack. "That's going to make it harder."

Jack was wearing a white handmade Irish cable-knit sweater and navy corduroy slacks. When he arrived at

Schwab House, Myles had opened the door for him, raised his eyebrows and said, "You two are going to look like Flossie and Freddie Bobbsey." He'd stood aside to let Jack in, and Jack faced Neeve, who was also wearing an Irish white cable-knit sweater and navy corduroy slacks. They'd laughed together, and Neeve had quickly changed to a navy-and-white cardigan.

The coincidence had lightened Neeve's dread of handling Ethel's personal effects. Now that dread was lost in her dismay at the careless handling of Ethel's treasured wardrobe.

"Harder but not impossible," Jack said calmly. "Tell me the best way to go about this."

Neeve gave him the file with the carbons of Ethel's bills. "We'll start with the latest purchases first."

She pulled out the brand-new clothing Ethel had never worn, laid it on the bed, then worked backward, reeling off to Jack the dresses and suits that were still in the closet. It soon became obvious that the missing garments were only suitable for cold weather. "So that eliminates any idea that she might have been planning to go to the Caribbean or whatever and deliberately didn't bring a coat," Neeve murmured as much to herself as to Jack. "But Myles may be right. The white blouse that went with the suit she had on when they found her isn't here. Maybe it *is* at the cleaners—Wait a minute!"

Abruptly she stopped speaking and reached far back into the closet to pull out a hanger that had been jammed between two sweaters. On it was a white silk blouse with a jabot neck and lace-trimmed sleeves. "That's what I was looking for," Neeve told Jack triumphantly. "Why didn't Ethel put it on? And if she did decide to wear the blouse that came with the outfit, why didn't she pack this one as well?"

They sat together on the chaise longue while Neeve copied from Jack's notes until she had a precise listing of the clothing that was missing from Ethel's closet. As Jack waited in silence, he looked around the room. Grimy, probably because of the police search. Good furniture. Expensive spread and decorative pillows. But it lacked identity. There were no personal touches, no framed snapshots, no special knickknacks. The few paintings scattered on the wall were totally unimaginative, as though they had been chosen only to fill space. It was a depressing room, empty rather than intimate. Jack realized he was beginning to feel an enormous sense of pity for Ethel. His mental image of her had been so different. He'd always thought of her as a self-propelled tennis ball, bobbing from one side of the court to the other in frenzied, unstopping motion. The woman this room suggested had been a rather pathetic loner.

They went back to the living room in time to watch Tse-Tse go through the stacks of mail on Ethel's desk. "It isn't here," she said.

"What isn't there?" O'Brien asked sharply.

"Ethel had an antique dagger as a letter opener, one of those Indian jobs with a fancy red-and-gold handle."

Neeve thought that Detective O'Brien suddenly had the look of a bird dog picking up a scent.

"Do you remember the last time you saw the dagger, Tse-Tse?" he demanded.

"Yes. It was here both days this week when I cleaned, Tuesday and Thursday."

O'Brien looked at Douglas Brown. "The dagger letter

opener wasn't here when we dusted yesterday. Any idea where we can find it?"

Douglas swallowed. He tried to look as though he were deep in thought. The letter opener had been on the desk on Friday morning. No one had come in except Ruth Lambston.

Ruth Lambston. She'd threatened to tell the police that Ethel was going to disinherit him. But he had already told the cops that Ethel was always finding the money she claimed he'd taken. That had been a brilliant answer. But now should he tell them about Ruth or just say he didn't know?

O'Brien was repeating the question, this time persistently. Douglas decided it was time to get the cops' attention off him. "Friday afternoon Ruth Lambston came over. She took back a letter Seamus had left for Ethel. She threatened to tell you people that Ethel was sore at me if I said one word about Seamus to you." Douglas paused, then piously added, "That letter opener was here when she came. She was standing next to the desk when I went into the bedroom. I haven't seen it since Friday. You better ask *her* why she decided to steal it."

When Ruth received the frantic call from Seamus on Saturday afternoon, she'd managed to contact the personnel director of her company at home. It was she who sent the lawyer, Robert Lane, to the police station.

When Lane brought Seamus home, Ruth was sure her husband was on the verge of a heart attack, and she wanted to take him to the emergency room of the hospital. Seamus vehemently refused, but did agree to go to bed. His eyes red-rimmed, welling with tears, he shuffled into the bedroom, a crushed and broken man.

Lane waited in the living room to talk to Ruth. "I'm not a criminal lawyer," he said bluntly. "And your husband is going to need a good one."

Ruth nodded.

"From what he told me in the cab, he might stand a chance of acquittal or reduced charges on a temporary insanity defense."

Ruth went cold. "He admitted killing her?"

"No. He told me he punched her, that she reached for the letter opener, that he grabbed it from her and in the scuffle that her right cheek was cut. He also told me that he hired some character who hangs out in his bar to make threatening phone calls to her."

Ruth's lips were stiff. "I just learned that last night."

Lane shrugged. "Your husband won't stand up under intense questioning. My advice is that he come clean and try to plea-bargain. You believe he killed her, don't you?"

"Yes, I do."

Lane stood up. "As I've said, I'm not a criminal lawyer, but I'll ask around and see who I can find for you. I'm sorry."

For hours Ruth sat quietly, the quiet of total despair. At ten o'clock she watched the news and heard the report that Ethel Lambston's ex-husband was being questioned about her death. She ran to snap off the set.

The events of the past week ran over and over again through her mind like a tape in a constant replay position. Ten days ago, the tearful call from Jeannie—"Mom, I was so humiliated. The check bounced. The bursar sent for me"—had started it all. Ruth remembered the way she had screamed and ranted at Seamus. I pushed him to the point where he went crazy, she thought.

Plea-bargain. What did that mean? Manslaughter? How many years? Fifteen? Twenty? But he had buried her body. He had gone to such trouble to conceal the crime. How had he managed to stay that calm?

Calm? Seamus? That letter opener in his hand, staring down at a woman whose throat he had cut? Impossible.

A new memory came back to Ruth, one that had been a family joke in the days when they were still able to laugh. Seamus had come into the delivery room when Marcy was born. And fainted. At the sight of the blood, he'd passed out cold. "They were more worried about your father than about you and me," Ruth used to tell Marcy. "That was the first and last time I let Dad set foot in the delivery room. He was better off standing drinks at the bar than getting in the doctor's way."

Seamus watching blood spurt from Ethel's throat, putting her body into a plastic bag, sneaking it out of her apartment. Ruth thought of the news report that the labels had been ripped from Ethel's clothes. Seamus having the cold courage to do that, then burying her in that cave in the park? It simply wasn't possible, she decided.

But if he didn't kill Ethel, if he'd left her as he claimed, then by scrubbing and disposing of the letter opener she might have destroyed evidence that might have led to someone else. . . .

It was too overwhelming for her to even consider any longer. Wearily, Ruth got up and went into the bedroom. Seamus was breathing evenly, but he stirred. "Ruth, stay with me." When she got into bed, he put his arms around her and fell asleep, his head on her shoulder.

At three o'clock, Ruth was still trying to decide what to do. Then, almost as in response to an unspoken prayer, she thought of how often she'd run into former Police Commissioner Kearny in the supermarket since he retired. He always smiled so pleasantly and said, "Good morning." Once when her bag of groceries had broken, he'd stopped to help her. She'd liked him instinctively, even though to see him was to remember that at least some of the alimony money was spent in his daughter's fancy shop.

The Kearnys lived in Schwab House on Seventy-fourth Street. *Tomorrow she and Seamus were going to go and ask to see the Commissioner. He'd know what they should do. She could trust him.* Ruth finally fell asleep thinking, I've got to trust somebody.

For the first time in years, she slept Sunday morning away. Her watch read quarter of twelve when she pulled herself up on one arm and glanced at it. The bright sunshine radiated into the room around the ill-fitting outlet-store shades. She looked down at Seamus. In sleep, he lost the anxious, fearful expression that so irritated her, and his even features retained the traces of a once handsome man. The girls get their looks from him, Ruth thought, and their humor. In the early days, Seamus had been witty and confident. And then the downspin began. The rent for the pub increased astronomically, the neighborhood became gentrified, and the old customers disappeared one by one. And every month the alimony check.

Ruth slipped out of bed and went to the bureau. The

sun mercilessly revealed the scars and nicks on it. She tried to open the drawer quietly, but it stuck and screeched in protest. Seamus stirred.

"Ruth." He was not quite awake.

"Stay there," she said, her voice soothing. "I'll call you when breakfast is ready."

The phone rang just as she took the bacon from the broiler. It was the girls. They had heard about Ethel. Marcy, the oldest, said, "Mama, we're sorry for her, but it does mean that Dad is off the hook, isn't he?"

Ruth tried to sound cheery. "It looks like that, doesn't it? We still haven't gotten used to the idea." She called Seamus, and he came to the phone.

Ruth knew the effort he was making as he said, "It's a terrible thing to be glad someone is dead, but it's not terrible to be glad a financial burden has been lifted. Now tell me. How are the Dolly sisters doing? None of the boys getting fresh, I hope."

Ruth had prepared fresh-squeezed orange juice, bacon, scrambled eggs, toast and coffee. She waited until Seamus had finished eating and she had poured a second cup of coffee for him. Then she sat opposite him, across the heavy oak dining-room table that had been an unwanted donation from his maiden aunt, and said, "We've got to talk."

She leaned her elbows on the table, clasped her hands under her chin, saw her reflection in the spotted mirror over the china cupboard and had a fleeting realization that she looked and was drab. Her housecoat was faded; her always fine light-brown hair had become thin and mousy; her round glasses made her small face seem pinched. She dismissed the thoughts as irrelevant and continued to speak. "When you told me you had punched Ethel, that she'd been nicked with the letter opener, that you'd paid someone to threaten her, I believed that you had gone one step further. I believed that you had killed her."

Seamus looked down into the coffee cup intently. You'd think it held the secrets of the universe, Ruth thought. Then he straightened up and stared into her eyes. It was as though a good night's sleep, talking to the girls, and a decent breakfast had set him straight. "I did not kill Ethel," he said. "I frightened her. Hell, I frightened myself. I never knew I was going to punch her, but maybe that came instinctively. She got cut because she went for the letter opener. I got it from her and threw it back on the desk. But she was scared. That's when she said, 'All right, all right. You can keep your damn alimony.' "

"That was Thursday afternoon," Ruth said.

"Thursday about two o'clock. You know how quiet the place gets around that time. You know the state you were in about the bounced check. I left the bar at one-thirty. Dan was there. He'll back me up."

"Did you go back to the bar?"

Seamus finished the coffee and set the cup back on the saucer. "Yes. I had to, then I came home and got drunk. And I stayed drunk over the weekend."

"Who did you see? Did you go out for the paper?"

Seamus smiled, a hollow, mirthless smile. "I wasn't in any condition to read." He waited for her reaction, then Ruth saw tentative hope coming into his face. "You believe me," he said, his tone humble and surprised.

"I didn't believe you yesterday or Friday," Ruth said.

"But I believe you now. You're a lot of things and you're *not* a lot of things, but I do know you could never take a knife or a letter opener in your hands and cut a throat."

"You got yourself some prize in me," Seamus said quietly.

Ruth's tone became brisk. "I could have done worse. Now let's get practical. I don't like that lawyer, and he admitted you need someone else. I want to try something. For the last time, swear on your life that you did not kill Ethel."

"I swear on my life." Seamus hesitated. "On the lives of my three girls."

"We need help. Real help. I watched the news last night. They talked about you. That you were being questioned. They're anxious to prove you did this. We need to tell the full truth to someone who can advise us what to do or send us to the right lawyer."

It took all afternoon of arguing, debating, cajoling, reasoning to get Seamus to agree. It was four-thirty when they put on their all-weather coats, Ruth sturdy and compact in hers, Seamus with the middle button straining on his, and walked the three blocks to Schwab House. Along the way, they spoke little. Even though the day was unseasonably brisk, people were reveling in the strong sunshine. Young children holding balloons, followed by exhausted-looking parents, made Seamus smile. "Remember when we took the girls to the zoo on Sunday afternoons? It's nice it's open again."

At Schwab House the doorman told them that Commissioner Kearny and Miss Kearny were out. Hesitantly,

Ruth asked permission to wait. For half an hour they sat side by side on a lobby sofa, and Ruth began to doubt the wisdom of her decision to come here. She was just about to suggest that they leave when the doorman held open the main door and a party of four people came in. The Kearnys and two strangers.

Before she lost her courage Ruth rushed to confront them.

"Myles, I wish you had let them talk to you." They were in the kitchen of the apartment. Jack was making a salad. Neeve was defrosting the remainder of the pasta sauce from Thursday night's dinner.

Myles was preparing a very dry martini for himself and Jack. "Neeve, there's no way I can let them spill their guts to me. You're a witness in this case as it is. I let him tell me he killed Ethel in a struggle, and I've got a moral obligation to report it."

"I'm sure that's not what he wanted to tell you."

"Be that as it may, I can promise you that both Seamus Lambston and his wife Ruth are facing hard questioning at headquarters. Don't forget, if that slimy nephew is telling the truth Ruth Lambston stole that letter opener, and you can bet she didn't want it as a souvenir. I did the best I could. I called Pete Kennedy. He's a hell of a good criminal lawyer, and he'll see them in the morning."

"And can they afford a hell of a good criminal lawyer?"

"If Seamus Lambston has clean hands, Pete will show our guys that they're barking up the wrong tree. If he's guilty, anything Pete charges will be worth it to get the count reduced from murder two to aggravated man-slaughter."

At dinner, it seemed to Neeve that Jack deliberately steered the conversation away from Ethel. He asked Myles about some of his famous cases, a subject Myles never tired of discussing. It was only when they were clearing the table that Neeve realized Jack knew a lot about cases that certainly never would have been publi-cized in the Midwest. "You looked up Myles in back news-papers," she accused.

He did not seem abashed. "Yes, I did. Hey, leave those pots in the sink. I'll do them. You'll ruin your nails."

It is impossible, Neeve thought, that so much has hap-pened in a week. It felt as though Jack had always been around. What was going on?

She knew what was going on. Then an aching cold came over her. Moses glimpsing the Promised Land and knowing he will never enter it. Why did she feel like that? Why did she feel as though somehow she was winding down? Why, when she looked at the mournful snapshot of Ethel, did she see something else in it today, some-thing secretive, as though Ethel were saying, "Wait till you see what it's like."

What is 'it'? Neeve wondered.

Death.

The ten-o'clock news was filled with more stories about Ethel. Someone had pieced together footage on her vivid background. The media had been short on exciting, headline-making news, and Ethel was helping to fill the void.

The program was just going off when the phone rang.

It was Kitty Conway. Her clear, almost musical voice sounded a bit hurried. "Neeve, I'm sorry to bother you, but I just got home. When I hung up my coat I realized that your father left his hat in the closet. I'm coming into the city tomorrow in the late afternoon, so maybe I could drop it somewhere for him."

Neeve was astonished. "Wait a minute, I'll get him." As she turned the phone over to Myles, she murmured, "You never forget anything. What's up?"

"Oh, it's pretty Kitty Conway." Myles sounded delighted. "I was wondering if she'd ever find the damned hat." When he hung up the phone, he looked sheepishly at Neeve. "She's going to stop by around six o'clock tomorrow. Then I'll take her out for dinner. Want to come?"

"Certainly not. Unless you think you need a chaperone. Anyhow, I have to get to Seventh Avenue."

At the door, Jack asked, "Tell me if I'm making a pest of myself. If I'm not, how about dinner tomorrow night?"

"You know darn well you're not making a pest of yourself. Dinner's fine if you don't mind waiting until I phone you. I don't know what time that would be. I usually make my last stop at Uncle Sal's, so I'll call you from there."

"I don't mind. Neeve, just one thing. Be careful. You're an important witness in Ethel Lambston's death, and seeing those people, Seamus Lambston and his wife, made me pretty uneasy. Neeve, they're desperate. Guilty or innocent, they want this investigation stopped. Their desire to spill to your father may be spontaneous or it may be pretty calculated. The point is, murderers don't hesitate to kill again if someone gets in the way."

# 11

Since Monday was Denny's day off from the delicatessen, his absence there would not be suspect, but he also wanted to establish the alibi that he'd spent the day in bed. "I guess I got flu," he mumbled to the disinterested clerk in the lobby of his rooming house. Big Charley had called him on the phone in this lobby yesterday. "Get rid of her now or we'll find someone who can."

Denny knew what that meant. He wouldn't be left around in case he ever tried to use his knowledge of the hit as a plea bargain. Besides, he wanted the rest of the money.

Carefully he laid his plans. He went to the corner drug-store and, coughing his way through the questions, asked the pharmacist to suggest over-the-counter medication. Back in the rooming house, he made it a point to talk to the stupid old broad who lived two doors down from him and was always trying to get friendly. Five minutes later, he left her room with a cup of evil-smelling tea in a bat-tered mug.

"It'll cure anything," she told him. "I'll look in on you later."

"Maybe you'd make more tea for me around noon," Denny whined.

He went to the bathroom that serviced the tenants on the second and third floors and complained of cramps to the old wino who was waiting patiently for the door to open. The wino refused to give up his place on line.

In his own room, Denny carefully packed all the shabby clothes he had used when following Neeve. You never knew who among doormen might have sharp eyes and be able to describe someone who'd been hanging around Schwab House. Even that old busybody with the dog. She'd gotten a good look at him. Denny did not doubt that when the ex–Police Commissioner's daughter was wasted, the cops would be swarming for leads.

He would drop the clothes into a nearby dumpster.

That was easy. The tough part was following Neeve Kearny from her shop to Seventh Avenue. But he had figured out a way. He had a new gray sweatsuit. No one around here had ever seen him wear it. He had a punk-rock wig and wide space-cadet glasses. In that outfit, he'd look like the messengers running all over town on their bikes knocking people down. He'd get a big manila envelope, watch for Neeve Kearny to come out. She'd probably cab to the fashion district. He'd follow her in another cab. He'd give the cabbie a cock-and-bull story about his bike being stolen and that lady needing the papers he was delivering.

With his own ears, he'd heard Neeve Kearny discuss a one-thirty appointment with one of those rich broads who could afford to spend big bucks for clothes.

Always leave margin for error. He'd be across the street from her place before one-thirty.

It wouldn't matter if the cabbie put two and two together after Kearny was wasted. They'd be looking for a guy with a punk-rock cut.

His plans made, Denny shoved the bundle of old clothes under the sagging bed. What a dump, he thought as he stared around the tiny room. Alive with cockroaches. Smelly. A bureau that wasn't much more than an orange crate. But when he finished the job and got the other ten thousand, he'd only have to hang around till his parole was up and then he'd take off. Boy, would he take off.

For the rest of the morning, Denny made frequent trips to the toilet, complaining about his pains to anyone who would listen. At noon, the hag down the hall knocked on his door and handed him another cup of tea and a stale roll. He made more trips to the toilet, standing inside the locked door, trying not to inhale the noxious odors and keeping others waiting until there were grumbled protests.

At quarter of one, he shuffled out and said to the old wino, "I think I feel better. I'm gonna get some sleep." His room was on the second floor and faced an alley. There was an overhang from the steep roof that jutted over the lower floors. Minutes after he had changed into the gray sweats, pulled on the punk wig and adjusted the glasses, he'd tossed the bag of beggar clothes into the alley and vaulted down.

He dropped the bundle deep into a rat-infested dumpster behind an apartment building on One Hundred and Eighth Street, caught the subway to Lexington and Eighty-sixth, picked up a large manila envelope and crayons in the five-and-ten, marked the envelope "Rush" and took up a vigil opposite Neeve's Place.

At ten o'clock on Monday morning, a Korean cargo plane, Flight 771, was cleared for landing at Kennedy Airport. Trucks from Gordon Steuber Textiles were waiting to pick up the crates of dresses and sportswear to be transported to Long Island City warehouses; warehouses that did not appear anywhere in the company records.

Others were waiting for that shipment: law-enforcement officers aware that they were about to make one of the biggest drug busts of the past ten years.

"A hell of an idea," one observed to the other as he waited in a mechanic's uniform on the tarmac. "I've seen the stuff stashed in furniture, in Kewpie dolls, in dog collars, in babies' diapers, but never in designer clothes."

The plane circled, landed, braked to a stop in front of the hangar. In an instant the field was swarming with Federal officers.

Ten minutes later, the first crate had been pried open. The seams of an exquisitely tailored linen jacket were slashed. Pure, uncut heroin poured into a plastic bag held open by the chief of the task force. "Christ," he said in awe, "there must be two million bucks' worth in this box alone. Tell them to pick up Steuber."

At 9:40 A.M., Federal officers burst into Gordon Steuber's office. His secretary tried to bar the way, but was firmly put aside. Steuber listened impassively as the Miranda warning was read to him. Without a trace of visible emotion, he watched as handcuffs were clasped around his wrists. Inwardly he was raging, a deadly, furious rage, and the target was Neeve.

As he was being led out he paused to speak to his weeping secretary. "May," he told her, "you'd better cancel all my appointments. Don't forget."

The expression in her eyes told him that she understood. She would not mention that twelve days ago, on Wednesday evening, Ethel Lambston had barged into his office and told him she was wise to his activities.

Douglas Brown did not sleep easily on Sunday night. As he tossed restlessly on Ethel's fine percale sheets, he dreamt of her, fitful dreams in which Ethel was brandishing a glass of Dom Pérignon at San Domenico: "Here's to Seamus the wimp." Dreams that portrayed

Ethel saying coldly to him, "How much did you help yourself to this time?" Dreams in which the police came to take him away.

At ten o'clock on Monday morning, the Medical Examiner's Office of Rockland County phoned. As next of kin, Doug was queried about his plans for the disposal of the mortal remains of Ethel Lambston. Doug tried to sound solicitous. "It was my aunt's wish that she be cremated. Can you suggest what I should do?"

Actually Ethel had said something about being buried with her parents in Ohio, but it would be a lot cheaper to mail an urn than a casket.

He was given the name of a mortuary. The woman who answered was cordial and solicitous and inquired about financial responsibility. Doug promised to get back to her and phoned Ethel's accountant. The accountant had been away for a long weekend and had just heard the dreadful news.

"I witnessed Miss Lambston's will," the accountant said. "I have a copy of the original. She was very fond of you."

"And I loved her dearly." Doug hung up. It still took getting used to, knowing that he was a rich man. Rich by his standards, anyhow.

If only it doesn't all get screwed up, he thought.

He had instinctively been expecting the cops, but, even so, the brisk rap on the door, the invitation to step down to headquarters for questioning, unnerved him.

At the precinct, he was startled when he received the Miranda warning. "You gotta be kidding."

"We tend to be overcautious," Detective Gomez said soothingly. "Remember, Doug, you don't need to answer questions. You can call a lawyer. Or, you can stop answering questions whenever you say the word."

Doug thought of Ethel's money; Ethel's co-op; the chick at work who had big eyes for him; throwing up his job; telling off that scum who was his immediate boss. He assumed a solicitous stance. "I'm perfectly agreeable to answering any questions."

That first one from Detective O'Brien threw him for a loop. "Last Thursday, you went to the bank and withdrew four hundred dollars which you took in hundred-dollar bills. No point in denying that, Doug. We checked it. That was the money we found in the apartment, wasn't it, Doug? Now, why would you put it there when you told us your aunt always found the money she accused you of taking?"

Myles slept from midnight till five-thirty. When he woke, he knew there was no chance of dozing off again. There was nothing he detested more than lying in bed on the off chance that he could slip back into the arms of Morpheus. He got up, reached for a bathrobe and went into the kitchen.

Over a cup of freshly perked decaffeinated coffee, he step-by-step examined the events of the week. His initial sense of release that had stemmed from Nicky Sepetti's death was fading. Why?

He glanced around the orderly kitchen. Last night he'd silently approved of the way Jack Campbell had assisted Neeve in clearing. Jack knew his way around a kitchen. Myles half smiled, thinking of his own father. A great guy. "Himself," his mother said when referring to him. But

God knows, Pop had never carried a dish to the sink or minded a child or pushed a vacuum around. Today's young husbands were different. And it was a good difference.

What kind of husband had he been to Renata? Good by most people's standards. "I loved her," Myles said now, his voice barely above a whisper, "I was proud of her. We had fun together. But I wonder how well I knew her. How much of my father's son was I during our marriage? Did I ever take her seriously outside of her role as wife and mother?"

Last night, or was it the night before, he'd told Jack Campbell that Renata had taught him about wine. I was busy clearing off my rough spots in those days, Myles thought, remembering how before he met Renata he had quietly set on a program of self-improvement. Tickets to Carnegie Hall. Tickets to the Met. Dutiful visits to the Museum of Art.

It was Renata who had changed those dutiful visits to exciting expeditions of discovery. Renata, who when she came home from an opera would hum the music in her strong clear soprano. "Milo, *caro,* are you the only Irishman in the world who is tone deaf?" she would tease.

*In the eleven wonderful years we had, we were only beginning to plumb all that we would have become to each other.*

Myles got up and poured a second cup of coffee. Why was this awareness so strong? What was eluding him? Something. Something. Oh, Renata, he begged: I don't know why, but I'm worried about Neeve. I've done my best for her these seventeen years. But she's your kid, too. Is she in trouble?

The second cup of coffee revived his spirits and he began to feel slightly foolish. When Neeve came yawning into the kitchen, he was sufficiently recovered to say, "Your publisher is a good pot-walloper."

Neeve grinned, bent down to kiss the top of Myles's head and replied, "So it's 'pretty Kitty Conway.' I approve, Commish. It's about time you started looking over the ladies. After all, you're not getting any younger." She ducked to avoid his swat.


Neeve chose a pale-pink-and-gray Chanel suit with gold buttons, gray leather pumps and a matching shoulder bag to wear to work. She pulled her hair into a smooth chignon.

Myles nodded his approval. "I like that kind of outfit. Better than Saturday's checkerboard. I must say, you have your mother's taste in clothes."

"Approbation from Sir Hubert is praise indeed." At the door, Neeve hesitated. "Commish, are you going to indulge me and ask the Medical Examiner if there's any chance Ethel's clothes were changed after she died?"

"I hadn't thought about it."

"Please think about it. And even if you don't approve, do it for my sake. Something else: Do you think Seamus Lambston and his wife were trying to sucker us?"

"Entirely possible."

"Fair enough. But, Myles, hear me out without hushing me up, just this once. The last person who admits to seeing Ethel alive was her ex-husband Seamus. We know that was Thursday afternoon. Can someone ask him what she was wearing? My bet is that it was a

multicolored light wool caftan that she just about
lived in when she was home. That caftan wasn't in
her closet. Ethel never traveled with it. Myles, don't
look at me like that. I know what I'm talking about. The
point is, suppose Seamus—or someone else—killed
Ethel while she was wearing that caftan and then changed her clothes."

Neeve opened the door. Myles realized that she was
expecting a derisive remark from him. He kept his tone
impersonal. "Meaning . . .?"

"Meaning that *if* Ethel's clothes were changed after she
died, there is no way that ex-husband is responsible for
her death. You saw the way he and his wife were dressed.
They have no more idea of fashion than I have of the
inner workings of the space shuttle. On the other hand,
there is a slimy bastard named Gordon Steuber who
would instinctively have chosen something that came
from his own company and dressed Ethel the way the
outfit was sold."

Just before she closed the door behind her, Neeve
added, "You're always talking about a killer leaving his
calling card, Commish."

Peter Kennedy, attorney at law, was frequently asked
whether he was related to *the* Kennedys. He did in fact
bear a strong resemblance to the late President. He was a
man in his early fifties with hair more rust than gray, a
square, strong face and a rangy body. Early in his career
he had been an assistant attorney general and formed a
lasting friendship with Myles Kearny. At Myles's urgent
phone call, Pete had canceled his eleven-o'clock appoint-

ment and agreed to meet Seamus and Ruth Lambston in his midtown office.

Now he listened to them incredulously as he observed their strained, weary faces. From time to time he interjected questions. "You are saying, Mr. Lambston, that you punched your former wife so violently that she fell backwards onto the floor, that she sprang up and grabbed the dagger she used as a letter opener, that in the struggle to wrench it from her hand her cheek was nicked."

Seamus nodded. "Ethel could see I'd been almost ready to kill her."

"Almost?"

"Almost," Seamuus said, his voice low and ashamed. "I mean, for one second if that punch had killed her, I'd have been glad. She made my life hell for more than twenty years. Then when she got up, I realized what could have happened. But she was scared. She told me to forget the alimony payments."

"And then . . ."

"I got out. I went to the bar. Then I went home, got drunk and stayed drunk. I knew Ethel. It woulda been just like her to file an assault charge against me. She tried to have me locked up three different times when I was late with the alimony." He laughed mirthlessly. "One of those times was the day Jeannie was born."

Pete continued his questioning and skillfully extracted the fact that Seamus had been afraid of Ethel's signing a complaint; sure that when she had time to think about it she'd demand the alimony; foolish enough to tell Ruth that Ethel had said it was all right to quit the payments; terrified when Ruth demanded he put it in writing to Ethel.

"And then you inadvertently left both the check and the letter in the mailbox and went back hoping to retrieve them?"

Seamus twisted his hands in his lap. To his own ears he sounded like a bumbling fool. Which was exactly what he was. And there was more. The threats. But somehow he couldn't bring himself to tell about them yet.

"You never saw or spoke to your former wife, Ethel Lambston, after Thursday, March thirtieth."

"No. I did not."

He hasn't told me everything, Pete thought, but it's enough for a start. He watched as Seamus Lambston leaned back on the maroon leather couch. He was beginning to relax. Soon he'd unwind enough to put everything on the table. Too much probing would be a mistake. Pete turned to Ruth Lambston. She was sitting primly next to her husband, her eyes wary. Pete realized that Ruth was becoming frightened at her husband's revelations.

"Is it possible for someone to charge Seamus with assault or whatever it is for punching Ethel?" she asked.

"Ethel Lambston's not alive to press a charge," Pete replied. Technically the police could file. "Mrs. Lambston, I think I'm a pretty good judge of character. You were the one who persuaded your husband to speak to Commissioner"—he corrected himself—"*former* Commissioner Kearny. I think you were right to know you needed help at this time. But the only way I can help you is if you tell me the truth. There is something that you are weighing and measuring, and I think I need to know what it is."

As her husband and this impressive-looking lawyer

stared at her, Ruth said. "I believe I threw away the murder weapon."

By the time they left an hour later, Seamus having agreed to offer to take a lie-detector test, Pete Kennedy was no longer sure of his instincts. At the very end of the session, Seamus admitted that he had hired some wet-brained goon who hung around his pub to threaten Ethel. Either he's only stupid and scared or he's playing a pretty shrewd hand, Pete decided, and made a mental note to let Myles Kearny know that not all the clients Myles sent him were his cup of tea.

The news of Gordon Steuber's arrest crashed like a tidal wave through the fashion center. Phone lines buzzed: "No, it isn't the illegal factories. Everybody does that. It's drugs." Then the big question: "Why? He makes millions. So he got a slap on the wrist for the sweatshops. So they're investigating him for income-tax evasion. A good team of lawyers could stall that for years. But drugs!" After an hour the black humor started. "Don't get Neeve Kearny mad at you. You'll trade your wristwatch for steel bracelets."

Anthony della Salva, surrounded by fluttering assistants, was working on the final details of the fashion show for his fall line, which was to be held the following week. It was an eminently satisfying collection. The new kid he'd hired fresh out of the Fashion Institute of Technology was a genius. "You're another Anthony della Salva," he told Roget, beaming. It was Sal's highest praise.

Roget, thin-faced, lank-haired, small-bodied, muttered under his breath, "Or a future Mainbocher." But he returned Sal's beatific smile. Within two years he was sure he'd have the backing to open his own place. He'd fought tooth and nail with Sal about his use of miniatures of the Pacific Reef design as accessories in the new collection, scarves and pocket handkerchiefs and belts in the brilliant tropical shades and intricate patterns that caught the magic and mystery of the aquatic world.

"I don't want it," Sal had said flatly.

"It's still the best thing you've ever done. It's your trademark." When the collection was complete, Sal admitted that Roget was right.

It was three-thirty when Sal heard the news about Gordon Steuber. And the jokes. He immediately phoned Myles. "Did you know this was coming?"

"No," Myles said, his voice testy. "I'm not on the ear for everything that's happening at One Police Plaza." Sal's worried tone flamed the abiding sense of oncoming disaster that had haunted him all day.

"Then maybe you should be," Sal retorted. "Listen, Myles, we've all known that Steuber has mob connections. It's one thing for Neeve to blow the whistle on him because of workers without green cards. It's a hell of another proposition when she's the indirect cause of a hundred-million-dollar drug bust."

"Hundred million. I hadn't heard that figure."

"Then turn on the radio. My secretary just heard it. The point is, maybe you should think about hiring a bodyguard for Neeve. *Take care of her!* I know she's your kid, but I claim a vested interest."

"You have a vested interest. I'll talk to the guys downtown and think about it. I just tried to call Neeve. She'd already left for Seventh Avenue. This is a buying day. Is she stopping in to see you?"

"She usually winds up here. And she knows I want her to preview the new line. She'll love it."

"Tell her to call me as soon as you see her. Tell her I'll wait for the call."

"Will do."

Myles started to say goodbye, then had a sudden thought. "How's the hand, Sal?"

"Not bad. Teaches me not to be so clumsy. Much more important, I feel crummy about ruining the book."

"Quit worrying. It's drying out. Neeve has a new beau, a publisher. He's going to take it to a restorer."

"No way. That's my problem. I'll send someone up for it."

Myles laughed. "Sal, you may be a good designer, but I think Jack Campbell is the right one for this job."

"Myles, I insist."

"See you, Sal."

At two o'clock, Seamus and Ruth Lambston returned to Peter Kennedy's law office for polygraph tests. Pete had explained to them, "If we're willing to stipulate that the police polygraph can be used in the event you come to trial, I think I can talk them into not pressing assault or tampering-with-evidence charges."

Ruth and Seamus had spent the intervening two hours having lunch in a small midtown coffee shop. Neither ate more than a few bites of the sandwiches the waitress placed before them. They both ordered more tea. Seamus broke the silence. "What do you think of that lawyer?"

Ruth did not look at him. "I don't think he believes us." She turned her head and stared straight into his eyes. "But if you're telling the truth, we did the right thing."

The test reminded Ruth of her last electrocardiogram. The difference was, these wires measured different impulses. The polygraph expert was impersonally cordial. He asked Ruth about her age, where she worked, her family. When she talked about the girls, she began to relax and a note of pride crept into her voice. "Marcy . . . Linda . . . Jeannie . . ."

Then the questions came about her visit to Ethel's apartment, about her tearing up the check, about taking the letter opener, bringing it home, washing it, dropping it into the basket in the Indian shop on Sixth Avenue.

When it was over, Peter Kennedy asked her to wait in the reception room and send Seamus in. For the next forty-five minutes she sat, dulled with apprehension. We've lost control of our lives, she thought. Other people will decide if we go to trial, go to jail.

The waiting room was impressive. The handsome leather couch, studded with gold nailheads. Must have cost at least six or seven thousand dollars. The matching loveseat; round mahogany drum table holding the latest magazines; excellent modernistic prints on the paneled walls. Ruth was aware that the receptionist was stealing curious glances at her. What did the smartly dressed young woman see? Ruth wondered. A plain woman in a plain green wool dress, sensible shoes, hair that was beginning to slip from the bun. She's probably thinking we can't afford the prices here, and she's right.

The door from the corridor that led to Peter Kennedy's private office opened. Kennedy was standing there, his face warm and smiling. "Won't you come in, Mrs. Lambston? Everything's fine."

When the polygraph expert left, Kennedy laid the cards on the table. "Normally I wouldn't want to move this swiftly. But you're concerned that the longer the media refers to Seamus as a suspect, the worse it will be for your daughters. I propose that I contact the homicide squad investigating the death. I demand an immediate polygraph test to clear the atmosphere of innuendo which you find intolerable. I warn you: In order to have them agree to an immediate test, we'll have to stipulate that if you ever came to trial the results of the test would be admissible. I think they'll go along with that. I think I can also persuade them to drop any other possible charges."

Seamus swallowed. His face was shiny, as though a perpetual glow of perspiration had been glossed onto it. "Go for it," he said.

Kennedy stood up. "It's three o'clock. We might still be able to get with them today. Would you mind waiting outside until I see what I can do?"

A half hour later, he came out. "We've got a deal. Let's go."

. . .

Monday was usually a slow day in retailing, but, as Neeve remarked to Eugenia, "You can't prove it by us." From the moment she unlocked the door at nine-thirty, the place was busy. Myles had passed on Sal's concern about bad publicity stemming from Ethel's death, but after working without a break until nearly twelve, Neeve said dryly, "Apparently a lot of people wouldn't mind being caught dead in a Neeve's Place outfit." Then she added, "Phone for coffee and a sandwich, okay?"

When the order was delivered to Neeve's office, she glanced up and raised her eyebrows. "Oh, I expected Denny. He didn't quit, did he?"

The delivery boy, a gangly nineteen-year-old, plunked the bag on her desk. "Monday's his day off."

When the door closed behind him, Neeve said wryly, "No room service with that one." Gingerly she removed the lid from the steaming container.

Jack phoned a few minutes later. "Are you okay?"

Neeve smiled into the speaker. "Sure I'm okay. In fact, I'm not only okay, I'm prosperous. It's been a great morning."

"Maybe you should plan on supporting me. I'm on my way to have lunch with an agent who isn't going to be happy with my offer." Jack dropped the bantering tone. "Neeve, take down this number. It's the Four Seasons. If you need me, I'll be there for the next couple of hours."

"I'm just about to attack a tuna-fish sandwich. Bring me a doggie bag."

"Neeve, I'm serious."

Neeve's voice became quiet. "Jack, I'm fine. Just save

some appetite for dinner. It'll probably be about six-thirty or seven when I call you."

Eugenia watched critically as Neeve hung up the phone. "The publisher, I gather."

Neeve opened the wrapping on the sandwich. "Uh-huh." She had just taken the first bite when the phone rang again.

It was Detective Gomez. "Miss Kearny, I've been studying the postmortem pictures of the deceased, Ethel Lambston. You have a pretty strong hunch that she may have been dressed after she died."

"Yes." Neeve felt her throat close and pushed away the sandwich. She was aware that Eugenia was staring at her; she could feel the color drain from her cheeks.

"Keeping that in mind, I had the pictures blown up pretty big. The tests aren't complete and we know the body had been moved, so it's pretty hard to be sure whether or not you're right, but tell me this: Would Ethel Lambston have left her home with a wide run in her stocking?"

Neeve remembered noticing that run when she identified Ethel's clothing. "Never."

"That's what I thought," Gomez agreed. "The autopsy report shows nylon fibers caught in a toenail. The run started when the stocking was being put on. That means if Ethel Lambston dressed herself, she went out in a designer outfit with a very unsightly-looking stocking. I'd like to talk about this in the next couple of days. You'll be around?"

As Neeve replaced the phone, she thought of what she had told Myles this morning. As far as she was concerned, Seamus Lambston, with his utter lack of fashion sense, had not dressed the bleeding corpse of his former wife. She remembered the rest of what she had told Myles. Gordon Steuber would instinctively have chosen the original blouse for the ensemble.

There was a perfunctory rap on the door, and the receptionist rushed in. "Neeve," she whispered, "Mrs. Poth is here. And, Neeve, did you know Gordon Steuber has been arrested?"

Somehow Neeve managed to keep a calm, attentive smile on her face as she helped her wealthy client select three Adolfo evening gowns that ranged in price from four to six thousand dollars apiece; two Donna Karan suits, one at fifteen hundred dollars, the other twenty-two hundred; slippers, shoes and handbags. Mrs. Poth, a strikingly chic woman in her midsixties, professed to be uninterested in the costume jewelry. "It's lovely, but I prefer my own real pieces." In the end she said, "These are more interesting," and accepted all Neeve's suggestions.

Neeve saw Mrs. Poth to her limousine, which was parked squarely in front of the shop. Madison Avenue was busy with shoppers and strollers. It seemed as though everyone was relishing the continuing sunshine and taking in stride the unusually chilly temperature. As Neeve turned back to the store, she noticed a man in a gray sweatsuit leaning against the building across the street. She had a fleeting sense of familiarity, which she disregarded as she hurried back into the shop and to her office. There she added fresh lip gloss and reached for her pocketbook. "Mind the store," she told Eugenia. "I won't be back, so lock up, please."

Smiling easily, pausing for a quick word with some of

the old customers, she made her way to the front door. The receptionist had a cab waiting. Neeve got into it quickly and did not notice that the man with the crazy punk hairstyle and the gray sweats had hailed a cab across the street.

Over and over again, from different angles, Doug answered the same questions. The time he had arrived at Ethel's. His decision to move into her apartment. The phone call threatening Ethel if she did not let Seamus off the hook. The fact that he had begun staying in the apartment from Friday the thirty-first but didn't begin to answer the phone for a week and then the first call he got was a threat. How come?

Repeatedly, Doug was told he was free to go. He could call for a lawyer; he could discontinue answering questions. His answer was, "I don't need a lawyer. I have nothing to hide."

He told them he hadn't answered the phone because he was afraid Ethel would call and order him to get out. "For all I knew, she was going to be gone for a month. I needed a place to stay."

Why had he made a bank withdrawal in hundred-dollar bills and then hidden them around his aunt's apartment?

"Okay. So I borrowed some of the bucks Ethel stashed around the apartment, and I put them back."

He had said he didn't know anything about Ethel's will, but his fingerprints were all over it.

Doug began to panic. "I just started to think that maybe something was wrong. I looked in Ethel's date book and saw that she'd canceled all her appointments after that Friday she was supposed to meet me at the apartment. That made me feel better. But the neighbor told me that dopey ex-husband of hers had had a fight with her and that he'd shown up while I was at work. Then his wife practically breaks in and tears up Ethel's alimony check. I started to think maybe something was wrong."

"And then," Detective O'Brien said, his voice laden with sarcasm, "you decided to answer the phone, and the first call you got was a threat to your aunt's life? And the second was the Rockland County District Attorney's office, notifying you that the body had been found?"

Doug felt perspiration soak his armpits. He moved restlessly, trying to find a comfortable spot in the straight-backed wooden chair. Across the table, the two detectives were observing him, O'Brien with his beefy thick-featured face, Gomez with his shiny dark hair and chipmunk chin. The mick and the spic. "I'm getting fed up with this," Doug said.

O'Brien's face hardened. "Then take a walk, Dougie. But if you're so inclined, give one more answer. The rug in front of your aunt's desk had been spattered with blood. Someone did a very thorough job of cleaning it up. Doug, before you got your present position, didn't you work in the carpet-and-furniture-cleaning department of Sears?"

Panic caused a reflex action in Doug. He jumped up, pushed the chair back so violently that it toppled over. "Screw you!" He spat out the words as he rushed to the door of the interrogation room.

. . .

Denny had taken a calculated risk in waiting to hail a cab just as Neeve Kearny got into hers. But he knew that cabbies were nosy. It made more sense to grab one, sound breathless and say, "Some creep stole my bike. Follow that cab, will ya? It's my head if this envelope don't get delivered to that broad."

The driver was a Vietnamese. He nodded indifferently and expertly cut off an approaching bus as he swung across, then up Madison Avenue and left on Eighty-fifth Street. Denny slouched in the corner, his head down. He didn't want the cabbie to have too much chance to observe him in the rearview mirror. The cabbie's only observation was, "Crackheads. If there was a market for farts, they'd steal them," The Nam's English was amazingly good, Denny thought sourly.

At Seventh Avenue and Thirty-sixth Street, the other cab made the light and they missed it. "Sorry," the driver apologized.

Denny knew that Neeve was probably getting off in the next block or so. Her cab would probably creep in this traffic. "So let them fire me. I tried." He paid off the driver and sauntered uptown. From sidelong glances, he was able to see when the cab started again, continuing down Seventh Avenue. Quickly, Denny reversed direction and sped from Seventh Avenue to Thirty-sixth Street.

As usual, the streets in the high Thirties, off Seventh Avenue, were milling with the hyperactivity of the Garment District. Outsize trucks in the process of being unloaded were double-parked along the road, snarling traffic into near-gridlock. Messengers on roller skates whizzed around the crowds of pedestrians; delivery men, indifferent to both pedestrians and vehicles, shoved cumbersome racks laden with clothing. Horns blared. Men and women in high-fashion outerwear strode rapidly, talking excitedly, totally indifferent to the people and traffic around them.

A perfect place for a hit, Denny thought with satisfaction. Halfway up the block, he saw a cab pull nearer to the curb and watched as Neeve Kearny emerged from it. Before Denny could get close to her, she rushed into a building. Denny took up an observation post across the street, shielded by one of the huge trucks. "While you're picking those fancy clothes, you better order yourself a shroud, Kearny," he mumbled to himself.

Jim Greene, at age thirty, had been recently promoted to detective. His ability to size up a situation and instinctively choose the correct course of action had recommended him to his superiors in the Police Department.

Now he had been assigned the boring but vital task of guarding the hospital bed of undercover detective Tony Vitale. It was not a desirable job. If Tony had been in a private room, Jim could have kept his vigil at the door. But in the intensive-care unit, it was necessary for him to sit in the nurses' station. There, for his eight-hour shift, he was constantly reminded of the fragility of life as monitors suddenly sounded alarms and the hospital staff rushed to stave off death.

Jim was wiry and of barely average height, a fact which

made it possible for him to be as unobtrusive as possible in the small, confined area. After four days the nurses had begun to treat him as a not unwelcome fixture. And they all seemed to have a particular concern for the tough young cop who was fighting for his life.

Jim knew the guts it took to be an undercover cop, to be at the table with cold-blooded killers, to know that at any moment your cover might be blown. He knew the concern that Nicky Sepetti might order a hit on Neeve Kearny; the relief when Tony managed to tell them, "Nicky . . . no contract, Neeve Kearny . . ."

Jim had been on duty when the PC came to the hospital with Myles Kearny and had had a chance to shake Kearny's hand. The Legend. Kearny had lived up to the title. After the way his wife died, his guts must have been shredded wondering if Sepetti would go for his daughter.

The PC had told them that Tony's mother thought he was trying to tell them something. The nurses had instructions to call Jim anytime Tony was able to speak.

It happened at four o'clock Monday afternoon. Vitale's parents had just left, the exhaustion in their faces brightened by hope. Barring the unexpected, Tony was out of danger. The nurse went in to check on him. Through the glass, Jim watched, then moved rapidly as she waved him in.

Glucose was dripping into Tony's arm and oxygen was being administered by tubes taped to his nostrils. Tony's lips were moving. He whispered a word.

"He's saying his own name," the nurse told Jim.

Jim shook his head. Bending, he put his ear to Tony's lips. He heard "Kearny." Then a faint "Nee . . ."

He touched Vitale's hand. "Tony, I'm a cop. You just said 'Neeve Kearny,' didn't you? Squeeze my hand if I'm right."

He was rewarded by the faintest pressure on his palm. "Tony," he said, "when you came in here, you tried to talk about a contract. Is that what you want to tell me?"

"You're disturbing the patient," the nurse protested.

Jim looked up at her briefly. "He's a cop, a good cop. He'll be better off if he communicates what he's trying to say." He repeated the question in Vitale's ear.

Again, a featherlike pressure on his palm.

"All right. You want to tell us something about Neeve Kearny and about a contract." Jim's mind raced over the words he knew Vitale had said upon admittance to the hospital. "Tony, you said 'Nicky, no contract.' Maybe that was only part of what you wanted to say." Jim had a sudden, chilling thought. "Tony, were you trying to tell us that Sepetti didn't put out a contract on Neeve Kearny but someone else did?"

An instant passed and then his hand was gripped convulsively.

"Tony," Jim begged. "Try. I'm watching your lips. If you know who ordered it, tell me."

It was as though the other cop's questions were echoing through a tunnel. Tony Vitale felt vast, overwhelming relief at having been able to give this much warning. Now the picture was so clear in his mind: Joey telling Nicky that Steuber ordered the hit. His voice simply wouldn't come, but he was able to move his lips slowly, pucker them to form the "Stu" syllable, release them for the "ber" sound.

Jim watched intently. "I think he's trying to say something like 'Tru . . .' "

The nurse interrupted. "To me it was "Stu-ber."

With a final effort before he fell back into a deep, healing sleep, undercover detective Anthony Vitale squeezed Jim's hand and managed to nod his head.


After Doug Brown stalked from the interrogation room, Detectives O'Brien and Gomez discussed the facts of the case as far as they were known. They jointly agreed that Doug Brown was a punk; that his story was thin; that he probably had been stealing from his aunt; that his cock-and-bull alibi for not answering the phone was an outright lie; that he must have panicked when he started the story of receiving threats to Ethel just as her corpse was found.

O'Brien leaned back in the chair and attempted to put his feet on the table, his "thinking" position at his desk. The table was too high for comfort, and, annoyed, he swung his feet to the floor, muttering about the crummy furniture and then adding, "That Ethel Lambston was some judge of character. Her ex-husband is a wimp; her nephew is a thief. But of the two scumbags, I say the ex-husband wasted her."

Gomez watched his partner cautiously. He had some thoughts of his own that he wanted to introduce gradually. When he began to speak, it was as though the idea had just floated through his mind. "Let's assume she was murdered at home."

O'Brien grunted in agreement.

Gomez continued, "If you and Miss Kearny are right,

somebody changed Ethel's clothes, somebody ripped out the labels, somebody probably dumped her suitcases and handbag."

Through half-closed but thoughtful eyes, O'Brien signaled agreement.

"Here's the point." Gomez knew it was time to unveil his theory. "Why would Seamus hide her body? It was only a fluke that it was discovered so soon. He'd have had to keep sending alimony to her accountant. Or, why would the nephew hide the body and rip off identification? If Ethel had rotted undisturbed, he'd have to wait seven years to get at her dough, and even then it would have involved a lot of expensive legal time. If one of them did it, they'd have *wanted* the body discovered, right?"

O'Brien raised his hand. "Don't credit these punks with brains. We just keep raking them over, making them nervous, and sooner or later one of them will say, 'I didn't mean to do it.' I still bet on the husband. For five bucks, you want the nephew?"

Gomez was saved from making the choice when the telephone in the interrogation room rang. The Police Commissioner wanted to see both detectives in his office immediately.

On the way downtown in a squad car, both O'Brien and Gomez tried to assess their activities on the case. The PC was on top of this one. Had they goofed? It was four-fifteen when they entered his office.


Police Commissioner Herbert Schwartz listened as the discussion progressed. Detective O'Brien was flat out against giving even limited immunity to Seamus Lambston. "Sir," he told Herb, his voice deferential, "I've been positive right along that the ex-husband did it. Hold off. Give me three days to solve this."

Herb was about to decide in O'Brien's favor when his secretary came in. Hurriedly, he excused himself and went to the outer office. Five minutes later he returned. "I have just been told," he said quietly, "that Gordon Steuber may have ordered a contract put on Neeve Kearny. We'll interrogate him immediately. Neeve blew the whistle on his illegal sweatshops, and that started the investigation that led to the drug bust, so it makes sense. But Ethel Lambston may also have gotten wind of his activities. So now there's a damn good chance that Steuber may have been involved with Ethel Lambston's death. I want to either pin down or eliminate the ex-husband in that murder. Go ahead with the deal his lawyer requested. And get the polygraph today."

"But . . ." O'Brien saw the expression on the PC's face and did not finish the sentence.


An hour later, in two separate interrogation rooms, Gordon Steuber, who had not yet raised ten million dollars in bail, and Seamus Lambston were being questioned. Steuber's lawyer hovered beside him as the questions crackled from Detective O'Brien.

"Do you have any knowledge of a contract put out on Neeve Kearny?"

Gordon Steuber, immaculate despite his hours in the detention pen, still assessing the seriousness of his situation, burst out laughing. "You gotta be kidding. But what a great idea."

In the next room, Seamus, under limited immunity, having told his story, was hooked up to a polygraph machine for the second time that day. Seamus kept reminding himself that this was the same as the other and he'd passed the first one. But it *wasn't* the same. The hard, unfriendly faces of the detectives, the claustrophobic smallness of the room, the realization that they were sure he'd killed Ethel, terrified him. The encouraging comments of his lawyer, Kennedy, didn't help. He knew he had made a mistake agreeing to the test.

Seamus was barely able to answer the early, simple questions. When he got to that last meeting with Ethel, it was as though he were there with her again, watching her mocking face, knowing she was enjoying his misery, knowing that she'd never let go. The rage built in him as it had that night. The questions became incidental.

"You punched Ethel Lambston."

His fist hitting her jaw. Her head snapping back. "Yeah. Yes."

"She picked up the letter opener and tried to attack you."

The hatred in her face. No. It had been *scorn*. She knew she had him. She'd shouted, "I'll have you arrested, you ape." She'd reached for the letter opener and thrust it at him. He'd twisted it from her hand and cut her face when they grappled for it. Then she'd seen what was in his eyes. She'd said, "All right, all right, no more alimony."

Then . . .

"Did you kill your former wife, Ethel Lambston?"

Seamus closed his eyes. "No. No . . ."

Peter Kennedy did not need confirmation from Detective O'Brien to tell him what he had already sensed. He had lost the gamble.

Seamus had failed the lie-detector test.

Herb Schwartz listened, his face impassive, his eyes wary, as for the second time that afternoon he conferred with Detectives O'Brien and Gomez.

In the past hour, Herb had agonized about whether or not to tell Myles that they suspected Gordon Steuber had ordered a contract on Neeve. He knew it might be enough to trigger another heart attack.

If Steuber had ordered a contract on Neeve, was it too late to stop it? Herb felt his guts wrench as he realized the probable answer. No. If Steuber had set it in motion, it would have filtered through five or six hoods before the arrangements were made. The hit man would never know who had ordered it. Likely as not, some out-of-town goon would be brought in and would be rushed away as soon as the execution had taken place.

Neeve Kearny. God, Herb thought, I can't let it happen. He'd been a thirty-four-year-old deputy commissioner when Renata was murdered. Till the day he died, he'd never forget the look on Myles Kearny's face as he knelt beside the body of his wife.

And now his daughter?

The line of inquiry that might have linked Steuber to

Ethel Lambston's death no longer seemed valid. The ex-husband had failed the lie-detector test, and O'Brien made no secret that he thought Seamus Lambston had cut his former wife's throat. Herb asked O'Brien to present his reasons again.

It had been a long day. Irritated, O'Brien shrugged, then, at a steely glance from the PC, assumed a respectful demeanor. As precisely as though he were on the witness stand, he made a forceful argument damning Seamus Lambston. "He's broke. He's desperate. He had a huge fight with his wife over a bounced tuition check. He goes up to see Ethel, and the neighbor four stories up can hear them quarreling. He doesn't go to his bar all weekend. Nobody sees him. He knows Morrison State Park like his own backyard. He and his kids used to spend Sundays there. A couple of days later, he drops off a letter to Ethel saying thanks for letting me off the hook, and with that he encloses the check he's not supposed to send. He goes back to retrieve it. He admits punching and cutting Ethel. He probably confessed everything to his wife, because she stole the murder weapon and got rid of it."

"Have you found it?" Schwartz cut in.

"Our guys are looking for it now. And, sir, the bottom line is—he failed the polygraph."

"And passed the one he took in his lawyer's office," Gomez interjected. Without looking at his partner, Gomez decided he had to tell what he thought. "Sir, I spoke with Miss Kearny. She is sure that there's something wrong about the outfit Ethel Lambston was wearing. The autopsy shows the victim tore her stocking when she put it on. When that pantyhose was pulled over her right foot, her toe caught and caused a huge run clear up the front. Miss Kearny believes Ethel Lambston would not have walked out looking like that. I respect Miss Kearny's opinion. A fashion-conscious woman would not leave her home dressed like that when in ten seconds she can grab other stockings."

"Have you got the autopsy report and the morgue shots?" Herb asked.

"Yes, sir."

When the envelope was produced, Herb studied the pictures with clinical detachment. The first picture, the hand protruding from the ground; the body after it had been removed from the cavelike opening, frozen by rigor mortis into a doubled-over ball of rotting flesh. The close-ups of Ethel's jaw, purple and black and blue. The bloody nick on her cheek.

Herb turned to another print. This depicted only the area between Ethel's chin and the bottom of her throat. The ugly jagged opening made Herb wince. No matter how many years he'd been in police work, the terrible proof of man's cruelty to his fellow beings still saddened him.

It was more than that.

Herb grasped the print convulsively. The way the throat had been cut. That long slash down, then the precise line from the base of the throat up to the left ear. He'd seen that exact thrust one time before. He reached for the phone.

Waves of shock did not affect the timbre of Police Commissioner Schwartz's voice as he calmly ordered a particular file from the archives.

. . .

Neeve quickly realized that her mind was not on ordering sportswear. Her first stop was Gardner Separates. The shorts and T shirts with contrasting loose jackets were amusing and well cut. She could visualize doing the front window of the shop with these outfits in a beach-scene motif in early June. But after that decision had been made, she found herself unable to focus on the rest of the line. Pleading the pressure of time, she made an appointment for the following Monday and hastened from the overly eager clerk who pleaded to "show the new swimwear. You'll flip, it's so great."

When she reached the street, Neeve hesitated. For two cents, I'd go home, she thought. I need some quiet time. She realized she had the beginnings of a headache, a faint sense of pressure like a band around her forehead. I never get headaches, she told herself as she stood indecisively in front of the building.

She could not go home. Just before she stepped into her car, Mrs. Poth had asked her to look for a simple white gown that would do for a small family wedding. "Nothing too elaborate," she'd explained. "My daughter has already broken two engagements. The minister marks her wedding dates in pencil. But this time it just may happen."

There were several houses where Neeve planned to search for the gown. She started to turn right, then paused. The other place was probably the better choice. As she reversed direction, she glanced directly across the street. A man in a gray sweatsuit, a large envelope under his arm, a man with heavy dark glasses and a freakish punk-rock hairstyle, was rushing toward her through the stalled traffic. For an instant they had eye contact and

Neeve felt as though an alarm had sounded. The sense of pressure along her forehead was accentuated. A truck pulled out, blocking the messenger from view, and, suddenly annoyed with herself, Neeve began to walk rapidly down the block.

It was four-thirty. The sunlight was hiding behind long, slanting shadows. Neeve found herself almost praying that she'd find a gown at the first stop. Then she thought, I'll quit and go see Sal.

She had given up trying to convince Myles that the blouse Ethel was wearing in death was important. But Sal would understand.


Jack Campbell went directly from his luncheon to an editorial meeting. It lasted until four-thirty. Back in his office, he tried to concentrate on the mountain of mail that Ginny had separated for him, but it was impossible. The sense of something being terribly wrong was overpowering him. Something he had missed. What was it?

Ginny stood at the door that separated Jack's office from the cubicled area where she worked, and studied him thoughtfully. In the month since Jack had taken over the presidency of Givvons and Marks, she had come to admire and like him tremendously. After twenty years of working for his predecessor, she had been afraid that she might not be able to adjust to the change, or that Jack might not want a holdover.

Both concerns were invalid. Now as she studied him, unconsciously approving of the casual good taste of his dark-gray suit and amused by the boyish way he had loosened his tie and the top button of his shirt, she realized that he was seriously worried. His hands were locked under his chin. He was staring at the wall. His forehead was furrowed. Had the editorial meeting gone well? she wondered. She knew there were still some noses out of joint that Jack had been tapped for the top job.

She knocked on the open door. Jack looked up and she watched as his eyes refocused. "Are you in deep meditation?" she asked easily. "If so, the mail can wait."

Jack attempted a smile. "No. It's just this Ethel Lambston business. There's something I've been missing about it, and I've racked my brains trying to figure it out."

Ginny sat at the edge of the chair opposite Jack's. "Maybe I can help. Think about the day Ethel came in here. You only spent about two minutes with her and the door was open, so I heard her. She was yapping about a fashion scandal but gave absolutely no specifics. She wanted to talk big money and you threw a figure at her. I don't think you missed anything."

Jack sighed. "I guess not. But tell you what. Let me look over that file Toni sent. Maybe there's something in Ethel's notes."

At five-thirty when Ginny looked in to say good night, Jack nodded absently. He was still poring over Ethel's voluminous research. For every designer mentioned in her article, she had apparently put together a separate file containing biographical information and Xerox copies of dozens of fashion columns from newspapers and magazines like the *Times, W, Women's Wear Daily, Vogue* and *Harper's Bazaar.*

She had obviously been a meticulous researcher. Interviews with the designers contained frequent notations: "Not what she said in *Vogue.*" "Check these figures." "Never won that prize." "Try to interview govern-ess about her claim she sewed clothes for her dolls." . . .

There were a dozen different drafts of Ethel's final ar-ticle, with slashes and inserts in each version.

Jack began to skim the material until he saw the name "Gordon Steuber." Steuber. Ethel had been wearing a suit he designed when she was found. Neeve had been so insistent about the fact that the blouse taken from Eth-el's body had been sold with that suit but that Ethel wouldn't have deliberately worn it.

With minute care he analyzed the material on Gordon Steuber and was alarmed to see how frequently his name was mentioned in newspaper clippings of the past three months showing he was under investigation. In the arti-cle, Ethel had credited Neeve for pointing the finger at Steuber. The next-to-final draft of her article not only dealt with the exposure of his sweatshops, his income-tax problems, but contained a sentence: "Steuber got his start in his father's business, making linings for fur coats. The word is that nobody else in the history of fash-ion has made more money with linings and seams in the last few years than the dapper Mr. Steuber."

Ethel had bracketed that sentence and marked it "Save." Ginny had told Jack about Steuber's arrest after the drug bust. Had Ethel discovered several weeks ago that Steuber was smuggling heroin in the linings and seams of his imports?

It ties in, Jack thought. It ties in with Neeve's theory about the clothes Ethel was wearing. It ties in with Eth-el's "big scandal."

Jack debated about calling Myles, then decided to show the file to Neeve first.

Neeve. Was it really possible that he'd known her for only six days? No. Six years. He'd been looking for her since that day on the plane. He glanced at the phone. His need to be with her was overpowering. He hadn't even once held her in his arms, and now they ached for her. She'd said she'd phone him from her Uncle Sal's place when she was ready to leave.

Sal. Anthony della Salva, the famous designer. The next pile of clippings and fashion sketches and articles were about him. Glancing at the phone, willing Neeve to call *now,* Jack began to go through the file on Anthony della Salva. It was thick with illustrations of the Pacific Reef collection. I can see why people went for it, Jack thought, and I don't know beans about fashion. The dresses and gowns seemed to float from the pages. He skimmed the write-ups of the fashion reporters. "Slender tunics with drifting panels that fall like wings from the shoulders . . ."; ". . . soft, pleated sleeves on gossamer-like chiffon . . ."; ". . . simple wool daytime dresses that drape the body in understated elegance . . ." The reporters were lyrical in their praise of the colors.

Anthony della Salva visited the Chicago Aquarium early in 1972 and found his inspiration there in the aquatic beauty of the magnificent Pacific Reef exhibit.

For hours he walked through the rooms and sketched the underwater kingdom where the brilliantly beautiful creatures of the sea vie with the wondrous plant life, the clusters of coral trees and the hundreds of exquisitely colored shells. He sketched those colors in the patterns and combinations that nature had decreed. He studied the movement of the ocean dwellers so that he might capture with his scissors and fabric the floating grace that is their birthright.

Ladies, put those man-tailored suits and those evening gowns with their ruffled sleeves and voluminous skirts in the back of your closet. This is your year to be beautiful. Thank you, Anthony della Salva.

I guess he *is* good, Jack thought, and started to stack the della Salva file together, then wondered what was bothering him. There was something he had missed. What was it? He had read Ethel's final draft of her article. Now he looked at the next-to-the-last version.

It was deeply annotated. "Chicago Aquarium—check date he visited it!" Ethel had clipped one of the fashion sketches of the Pacific Reef collection to the top of her working draft. Next to it she had drawn a sketch.

Jack's mouth went dry. He had seen that sketch in the last few days. He had seen it in the stained pages of Renata Kearny's cookbook.

And the Aquarium. "Check date." Of *course!* With dawning horror, he began to understand. He had to be sure. It was nearly six o'clock. That meant that in Chicago it was nearly five. Rapidly he dialed Chicago area code information.

At one minute to five, Chicago time, the number he dialed was answered. "Please call the director in the morning," an impatient voice told him.

"Give him my name. He knows me. I must speak to him immediately, and let me tell you, lady, if I find out he's there and you don't put me through, I'll get your job."

"I'll connect you, sir."

A moment later, a surprised voice asked, "Jack, what's going on?"

The question tumbled from Jack's lips. He realized his hands were clammy. Neeve, he thought, Neeve, be careful. He stared down at Ethel's article and noticed where she had written, "We salute Anthony della Salva for creating the Pacific Reef look." Ethel had crossed out della Salva's name and over it written: "the designer of the Pacific Reef look."

The answer from the curator of the Aquarium was even more frightening than he had anticipated. "You're absolutely right. And you know what's crazy? You're the second person to call about that in the last two weeks."

"Do you know who the other one was?" Jack asked, knowing what he would hear.

"Sure I do. Some writer. Edith . . . Or no, Ethel. Ethel Lambston."


Myles had an unexpectedly busy day. At ten o'clock, the phone rang. Would he be available at noon to discuss the position he was being offered in Washington? He agreed to luncheon in the Oak Room of the Plaza. In the late morning, he went to the Athletic Club for a swim and massage and secretly was delighted at the confirmation the masseur gave him: "Commissioner Kearny, your body's in great shape again."

Myles knew that his skin had lost that ghastly pallor. But it wasn't just appearance. He *felt* happy. I may be sixty-eight, he thought as he knotted his tie in the locker room, but I look all right.

I look all right to myself, he decided ruefully as he waited for the elevator. A woman may see it differently. Or, more specifically, he acknowledged as he stepped from the lobby onto Central Park South and turned right toward Fifth Avenue and the Plaza, Kitty Conway may see me in a less flattering light.

The luncheon with a Presidential aide had one purpose. Myles must give his answer. Would he accept the chairmanship of the Drug Enforcement Agency? Myles promised to make his decision in the next forty-eight hours. "We're hoping it's affirmative," the aide told him. "Senator Moynihan seems to think it will be."

Myles smiled. "I never cross Pat Moynihan."

It was when he returned to the apartment that the sense of well-being vanished. He had left a window in the den open. As he entered the room, a pigeon flew in, circled, hovered, perched on the windowsill and then flew out over the Hudson. "A pigeon in the house is a sign of death." His mother's words pounded in his ears.

Crazy, superstitious rot, Myles thought angrily, but the persistent sense of foreboding could not be shaken. He realized he wanted to talk to Neeve. Quickly he dialed the shop.

Eugenia got on. "Commissioner, she just left for Seventh Avenue. I can try to track her down."

"No. Not important," Myles said. "But if she happens to phone, tell her to give me a call."

He had just put the receiver down when the phone rang. It was Sal confirming that he too was worried about Neeve.

For the next half hour, Myles debated about calling Herb Schwartz. But for what? It wasn't that Neeve would be a witness against Steuber. It was just that she'd pointed the finger at him and set the investigation in motion. Myles acknowledged that a hundred-million-dollar drug bust was enough reason for Steuber and his cohorts to exact revenge.

Maybe I can persuade Neeve to move down to Washington with me, Myles thought, and rejected the idea as ridiculous. Neeve had her life in New York, her business. Now, if he was any judge of human events, she had Jack Campbell. Then forget Washington, Myles decided as he paced the den. I've got to stay here and keep an eye on her. Whether she liked it or not, he would hire a bodyguard for her.

He expected Kitty Conway at about six o'clock. At five-fifteen he went into his bedroom, stripped, showered in the adjoining bathroom and carefully selected the suit, shirt and tie he would wear to dinner. At twenty of six, he was fully dressed.

Long ago, he'd discovered that working with his hands had a calming effect on him when he was facing an intolerable problem. He decided that for the next twenty minutes or so he'd see whether he could fix the handle that had broken off the coffeepot the other night.

Once again, he realized he was looking with anxious appraisal into the mirror. Hair pure white now but still plenty thick. No monk's tonsures in his family. What difference did that make? Why would a very pretty woman ten years his junior have any interest in an ex–police commissioner with a bum heart?

Avoiding that train of thought, Myles glanced around the bedroom. The four-poster bed, the armoire, the dresser, the mirror, were antiques, wedding gifts from Renata's family. Myles stared at the bed, remembering Renata, propped up on pillows, an infant Neeve at her breast. *"Cara, cara, mia cara,"* she would murmur, her lips brushing Neeve's forehead.

Myles grasped the footboard as he again heard Sal's worried warning, "Take care of Neeve." God in heaven! Nicky Sepetti had said, "Take care of your wife and kid."

Enough, Myles told himself as he left the bedroom and headed for the kitchen. You're turning into a nervous old biddy who'd jump at the sight of a mouse.

In the kitchen, he fished among the pots and pans until he'd pulled out the espresso pot that had scalded Sal on Thursday night. He brought it into the den, laid it on his desk, got his tool kit out of the storage closet and settled down to the role Neeve dubbed "Mr. Fixit."

A moment later, he realized that the reason the handle was off was not a matter of loose or broken screws. Then he said aloud, "This is absolutely crazy!"

He tried to remember just exactly what had happened the night Sal had burned himself. . . .

On Monday morning, Kitty Conway awoke with a sense of anticipation she had not felt for a long time. Gamely refusing the temptation to grab another forty winks, she dressed in a jogging outfit and ran through Ridgewood from seven until eight o'clock.

The trees along the lovely wide avenues had that special reddish haze that signaled spring was coming. Only last week when she had run here, she'd noticed the budding, thought of Mike and remembered a fragment of a poem: "What can spring do; except renew; my need for you?"

Last week she had looked with nostalgia at the sight of the young husband down the block waving goodbye to his wife and toddlers as he backed his car out of the driveway. It seemed only yesterday that she was holding Michael and waving goodbye to Mike.

Yesterday and thirty years ago.

Today she smiled absently at her neighbors as she approached her house. She was due at the museum at noon. She'd get home at four, just in time to dress and start for New York. She debated about getting her hair done and decided she did a better job on it herself.

Myles Kearny.

Kitty fished in her pocket for the house key, let herself in, then exhaled a long sigh. It felt good to jog, but, oh Lord, it sure made her feel her fifty-eight years.

Impulsively she opened the hall closet and looked up at the hat Myles Kearny had "forgotten." The moment she'd discovered it last night, she'd known that it was his excuse to see her again. She thought of the chapter in *The Good Earth* where the husband leaves his pipe as a sign he plans to return to his wife's quarters that night. Kitty grinned, saluted the hat and went upstairs to shower.

The day went quickly. At four-thirty, she debated between two outfits, a simply cut square-necked black wool that accentuated her slenderness and a two-piece blue-green print that played up her red hair. Go for it, she decided, and reached for the print.

At five past six, the concierge announced her arrival and gave her Myles's apartment number. At seven past six she was getting off the elevator and he was waiting in the hallway.

She knew immediately there was something wrong. His greeting was almost perfunctory. And yet she instinctively knew that the coolness was not directed at her.

Myles put his hand under her arm as they walked down the hall to his apartment. Inside, he took her coat and absentmindedly laid it on a chair in the foyer. "Kitty," he said, "bear with me. There's something I'm trying to dope out and it's important."

They went into the den. Kitty glanced around the lovely room, admiring its comfort and warmth and intrinsic good taste. "Don't worry about me," she said. "Get on with what you're doing."

Myles went back to his desk. "The point," he said, thinking aloud, "is that this handle didn't just come loose. It was *forced* off the pot. It was the first time Neeve used that coffeepot, so maybe it came that way, the way things are made these days. . . . But, for God's sake, wouldn't she have noticed the damn handle was hanging by a thread?"

Kitty knew Myles was not expecting an answer. She walked around the room quietly, admiring the fine paintings, the framed family pictures. She smiled unconsciously at the sight of the three scuba divers. Through the masks it was almost impossible to detect the faces, but it was undoubtedly Myles, his wife and a seven- or eight-year-old Neeve. She and Mike and Michael used to scuba-dive in Hawaii, too.

Kitty looked at Myles. He was holding the handle against the pot, his expression intent. She walked over to stand beside him. Her glance fell on the open cookbook. The pages were stained with coffee, but the sketches were

299

accentuated rather than diminished by the discoloration. Kitty bent over and examined them closely, then reached for the magnifying glass next to them. Again she studied the sketches, concentrating on one of them. "How charming," she said. "That's Neeve, of course. She must have been the first child to wear the Pacific Reef look. How chic can you get?"

She felt a hand snap around her wrist. "What did you say?" Myles asked. *"What did you say?"*

When Neeve arrived at Estrazy's, her first stop in her search for the white gown, she found the showroom crowded. Buyers from Saks and Bonwit's and Bergdorf as well as others like her with small private shops were there. She quickly realized that everyone was discussing Gordon Steuber.

"You know, Neeve," the buyer from Saks confided, "I'm stuck with a load of his sportswear. People are funny. You'd be amazed at how many got turned off Gucci and Nippon when they were convicted of sales-tax evasion. One of my best customers told me she won't patronize greedy felons."

A sales clerk whispered to Neeve that her best friend, who was Gordon Steuber's secretary, was frantic. "Steuber's been good to her," she confided, "but now he's in big trouble and my friend is afraid she could be, too. What should she do?"

"Tell the truth," Neeve said, "and please warn her not to have misplaced loyalty to Gordon Steuber. He doesn't deserve it."

The sales clerk managed to find three white gowns.

One of them, Neeve was sure, would be perfect for Mrs. Poth's daughter. She ordered the one, took the other two on consignment.

It was five minutes past six when she arrived at Sal's building. The streets were becoming quiet. Between five and five-thirty the uproar of the Garment District ended abruptly. She went into the lobby and was surprised to see that the guard was not at his desk in the corner. Probably went to the john, she thought as she walked to the bank of elevators. As usual after six o'clock, only one elevator was in service. The door was closing when she heard footsteps scurrying down the marble floor. Just before the door snapped shut and the elevator began to rise, she caught a glimpse of a gray sweatsuit and a punk-rock haircut. Eyes met.

The messenger. In a moment of total recall, Neeve remembered noticing him when she'd escorted Mrs. Poth to her car; noticing him when she'd left Islip Separates.

Her mouth suddenly dry, she pushed the twelfth-floor button, then all the buttons of the remaining nine upper floors. At the twelfth floor she got out and rushed down the corridor the few steps to Sal's place.

The door to Sal's showroom was open. She ran in and closed it behind her. The room was empty. "Sal!" she called, almost panicked. "Uncle Sal!"

He hurried from his private office. "Neeve, what's the matter?"

"Sal, I think someone is following me." Neeve grasped his arm. "Lock the door, please."

Sal stared at her. "Neeve, are you sure?"

"Yes. I've seen him three or four times."

*Those dark deep-set eyes, the sallow skin.* Neeve felt

the color drain from her face. "Sal," she whispered, "I know who it is. He works in the coffee shop."

"Why would he be following you?"

"I don't know." Neeve stared at Sal. "Unless Myles was right all along. Is it possible Nicky Sepetti wanted me dead?"

Sal opened the outside door. They could hear the whirring of the elevator as it made its way down. "Neeve," he said, "are you game to try something?"

Not knowing what to expect, Neeve nodded.

"I'm going to leave this door open. You and I can be talking. If someone is after you, it's better if he doesn't get scared off."

"You want me to stand where someone can see me?"

"The hell I do. Get behind that mannequin. I'll be in back of the door. If someone comes in, I can get a drop on him. The point is to detain him, to find out who sent him."

They stared at the indicator. The elevator was on the lobby floor. It began to rise.

Sal rushed into his office, opened his desk drawer, pulled out a gun and hurried back to her. "I've had a permit since I was robbed years ago," he whispered. *"Neeve, get behind that mannequin."*

As though in a dream, Neeve obeyed. The lights had been dimmed in the showroom, but, even so, she realized that the mannequins were dressed in Sal's new line. Dark fall colors, cranberry and deep blue, charcoal brown and midnight black. Pockets and scarves and belts blazoned with the brilliant colors of the Pacific Reef collection. Corals and reds and golds and aquas and emeralds and silvers and blues combined in microscopic versions of the delicate patterns as Sal had sketched them in the Aquarium so long ago. Accessories and accents, signatures of his great classic design.

She stared at the scarf that was brushing her face. *That pattern.* Sketches. *Mama, are you drawing my picture? Mama, that's not what I'm wearing....Oh, bambola mia, it's just an idea of what could be so pretty...*

Sketches—Renata's sketches drawn three months before she died, a year before Anthony della Salva stunned the fashion world with the Pacific Reef look. Only last week Sal had tried to destroy the book because of one of those sketches.

"Neeve, say something to me." Sal's whisper pierced the room, an urgent command.

The door was ajar. From the corridor outside, Neeve heard the elevator stop. "I was thinking," she said, trying to make her voice sound normal, "I love the way you've incorporated the Pacific Reef look in the fall line."

The elevator door slid open. The faint sound of footsteps in the hall.

Sal's voice sounded genial. "I let everybody go early. They've all been breaking their necks getting ready for the show. I think this is my best collection in years." With a reassuring smile in her direction, he stepped behind the partially open door. The dimmed lights sent his shadow looming against the far wall of the showroom, the wall that was decorated with a Pacific Reef mural.

Neeve stared at the wall, touched the scarf on the mannequin. She tried to answer, but words would not come.

The door opened slowly. She saw the silhouette of a hand, the muzzle of a gun. Cautiously Denny walked into the room, his eyes darting in search of them. As Neeve watched, Sal stepped noiselessly from behind the door. He raised the gun. "Denny," he said softly.

As Denny spun around, Sal fired. The bullet went through Denny's forehead. Denny dropped the pistol and fell to the floor, without making a sound.

Stupefied, Neeve watched as Sal pulled a handkerchief from his pocket and, holding it, reached down and picked up Denny's gun.

"You shot him," Neeve whispered. "You shot him in cold blood. You didn't have to do that! You never gave him a chance."

"He would have killed you." Sal dropped his own gun on the receptionist's desk. "I was only protecting you." He began to walk toward her, Denny's pistol in his hand.

"You *knew* he was coming," Neeve said. "You *knew* his name. You planned this."

The warm, jovial mask that had been Sal's permanent expression was gone. His cheeks were puffy, and shiny with perspiration. The eyes that always seemed to twinkle were narrowed into slits that disappeared into the fleshiness of his face. His hand, still blistered and red, raised the gun and pointed it at her. Spatters of Denny's blood glistened on the shiny fabric of his suit jacket. On the carpet a widening pool of blood encircled his feet. "Of course I did," he said. "The word is out that Steuber ordered you hit. What nobody knows is that *I'm* the one who started that word and *I'm* the one who gave the contract. I'll tell Myles that I managed to get your killer, but too late to save you. Don't worry, Neeve. I'll comfort Myles. I'm good at that."

Neeve stood, rooted, unable to move, beyond fear. "My mother designed the Pacific Reef look," she told him.

"You stole it from her, didn't you? And somehow Ethel found out. You're the one who killed *her! You* dressed her, not Steuber! *You* knew which blouse belonged with the ensemble!"

Sal began to laugh, a mirthless chuckle that shook his body. "Neeve," he said, "you're a lot smarter than your father. That's why I have to get rid of you. You knew there was something wrong when Ethel didn't show up. You caught on that all her winter coats were still in her closet. I figured you would. When I saw a Pacific Reef sketch in the cookbook I knew I had to get rid of it any way I could, even if it meant burning my hand. You'd have made the connection, sooner or later. Myles wouldn't have recognized it blown up to billboard size. Ethel found out that my story about getting inspiration for the Pacific Reef look in the Chicago Aquarium was a lie. I told her I could explain it and went to her place. She was smart all right. She told me she knew I'd lied, and *why* I lied—that I'd stolen that design. And she was going to prove it."

"Ethel saw the cookbook," Neeve said numbly. "She copied one of the sketches into her appointment book."

Sal smiled. "Was that how she made the connection? She didn't live long enough to tell me. If we had time, I'd show you the portfolio your mother gave me. The whole collection is there."

This wasn't Uncle Sal. This wasn't her father's boyhood friend. This was a stranger who hated her, hated Myles. "Your father and Dev, treating me like I was a big joke from the time we were kids. Laughing at me. Your mother. High-class. Beautiful. Understanding fashion the way you only can when it's born in you. Wasting all that knowledge on a clod like your father who can't tell a housedress from a coronation robe. Renata always looked down her nose at me. She knew I didn't have it, the gift. But when she wanted advice about where to take her designs, guess who she came to!

"Neeve, you still haven't figured the best part of it. You're the only one who'll ever know, and you won't be around to tell. Neeve, you damn fool, I didn't just *steal* the Pacific Reef look from your mother. *I cut her throat for it!*"

"It's Sal!" Myles whispered. "He ripped the handle off the coffeepot. He tried to ruin those sketches. And Neeve may be with him now."

"Where?" Kitty grasped Myles's arm.

"His office. Thirty-sixth Street."

"My car is outside. It has a phone."

Nodding, Myles ran for the door and down the corridor. An agonizing minute passed before the elevator came. It stopped twice to pick up passengers before the ground floor. Holding Kitty's hand, he ran across the lobby. Heedless of traffic, they dashed across the street.

"I'll drive," Myles told her. With a screeching U-turn he raced down West End Avenue, willing a squad car to see him, to follow him.

As always in a crisis, he felt himself go icy cold. His mind became a separate entity, weighing what he must do. He gave Kitty a number to dial. Silently she obeyed, and handed the phone to him.

"Police Commissioner's office."

"Myles Kearny. Put the Commissioner on."

Frantically Myles steered around the heavy evening

traffic. Ignoring red lights, he left in his wake a snarl of angry motorists. They were at Columbus Circle.

Herb's voice. "Myles, I just tried to reach you. Steuber put a contract out on Neeve. We've got to protect her. And, Myles, I think there's a connection between Ethel Lambston's murder and Renata's death. The V-shaped slash in Lambston's throat—it's exactly the same as the wound that killed Renata."

*Renata, her throat slashed. Renata, lying so quietly in the park. No sign of struggle. Renata who had not been mugged but who had met a man she trusted, her husband's boyhood friend.* Oh Jesus, Myles thought. Oh Jesus.

"Herb, Neeve is at Anthony della Salva's place. Two-fifty West Thirty-sixth. Twelfth floor. Herb, send our guys there fast. Sal is a murderer."

Between Fifty-sixth and Forty-fourth streets, the right lanes of Seventh Avenue were being repaved. But the workers had left. Recklessly Myles drove behind the stanchions, over the still-damp tarmac. They were passing Thirty-eighth Street, Thirty-seventh . . .

Neeve. Neeve. Neeve. Let me be on time, Myles prayed. Grant me my child.


Jack laid down the phone, still absorbing what he had just heard. His friend the director of the Chicago Aquarium had confirmed what he suspected. The new museum had opened eighteen years ago, but the magnificent display on the top floor that reproduced the dazzling sense of walking the bottom of the ocean at the Pacific Reef had not been completed until *sixteen* years ago. Not too many people were aware that there had been a problem with the tanks and the Pacific Reef floor had not been open to the public for nearly two years after the rest of the Aquarium was completed. It was not something that the director cared to include in the public-relations releases. Jack knew because he'd gone to Northwestern and used to visit the museum regularly.

Anthony della Salva had claimed that his inspiration for the Pacific Reef look had been occasioned by a visit to the Chicago Aquarium *seventeen* years ago. Impossible. Then why had he lied?

Jack stared down at Ethel's voluminous notes; the clip sheets of the interviews and write-ups about Sal; the bold question marks over Sal's rhapsodic descriptions of his first experience seeing the Pacific Reef exhibition at the Aquarium; the copy of the sketch from the cookbook. Ethel had picked up the discrepancy and pursued it. Now she was dead.

Jack thought of Neeve's absolute insistence that there was something odd about the way Ethel was dressed. He thought about Myles saying, "Every killer leaves a calling card."

Gordon Steuber wasn't the only designer who might have mistakenly clothed his victim in a seemingly appropriate outfit.

Anthony della Salva might have made exactly the same mistake.

Jack's office was silent, the silence that comes when a room that is used to the activity of visitors and secretaries and ringing phones is suddenly hushed.

Jack grabbed the phone book. Anthony della Salva had six different office addresses. Frantically, Jack tried the first one. There was no answer. The second and third had an answering machine: "Business hours are eight-thirty till five P.M. Please leave a message."

He tried the apartment at Schwab House. After six rings he gave up. As a last resort he phoned the shop. Somebody answer, he prayed.

"Neeve's Place."

"I've got to reach Neeve Kearny. This is Jack Campbell, a friend."

Eugenia's voice was warm."You're the publisher—"

Jack interrupted. "She's meeting della Salva. Where?"

"His main office. Two-fifty West Thirty-sixth Street. Is anything wrong?"

Without answering, Jack slammed down the phone.

His office was at Park and Forty-first Street. He ran through the deserted corridors, managed to catch an elevator that was just descending and hailed a cruising cab. He threw twenty dollars at the driver and shouted out the address. It was eighteen minutes past six.


Is this the way it was for Mother? Neeve thought. Did she look up at him that day and see the change come over his face? Did she have any warning?

Neeve knew she was going to die. She had felt all week that her time was running out. Now that she was beyond hope, it seemed suddenly vital to have those questions answered.

Sal had moved closer to her. He was less than four feet away. Behind him, near the door, the crumpled body of Denny, the delivery man who would fuss to open the coffee container for her, was sprawled on the floor. From the corner of her eye, Neeve could see the blood that was oozing from the wound in his head; the outsized manila envelope that he had been carrying was spattered with blood, the punk-rock haircut that had been a wig was mercifully half covering his face.

It seemed an age ago since Denny had burst into this room. How long had it been? A minute? Less than a minute. The building had felt deserted, but it was possible someone had heard the shot. Someone might investigate. . . . The guard was *supposed* to be downstairs. . . . Sal didn't have time to waste, and they both knew it.

From far off Neeve heard a faint whir. An elevator was moving. Someone might be coming. Could she delay the instant when Sal pulled the trigger?

"Uncle Sal," she said quietly, "will you tell me just one thing? Why was it necessary for you to kill my mother? Couldn't you have worked with her? There isn't a designer going who doesn't pick the brains of apprentices."

"When I see genius, I don't share, Neeve," Sal told her flatly.

The sliding of an elevator door in the hallway. Someone was there. To keep Sal from hearing the sound of footsteps, Neeve shouted. "You killed my mother because of your greed. You comforted us and cried with us. At her casket you told Myles, 'Try to think your pretty one is sleeping.' "

"Shut up!" Sal stretched out his hand.

The muzzle of the pistol loomed before Neeve's face. She turned her head and saw Myles standing in the doorway.

"Myles, run, he'll kill you!" she screamed.

Sal spun around.

Myles did not move. The absolute authority in his voice rang through the room as he said, "Give me the gun, Sal. It's all over."

Sal held the pistol on both of them. His eyes wild with fear and hatred, he stepped back as Myles began to approach him. "Don't come any further," he cried. "I'll shoot."

"No you won't, Sal," Myles said, his voice deadly quiet now, not a trace of fear or doubt in it. "You killed my wife. You killed Ethel Lambston. In another second you would have killed my daughter. But Herb and the cops will be here any minute. They know about you. You can't lie your way out of this one. So *give me that gun.*"

His words became measured and were spoken with awesome force and contempt. He paused for a moment before speaking again. "Or else do yourself and all of us a favor and put the muzzle of that pistol in your lying mouth and blow your brains out."


Myles had told Kitty not to leave the car. Agonized, she waited. Please—please help them. From down the block she heard the insistent scream of sirens. Directly in front of her a cab stopped and Jack Campbell rushed out.

"Jack." Kitty pushed open the car door and ran after him into the lobby. The guard was on the phone.

"Della Salva," Jack snapped.

The guard held up his hand. "Wait a minute."

"The twelfth floor," Kitty said.

The one elevator in service was not there. The indicator showed that it was on the twelfth floor. Jack grabbed the guard by the neck. "Turn on another elevator."

"Hey, what do you think . . ."

Outside the building, squad cars screeched to a halt. The guard's eyes widened. He threw Jack a key. "This'll unlock them."

Jack and Kitty were on the way up before the police burst into the lobby. Jack said, "I think della Salva—"

"I know," Kitty said.

The elevator lumbered to the twelfth floor, stopped. "Wait here," Jack told her.

He was in time to hear Myles say in a quiet, disciplined voice: "If you're not going to use it on yourself, Sal, *hand me that gun.*"

Jack stood in the doorway. The room was heavily shadowed and the scene like a surrealistic painting. The body on the carpet. Neeve and her father with the pistol pointed at them. Jack saw the glint of metal on the desk near the door. A gun. Could he reach it in time?

Then, as he watched, Anthony della Salva dropped his hand to his side. "Take it, Myles." He pleaded, "Myles, I didn't *mean* it. I never meant it." Sal fell to his knees and put his arms around Myles's legs. "Myles, you're my best friend. Tell them I didn't mean it."

For the last time that day, Police Commissioner Herbert Schwartz conferred in his office with Detectives O'Brien and Gomez. Herb had just returned from Anthony della Salva's office. He had arrived there just behind the first squad car. He'd spoken to Myles after they'd taken that scum della Salva out. "Myles, you've tortured yourself for seventeen years thinking you didn't take Nicky Sepetti's threat seriously. Isn't it time you let go of the guilt? Do you think if Renata had come to you with the Pacific Reef design, you'd have been able to say it was genius? You may be a smart cop, but you're also somewhat color-blind. I remember Renata saying she laid out your ties for you."

Myles would be all right. What a shame, Herb thought, that "An eye for an eye and a tooth for a tooth" wasn't acceptable anymore. The taxpayers would support della Salva for the rest of his life. . . .

O'Brien and Gomez waited. The PC looked exhausted. But it had been a good day. Della Salva had admitted to murdering Ethel Lambston. The White House and the Mayor would be off their backs.

O'Brien had a few things to tell the PC. "Steuber's secretary came in on her own about an hour ago. Lambston went to see Steuber ten days ago. In effect, told him she was going to get him busted. She was probably onto his drug operation, but it doesn't matter. He didn't hit Lambston."

Schwartz nodded.

Gomez spoke up. "Sir, we know now that Seamus Lambston is innocent of his ex-wife's murder. Do you want to press the assault charge against him and the tampering-with-evidence charge against his wife?"

"Did you find the murder weapon?"

"Yes. In that Indian shop just as she told us."

"Let's give the poor bastards a break." Herb got up. "It's been a long day. Good night, gentlemen."


Devin Stanton was having a pre-dinner cocktail with the Cardinal at the Madison Avenue residence and watching the evening news. Old friends, they were discussing Devin's forthcoming red hat.

"I'll miss you, Dev," the Cardinal told him. "Sure you want the job? Baltimore can be a bathhouse in the summer."

The bulletin broke just before the program went off. Famed designer Anthony della Salva was being arraigned for the murders of Ethel Lambston, Renata Kearny and Denny Adler, and for the attempted murder of former Police Commissioner Kearny's daughter, Neeve.

The Cardinal turned to Devin. "Those are your friends!"

Devin jumped up. "If you'll excuse me, Eminence . . ."

Ruth and Seamus Lambston listened to the NBC six-o'clock news sure they would hear that Ethel Lambston's ex-husband had failed the lie-detector test. They had been astonished when Seamus was allowed to leave police headquarters, both convinced that his arrest was only a matter of time.

Peter Kennedy had tried to offer some encouragement. "Polygraph tests are not infallible. If it comes to trial, we'll have the evidence that you passed the first one."

Ruth had been taken to the Indian shop. The basket where she'd dropped the dagger had been moved. That was why the cops hadn't found it. She dug it out for them, watched the impersonal way they slipped it into a plastic bag.

"I scoured it," she told them.

"Bloodstains don't always disappear."

How could it have happened? she wondered as she sat

in the heavy overstuffed velour chair that she had hated for so long but that now felt familiar and comfortable. How did we lose control over our lives?

The bulletin about the arrest of Anthony della Salva came just as she was about to turn off the set. She and Seamus stared at each other, for the moment unable to comprehend, then clumsily reached for each other.

Douglas Brown listened incredulously to the report on *The CBS Evening News,* then sat down on Ethel's bed— no, *his* bed—and held his head in his hands. It was over. Those cops couldn't prove he'd taken Ethel's money. He was her heir. He was rich.

He wanted to celebrate. He pulled out his wallet and reached for the phone number of the friendly receptionist from work. Then he hesitated. That kid who cleaned, the actress. There was something about her. That idiotic name. "Tse-Tse." She was listed in Ethel's personal telephone directory.

The phone rang three times, then was picked up. "Allo."

She must have a French roommate, Doug concluded. "May I speak to Tse-Tse, please? This is Doug Brown."

Tse-Tse, who was auditioning for the part of a French prostitute, forgot her accent. "Drop dead, twerp," she told him, and slammed down the receiver.

Devin Stanton, Archbishop designate of the Baltimore diocese, stood at the door of the living room and watched the silhouette of Neeve and Jack against the windows.

Beyond them a crescent moon had finally broken through the clouds. With rising anger, Devin thought of the cruelty, greed and hypocrisy of Sal Esposito. Before his clerical training recaptured Christian charity, he muttered to himself, "That murdering bastard." Then, as he watched Neeve in Jack's arms, he thought, Renata, I hope and pray you're aware.

Behind him in the den, Myles reached for the bottle of wine. Kitty was sitting in a corner of the couch, her red hair soft and shimmering under the glow of the Victorian table lamp. Myles heard himself say, "Your hair is a lovely shade of red. I think my mother would have called it strawberry blond. Would that be right?"

Kitty smiled. "At one time. Now nature is being helped along."

"In your case nature doesn't need any help." Myles felt suddenly tongue-tied. How do you thank a woman for saving your daughter's life? If Kitty had not connected the sketch to the Pacific Reef look, he would not have reached Neeve on time. Myles thought of how Neeve and Kitty and Jack had wrapped their arms around him after the cops took Sal away. He had sobbed, "I didn't listen to Renata. I never listened. And because of that, she went to him and died."

"She went to him for an expert's opinion," Kitty had said firmly. "Be honest enough to admit you couldn't have offered her that."

How do you tell a woman that because of her presence the terrible rage and guilt you've carried all these years is in the past, that instead of feeling empty and devastated, you feel strong and eager to really live the rest of your life? There was no way.

Myles realized he was still holding the wine bottle. He looked around for her glass.

"I'm not sure where it is," Kitty told him. "I guess I laid it down somewhere."

There *was* a way to tell her. Deliberately Myles filled his own glass to the brim and handed it to Kitty. "Have mine."

Neeve and Jack stood at the window and looked out over the Hudson River, the parkway, the outline of the apartment houses and restaurants that loomed on the waterfront of New Jersey.

"Why did you go to Sal's office?" Neeve asked quietly.

"Ethel's notes on Sal were annotated with references to the Pacific Reef look. She had a whole bunch of magazine ads showing that look, and next to them she'd done a sketch. The sketch reminded me of something and I realized I'd seen the same one in your mother's cookbook."

"And you knew?"

"I remembered you telling me how Sal created that look after your mother died. Ethel's notes showed that Sal claimed he'd gotten the inspiration for the Pacific Reef look at the Aquarium in Chicago. That simply wasn't possible. Everything fell into place when I realized that. Then, knowing you were with him, I almost went crazy."

All those years ago, Renata as a ten-year-old child, hurrying home in the midst of two armies shooting at each other, had, because of a "feeling," gone into church and saved a wounded American soldier. Neeve felt Jack's arm go around her waist. The movement was not tentative, but sure and steady.

"Neeve?"

All these years she'd been telling Myles that when it happened, she would know it.

As Jack drew her closer to him, she knew that that time had finally come.